LISA HENRY
HEIDI BELLEAU

BLISS

RIPTIDE
PUBLISHING

Riptide Publishing
PO Box 6652
Hillsborough, NJ 08844
www.riptidepublishing.com

Bliss

Cover Art by Kanaxa, http://www.kanaxa.com
Editor: Danielle Poiesz
Layout: L.C. Chase, lcchase.com/design.htm

ISBN: 978-1-62649-139-7

First edition
August, 2014

Also available in ebook:
ISBN: 978-1-62649-138-0

LISA HENRY
HEIDI BELLEAU

BLISS

RIPTIDE
PUBLISHING

TABLE OF
CONTENTS

CHAPTER ONE

Rory hadn't expected his fresh start to begin with a concussion.

After all, the city-state of Beulah had a reputation for being the safest in the world. More than that, it was a *community*. The kind of friendly, picket-fence place that used to exist only on syrupy old television programs. It was clean, energy efficient, and had a nearly negligible crime rate. It was Rory's fresh start, away from the polluted, crime-ridden place he'd grown up in. Beulah didn't even have graffiti or loitering teens, let alone the carjackings and rapes at knifepoint Rory had grown up with in Tophet. He had been lucky enough never to have been a victim of a violent crime at home, and he wasn't sure what had shocked him the most when the man had hit him: the sudden excruciating pain as something *crunched* inside his nose, or the sheer ludicrous fact that he'd come all the way to crime-free Beulah and *then* gotten mugged.

"Mr. James?"

Or not mugged, since apparently he still had his ID.

"Mr. James?" the voice repeated.

Rory squinted into the torchlight. He raised a hand to try to bat it away, but only succeeded in smacking himself in the chin.

"You're in the hospital, Mr. James. Can you tell me how you're feeling?"

"Like I should have stayed where I was."

The nurse circled his wrist with her fingers and drew his arm back down. "It's terrible, what happened. Just terrible."

"What *did* happen?" he asked, relieved when she finally moved the torch and he could see again. Well, see everything other than what was behind the floating blobs the torch had left in his vision.

"You were assaulted," the nurse said, her tone becoming almost breathless. "It's all over the news already."

"What?" Rory frowned and winced at the pain that shot through his forehead. "I'm newsworthy?"

"It *never* happens," the nurse told him. "I can't even remember the last time we had an assault victim brought in."

"Really?" The nurse's horror seemed genuine, like Beulah really was as safe as everyone said. Rory tried to take some comfort in that. Which was difficult, since his head hurt so much. And since he was the lucky exception to the rule.

"The police are waiting to talk to you," the nurse said, "but Mr. Lowell says they're not to bother you until you're ready."

"Mr. Lowell? He's here?" Rory struggled to sit up, but the nurse put a hand on his shoulder and eased him gently back down. "Why would he . . .?"

"It never happens," the nurse repeated in a low voice.

Rory had spoken to Jericho Lowell a few times by telephone when he'd applied for the job as the man's executive assistant. Lowell was the chief justice, both a judicial and political appointment in Beulah. Rory knew Lowell's position had helped secure his visa, so the nearest Rory could figure was that he was a cross between a judge and a mayor. Lowell had been impressed with his credentials—Rory had majored in political science and media relations at university and had the volunteer hours to prove he was no armchair expert—and the usually painstaking process of applying for residency in Beulah had been fast-tracked so that Rory could start work as soon as possible.

He was looking forward to meeting Lowell, but not like this. He was a mess. His shirt was bloodstained, and he hated to think what his face looked like.

"He came as soon as he heard," the nurse said, a note of pride in her voice. "He's a good man and, just between us, he's very upset about what happened to you."

Rory was pretty upset by it himself, even though he was sketchy on the details. He tried to remember the man who'd hit him, but everything was a blur. He'd been standing next to his stack of luggage at the train station, trying to figure out the way to the taxis and fumbling in his pocket for his paperwork at the same time. No point getting a taxi if he didn't know the address . . . He'd also been wondering if his house would be as nice as it looked in the pictures he'd been sent, and his stomach had been growling a bit. Shower or meal first, when he got to his new home? Suddenly he'd become aware of a flash of nearby movement, the shape of a man running toward him, and then that blinding shock of pain . . . and then the hospital.

The pain was bad enough, but he was more concerned that this might reflect badly on him in Lowell's eyes somehow. After all, if there was no crime in Beulah, then maybe Rory had brought this on himself. Brought the violence with him from Tophet like it was a contagion.

A worry that was very quickly vanquished when a man swept into the room. He was tall, broad, and in good shape for his age. He had a little extra weight around his middle, but he carried it well. His dark hair was graying at his temples and there were laugh lines around his eyes. He wasn't laughing at the moment. His face was strained with concern.

"Rory," he said warmly, reaching down to shake his hand. "Jericho Lowell. Son, I can't even begin to tell you how sorry I am that this happened. Please accept my sincerest apologies."

Rory tried to smile. "There's no need to apologize, Mr. Lowell. You weren't the one who hit me."

Lowell smiled and gripped his hand tighter. "Well, you'd better get used to hearing it because a lot of people are going to tell you the same thing. You see, here in Beulah we all take responsibility for everything that goes on in our community. The crime committed against you rests on all our shoulders, not just those of the man who attacked you."

"The man who attacked me," Rory interrupted, latching on to the topic. "Who was he? What did he want?"

"An outsider," Lowell said, grave. "Came here because he thought our lack of crime meant we must be easy targets, I'd wager. As to what he wanted, the police are talking to him now so you needn't worry about that."

"Will there be a trial? Will I have to go on the witness stand? I don't want to press charges if it's going to cause trouble for you. I'd like to just move on from the whole thing and start my job."

"These things rarely go to trial," Lowell said. "Not here. Here, men *confess* to their crime. It's what's right and just, after all."

Rory frowned. "But . . ."

"The incident was captured on camera at the train station," Lowell said. "I've seen the footage myself. Terrible stuff, and he'll surely face consequences for what he's done. As for you, you'll be able to start your job, I assure you, but when it comes to 'moving on' . . ."

Rory's heart leaped. He couldn't speak, couldn't even name the strange horror and fear rising inside him.

"Well, I suppose there's a trade-off, you could say. Where you come from, you do the trial and then you 'move on,' as you say. Part ways with the criminal and that's the end of it. But you likely never get justice, and he goes on to commit more crimes. Here, we require a long-term involvement on your part as the aggrieved."

"I don't understand."

"I imagine you wouldn't, growing up in Tophet." Lowell patted him on the arm. "The whole system would be completely foreign to you, what with that meat grinder system the rest of the world runs on. Well, there are no prisons in Beulah, Rory, because our convicted felons are expected to repay their debt to society through labor and service. Rehabilitation through restitution, as the sign in the Hall of Justice says. Which means, in practical terms, that in order to repay his crime against you, and to know his victim as a man, your assailant will be required to fulfill a period of service to you. In fact—" Lowell's eyes twinkled almost naughtily. "—I'd dare say that other than the injury, you're almost lucky this happened to you. Now you'll have your very own rezzy—that is, a person doing restitution labor—at your beck and call. Have him keep your house clean, cook you dinner, maintain your yard, run your errands, that sort of thing. Of course, it's not just about him paying back the price of your injury or else he could just pay your medical bills and be done with it. A personal relationship between victim and perpetrator, that's the ticket. Once he sees what a pleasant young man you are, his crime suddenly has a face."

Rory was stunned. He didn't know what to object to first. "But I don't want the man who hurt me in my life . . . or my house!"

"He'll be no danger to you at all," Lowell said. "He'll be assessed to make sure he's not violent."

Rory was pretty damn sure he *was* violent, and he was the living proof.

"It's difficult, I know," Lowell said. "You're conditioned to believe that most offenders are recidivists because that's what the prison system outside our borders makes them. You send a man to prison once and chances are he'll go there again and again. Prisons and punishments *create* criminals; they don't deter them. But you give him the chance to rehabilitate himself in a meaningful way and everyone wins. You do, he does, and so does society as a whole. I know it's not an easy thing to get on board with, particularly when you're still in pain, but the results speak for themselves."

Rory supposed they did, although it did nothing to ease the worry in him. The guy had *hit* him. For no reason. "I wouldn't even know what I'm supposed to do."

"Ah, see, that's why I hired you, Rory. You're self-sufficient. Hardworking. It's almost a relief to hear how uncomfortable you are with this proposition. But don't worry. Ask for help when you need it, and if you don't, the man should keep himself busy. He'll be fully educated on his duties and responsibilities as a part of his plea deal." Lowell smiled. "And I should add that this won't cost you a thing. Everything he needs, from food to clothing to medical expenses, is covered by the government."

Rory wondered if this would make any more sense when his concussion healed. "I don't feel very comfortable with this at all."

The understatement of the century.

"You wait and see," Lowell said, his tone warm. "In the meantime, maybe the fact that today's lead news story is a man getting punched for no reason will indicate to you just how well the system works. We're unused to violence here, Rory. It still shocks us, when I think the rest of the world has been unshockable for a very long time." He smiled. "Now, I've got a lot of work to do today. I was hoping my new executive assistant would be starting tomorrow, but I see that he needs at least a few days off. You get yourself better, and come in to the office when you're ready and not a minute before."

"Thank you," Rory said.

Lowell turned to the nurse. "Look after Mr. James for me. When he's ready to leave, call my office and I'll have a car sent to take him home."

"My luggage . . ."

"Is waiting at the police station to be collected," Lowell assured him. "I'll have it taken to your house so you don't need to worry about that."

Rory was relieved. Some good news, at last. "Thank you," he said again.

He closed his eyes.

Maybe shit would start making sense once he'd gotten some sleep. Or maybe it would take another punch to the face.

Tate could still feel the bruise on his spine where the cop with the bony knees had knelt on him. His shoulders hurt from having his arms wrenched back. He'd caught a glimpse of the poor bastard he'd hit, lying on the platform with blood pissing out of his nose, and then the cop had pushed Tate's face down again and scraped it across the rough concrete.

Six hours later it was still stinging, but Tate wasn't complaining.

He was in shock.

"What do you mean I should take the plea bargain?" He felt the blood drain from his face.

His lawyer, Cal Mitchell, leaned back in his chair and smiled. "I'm saying, Mr. Patterson, that I would strongly advise you not to go to trial."

It would have been smarter to look up the peculiarities of the Beulah legal system before arriving, but he hadn't really thought it would come to this. He knew there were no prisons in Beulah, and that was good enough for him. It hadn't occurred to him until he was talking to his government-appointed lawyer that maybe the locals had come up with a system of punishment altogether more cruel and unusual.

"Why not?"

Not that he was innocent in any way, shape, or form but surely he had a better chance with a jury.

"If you go to trial and you lose," Mitchell said, "you'll get life servitude. No parole."

Tate swallowed. "What?"

"That's how things work here in Beulah. Just as a man is rewarded for taking responsibility for his crimes early on, he is penalized for tying up the system with lies."

Tate's jaw dropped. Never in all his life, and in all his run-ins with the law, had he heard the right to trial referred to as *tying up the system.* What next? A perjury charge for pleading not guilty?

"If you take the plea bargain," Mitchell drawled, "you'll be free in seven years."

Seven years. Tate's vision swam. It was better than life though, wasn't it?

"But, um, what would my chances be at trial?" His chest hurt. Was he having a heart attack? Every breath stabbed him.

"Take the plea bargain, Mr. Patterson." Mitchell reached over the scratched surface of the table and patted Tate's cold hand. "You're young."

Tate tried another tactic. "But what if I'm innocent?"

"You do realize the attack was recorded by CCTV, don't you?" Mitchell raised his bushy eyebrows. "You're not innocent." He smiled slightly. "But then, nobody ever is. That's why they always take the plea bargain."

God. Tate squeezed his eyes shut. Not happening. Not happening.

Mitchell patted his hand again. "It's not so bad. You'll do your seven years, and then you'll be a free man. All will be forgiven."

Tate's guts twisted. He wanted to laugh, it was so absurd. So he'd hit some guy. How was that worth seven years? Or *life*? He clenched his jaw. Only in a self-proclaimed paradise like Beulah would that shit fly.

He'd been in Beulah for two days. In and out, that was the plan. And it had been working too, right up until the *out* part. Five grand wasn't a lot of money, but Beulah had been easy pickings. Shit, these people left their doors unlocked. *Unlocked.* They might as well have laid down the welcome mat. Tate had hit a few places and filled his bag up with cash and valuables, and then he'd headed for the station to catch a train to Tophet.

Why they'd chosen his bag to search, Tate didn't know and didn't much care. He'd concentrated on getting some distance between him and the cops when the bright idea had hit him: what he needed was a distraction. And there he'd been: a young guy standing on the platform staring at a piece of paper in his hand. So engrossed that he'd been chewing his lip.

Sorry, man.

Tate had punched him, seen him go down, and in the ensuing chaos had figured it had been a good plan. Until that bony cop had come out of nowhere and flattened him.

"What . . . what happens if I take the plea bargain?"

Mitchell smiled at him. "You'll undergo the induction program, and then you'll begin your sentence."

"Induction program?"

"It takes a couple of days," Mitchell said. "Then you're assigned to your restitutional duties."

"Like what?" Tate asked. "Like hard labor? Breaking rocks in a chain gang or something?"

Mitchell looked shocked. "Certainly not. This is to rehabilitate you, Mr. Patterson; it's not barbarous. You'll be expected to perform basic domestic tasks. Cooking, cleaning, perhaps some gardening . . ."

Tate raised his eyebrows. "Like a maid?" *Or a slave?*

"Like a functioning, contributing member of a family unit."

"What?" He was even more confused.

"You're not being punished, you're being rehabilitated. If you feel your duties are too onerous or that you're being mistreated, you always have the right of complaint." The lawyer smiled. "And what's worse, really? You'll get to live in a nice house and be treated with dignity. Seven years in Beulah sounds a lot better to me than seven years in the concrete torture boxes they have in Tophet."

Tate shifted uneasily. Yeah, there was that.

"All of the rezzies I've spoken to have been nothing but grateful for the chance to rehabilitate themselves. Even once they're free, they speak highly of the program. You should take the plea bargain, Mr. Patterson. That's my advice to you."

"I get to live in a house?" Tate had been picturing, well, not a prison since Beulah didn't have those, but some sort of labor camp. "With a *family?*"

Crazier and crazier.

"That's right. Well, I don't know if your sponsor has a family, but you'll get to live in his house."

"My *sponsor?*"

"The person who has agreed to oversee your rehabilitation, yes."

"No, I can't . . . Seven years *cannot* be my best option!" He slammed a fist on the table, his cuffs rattling.

"Once you get there, you're going to wish for longer than seven years." Mitchell sat back in his chair with a lazy slouch that spoke of absolute sureness. "But look. I'm your lawyer, and it's my job to defend you. I'll do my job if you want to take this to trial, I will. But seriously, confess. Take the plea bargain. It's only seven years, and they may well be the best seven years of your life."

Tate didn't believe that for a second.

But what if he went to trial and *lost*? Seven years or life. Right now they both sounded impossible. In seven years he'd miss so much . . . But life? He couldn't do life. Couldn't take that risk.

"Fine," he rasped. "I'll confess. Accept the plea bargain. All of it."

Mitchell's face lit up with a smile, and he shook both of Tate's hands. He seemed elated, ecstatic, a little like a guy who'd drunk seven cups of coffee in short order. "You won't regret this," he blabbered, rifling through the folders and papers that had half spilled out of his briefcase. "Now, just let me gather all of the required paperwork for you to sign, and you can be on your way to your new life."

Tate put his head in his hands.

Yeah, well, that had been the point of coming to Beulah in the first place, right? Get enough to pay off his debts, maybe even move away from Tophet. Five grand wasn't much, but it would have been *enough*. Enough for a new start someplace where the air didn't stink. Someplace where there was more to a neighborhood than concrete and razor wire and fucking dealers pushing their shit day in and day out.

And now what?

No fucking clue.

Seven years.

But he signed the papers anyway. He didn't have any other choice.

CHAPTER
TWO

"Hi!" The face that poked around the hospital room door was a little anxious, a little impish, and topped with spiky hair. "I'm Aaron. Mr. Lowell sent me to come get you. Wow, your face looks pretty bad."

And just when Rory had been telling himself that the swelling really was going down. "You're the driver?"

Aaron stepped inside. "Actually, I'm the intern. So I guess that makes me the driver. And the coffee boy. And the guy who does the photocopying." But he didn't seem disheartened by his long list of lowly, unpaid duties at all. Absolutely overjoyed, more like it.

"Wow, Mr. Lowell must be some kind of a boss."

Aaron smiled. "Yeah, he's *great*." He flushed. "Uh, I mean, it's an honor and a privilege to work for him. I mean, he buys the whole office pizza on Friday nights, and he's really cool and stuff. And smart. And so charismatic. I don't think Beulah could even exist without him, and— Oh God, I'm gushing, aren't I?"

Rory smiled. Lowell had seemed nice enough on his visit to the hospital, but Aaron was talking about the guy like he'd hung the moon. Someone had a touch of hero worship going on. It was a little . . . nice. Yes. Safer to go with nice than with weird. Maybe it was a cultural thing. Maybe people here were just . . . *happier*. Or maybe it was just Aaron.

"Mr. Lowell says I'm to take you home and help you unpack, and then I have to go get your groceries and whatever takeout you want." Aaron's smile grew. "He gave me his credit card."

"I don't think I need the taxpayers of Beulah to pay for my groceries just because I got hit in the face," Rory said, scrunching up his nose before he remembered how much it *hurt*.

"No, *his* credit card. Mr. Lowell is really careful about stuff like that," Aaron said proudly.

An honest judge? Beulah really was paradise.

"So have you got everything here? I've already got your luggage in the car."

"I guess," Rory replied. It wasn't like he'd come here with much. Nobody had much of anything in the outside world. What you had got stolen, or you pawned it to pay off your debts—to the protection rackets or the bank, depending on who had your balls in the tightest vice. The fact that his hospital room had a nice TV over the bed, one that hadn't been busted or stolen, was a whole new experience for Rory. And the fact that his stay here was free. No insurance reps lurking around like vultures, trying to convince him to sell blood or organs to pay his medical debts. Still not worth getting punched in the face, but it was nice to know that the things he'd read about Beulah hadn't been exaggerated. It really was close to perfect. A hell of a lot closer than anything Rory had ever known before.

Aaron held out a bag. "I got you a new shirt. Mr. Lowell worried your old one might have blood on it."

"Thanks." Rory shrugged off his hospital gown and pulled the shirt on. He wondered what had happened to his old shirt. Even if there was blood, he might be able to clean it. To throw it out seemed wasteful. Groceries, a shirt . . . Rory felt a little uneasy with this sort of generosity. *No such thing as a free lunch*, his grandmother had always said.

Aaron followed Rory to the nurses' station, where he signed his release form, and then they took the elevator down to the parking bays. Rory couldn't help smiling as they passed the rows of cars, every one a hybrid.

"These take ethanol, right?"

Aaron nodded, opening the passenger-side door for Rory and helping him in. "We make it ourselves, from sugarcane. It's not perfect, but it's cheap, and it's better than relying on oil. We're self-sufficient here in Beulah. We pretty much have to be, honestly. If we start tangling our economy up in the outside world's, pretty soon we'd inherit the rest of their baggage, too." He winced. "Sorry. Not trying to imply that you brought baggage with *you*. What happened to you was totally abnormal, I mean. Violence doesn't normally follow immigrants in, you know? Since the vetting process is so thorough.

All you people usually bring with you is new perspective and fresh ideas."

"No, I get what you mean," Rory said.

Protectionist. Elitist. Creepy perfect. A lot of people said a lot of sneering things about Beulah. But Beulah was also *safe*. Safe and clean and— Wow. *Green.* The car had pulled out of the parking garage, and Rory was stunned by the beautiful foliage lining the roads. Trees and shrubs and flowers, all well maintained and perfectly landscaped. People here didn't live in massive, towering apartment blocks; they lived in beautiful condos with green roofs or in houses with sprawling yards and riotous gardens. Solar panels gleamed and windmills spun in the breeze.

Rory'd never seen anything like it in his whole life. He wanted to know more. In fact, as a new citizen, it was practically his *duty* to know more. "Is all of your power solar or wind generated?"

"There's a big hydro scheme up north," Aaron said. "But most houses and businesses generate at least eighty percent of their own energy. It's better with the newer houses, but the technology wasn't as advanced twenty years ago."

"It doesn't look like a city at all," Rory marveled.

Aaron smiled. "No skyscrapers, you mean? We live densely for the good of the community and the planet, not because landlords are packing people into slums for maximum profit. That's why we have to keep a cap on immigration. Grow too fast and it gets messy. Overcrowding. Not enough resources to go around. And then there's the possibility of the *wrong* people coming in. Not like you, of course—Mr. Lowell says you came here with high recommendations and impressive credentials—I mean people like the man who assaulted you. Anyway, a few years of restitution and rehabilitation, and he'll be as valuable to the community as you are. But too many others like him, and the system gets strained. You know?"

"Makes sense," Rory acknowledged. It was brutally pragmatic, but he could see the point. If Beulah opened its borders, it'd be overrun. Already, people on the outside were banging down the city-state's door trying to get in. Rory knew; he'd been one of them.

"So," Aaron said, flashing him a smile, "your house is nice and new, with enough solar panels that you're feeding power back into the grid. It's over by the university. The train station is only about a block away. You'll need a card to use the transport system, but they don't cost very much. I think Mr. Lowell will be providing you with a company car anyway. As his assistant, you'll probably do near as much running and fetching as me. But you know, for a salary."

Rory laughed. "Are you still a student?"

"Yeah, I'm working for Mr. Lowell for the summer. I was really lucky to get an internship. My whole class put in for it, and I didn't even have the best results. I guess I just interviewed okay or something." He grinned. "You should have seen the look on Alexandra Holt's face when she found out I got it. She looked like she was gonna throw up! Or punch me in the head, but I guess she thought better of getting stuck as my rezzy for the next seven years."

"What are you studying?"

"Environmental law. Which is why I can rattle off statistics about solar panels. It's just . . . It makes me mad sometimes that we're doing so well here in Beulah and it makes no difference in the outside world. What I'd like to do, one day, is set up a program to send out *our* best and brightest as emissaries to teach the rest of the world, instead of always just letting *their* best and brightest in. Or hell, arrange a system where people like you come in but also return to where they came from periodically to bring back their learnings. Share the wealth of knowledge, you know?"

Rory smiled at the passing landscape. "Yeah, I think that's a great idea. They could use a lot of help out there."

They. Not *we.* Rory felt no sense of loss for the outside world, or for the life he'd had there. And what kind of life had it been anyway? Working sixteen-hour days in data entry for the Interim Government, removing people from the social security database. Criminals, loan defaulters, political agitators—the people the government felt were no longer eligible for assistance. Nothing to show for his degree except a piece of paper and a student debt that was rapidly bankrupting him. One of his former professors had told him about the job in Beulah, and Rory had applied. He hadn't expected to make the shortlist, let alone actually land the thing. Beulah was his salvation. He could be happy here.

They turned off the main road into a narrower street. They passed a school where kids ran around on the green playing fields. There were no chain-link fences, no battered old basketball hoops. Then a shopping mall and a street of restaurants.

"If we turn left here, that takes you to the university," Aaron said and turned right. Another right turn and then a left, and the car slowed to a crawl and pulled up outside a small house.

God. It was better than the pictures.

"This is mine?"

It was perfect. A sleek, modern design, set in a yard full of shady trees.

Aaron handed him a key. "I'll bring your bags in."

Rory's eyes stung as he walked up the front path. The lawn was a little overgrown compared to the neighbors' yards, but that was a luxury in itself. Thick green grass. Potted trees on either side of the door. Neat red flowers planted the whole way up the path to the house, bright and fresh. He could hear *birdsong*.

"You have a vegetable garden in the back, too. The more you grow yourself, the less you have to buy, right?" Aaron lugged a suitcase up the path behind him. "And you can keep a couple of chickens, if you like."

"Right," Rory said, a little dazed at the possibility. He unlocked the front door and pushed it open. The small house was light and airy. Louvers set around the ceiling allowed both the light and the breeze to enter. The living room and kitchen were open plan. He could see gleaming appliances and a polished stone countertop. There was a fireplace in the living room, and a big sectional sofa. Nothing looked cheap or like it had been made in a sweatshop.

"Is this a . . . *standard* house?"

Aaron nodded, his face falling. "Is it okay? Mr. Lowell doesn't like to play favorites. In fact, he lives just a couple of houses down in a pretty similar setup."

"Oh fuck." Rory sucked in a shaking breath. "Language. Sorry. No, it's perfect. It's better than I'd dared hope for."

Aaron beamed. "I'm glad you like it."

Rory wanted to cry. His last month in his old bed-sit, he'd had to sleep with his bed shoved up against the door because someone had broken the locks while he'd been at work. Lying there every night, listening to the doorknob rattle and people laughing in the hallway. *"Come out and play, neighbor."* He'd been terrified.

And now this. It couldn't be real.

"It's perfect," Rory repeated, gazing around in awe. "It's just perfect."

Would it still be perfect once he was sharing it with the man who'd nearly busted his head?

"Get the fuck off me!"

Right up until his lawyer had left, everyone had played nice, including Tate, more or less. But as soon as he'd signed the plea agreement, as soon as Cal Mitchell had shaken his hand, wished him well, and walked out the door, it'd started.

Tate didn't even know who these guys were. They weren't cops; their uniforms were wrong. More like doctors in a mental hospital, maybe. Some *One Flew Over the Cuckoo's Nest* kinda shit. But they'd barreled into the room, uncuffed him only long enough to pull his hands behind him and slap the cuffs on him again, and shoved him onto the floor. One of them was kneeling on the back of Tate's neck to keep him down.

"Get the fuck off me!" he yelled again, the noise muffled as his face was pressed into the concrete.

"Shut your mouth, rezzy."

Tate bucked but couldn't dislodge the guy. He should have known there was something fucking fake about how nicey-nice and perfect this place was.

"Hurts, doesn't it?" the guy said. "Not pleasant, is it? You'll learn to behave soon enough."

"Where's my lawyer?" Tate shouted. "He said this wasn't a punishment! He said I'd be okay!"

"You will, rezzy, you will," the man said. "Just as soon as the chip's in."

Tate froze. "The fucking *what*?"

The man stood up and pulled Tate to his knees. He grinned down at him. "Just a little chip. Goes in the back of your neck and turns you into a nice boy."

Tate knew about chips. They had them back in Tophet too, if you had the money. Chips to make you lose weight, chips to make you quit smoking, chips to make you a better public speaker. And then there were the black market versions: chips to make you a ruthless killer, chips to make you a shameless whore, chips to make you a card counter. But they were expensive and fucking patchy at best. Which explained the number of fat, smoking stammerers still around the place, right?

"That's fucking bullshit!"

The man grinned at the other two officials, then narrowed his eyes at Tate. "You kiss with that mouth, rezzy? Your master's not gonna like hearing language like that when your lips should be around his dick."

The blood drained out of Tate's face. "You're fucking kidding me. This is a fucking joke."

Master. My master? No. My sponsor. My sponsor! I'm supposed to be a member of the family, not—

God, why had he even fallen for that fucking sales pitch in the first place? Hadn't he told himself not to get caught up in any of Beulah's bullshit? Hadn't he decided it was all a front, all too good to be true?

"Oh, I'm not kidding. Maybe you get a master who likes his dick sucked, maybe you don't. Maybe you spend the next seven years on your knees, maybe you spend them at a sink washing dishes. Whatever. That's up to *him*, though, not you. And I ain't met anybody who didn't wind up using their rezzy to get off one way or another."

"Fuck you," Tate said. "I don't suck dick!"

The men laughed.

"If he tells you to, you'll fucking love it," the first man said. "You know what this is, rezzy? This is my favorite part of this job. Where I see some vicious, violent piece of shit like you and he swears he's gonna be different. That he's gonna keep his pride and his dignity and he's not gonna let the chip rule him, he's not gonna become some rezzy robot. And then we stick the chip in him, and you know what? He's just like every other piece of shit rezzy who went before. Picking up trash and sucking dick and begging to do it all day long, because guess what else? It feels good, rezzy. Feels good when you do what your master says."

"Fuck off. I don't believe you."

One of the other men grinned. "They always say that too."

"I want to see my lawyer," Tate managed, his voice hitching.

It couldn't be true. No way in hell. Cold dread filled him.

"You will," the first man said. "You'll see him in a few days, and you'll be so fucking happy to be a part of the rehabilitation program that you'll thank him for it. You'll even thank the cops that arrested you. Good guys, those cops. Makes them feel like they're doing a worthwhile job when a rezzy apologizes for all the trouble he gave them."

"Why . . ." Tate sucked in a shallow breath. "Why the fuck are you even telling me this?"

"Mostly to see the look on your face," the man said. "To see how fucking outraged you are, because you sure as hell won't be doing anything but smiling once you're doped up on the chip."

"I'm sorry," Tate babbled. "Please, I want to go to trial!" He'd throw himself on the fucking mercy of the court. Tell them what it was like out there, where life was filthy and squalid—not like here, where everything was open and so, so clean—and Tate had been *desperate*. Not just for himself, but for Emmy. "I want to tell the judge I'm sorry, and—"

"Tell what judge?" the man cut in. "The judge whose new assistant you punched unconscious at the station? You fucked up, rezzy. You came into Beulah, and you fucked up. Now you have to take the consequences. And I promise you, you'll be happier than you've ever been."

"Even if you are sucking dick," the second man leered. "Best place for an animal like you, on your knees for a decent man."

"Groveling," the third added with a laugh.

Tate's stomach clenched. He'd had nothing to eat or drink all day except for the weak coffee the cops had given him. Not enough in him to vomit back up but, shit, it was trying. "No . . . I can't . . . I'm not like that."

"Hey, it's not so bad," the first man said. "That's the smartest thing about the chip, rezzy. It doesn't care what you like and what you don't.

It rewards you for doing what your master says. Doesn't matter if you've never sucked dick in your life before. Your master tells you to do it, and doing it is gonna be the best feeling in the world. Best sex of your life, I bet."

"Impossible. It's fucking impossible." Tate couldn't meet the man's eyes anymore. He fixed his gaze on the floor. "It's *wrong*."

"What's that? A moral judgment from the piece of shit who punched a guy just for standing there?" The man reached down and gripped Tate's hair, twisting his head up. "You could have killed him, you know. It only takes one punch. What if it had been a woman or a child?"

Tate's voice rasped when he spoke. "I wouldn't have . . ."

"And why the fuck should I believe that? You've earned your punishment, rezzy. Men like you are the reason people in that shithole Tophet are afraid to leave their own homes. You're like a fucking cancer on society. You need to be cut out." The man wasn't grinning anymore. None of them were. "And you should be thankful that in Beulah we don't answer violence with violence. You should be thankful we're better than you."

Better? Tate wrenched his head free, not caring about the pain. These people actually thought they were *better*? Okay, so hitting that guy had been wrong, but no way in hell did that make *this* right. Fuck, he'd just wanted to get home, pay off all the money he owed, and move out of the city. Just wanted to be free of fucking debt collectors, free of threats of violence. And everyone said that Beulah didn't even have prisons . . .

Stupid of him. Unbelievably fucking stupid.

"Please . . ." He swallowed and looked at the floor again. "I'm sorry. Please."

"That's good. Begging. Apologizing. You'll be doing a lot of that over the next seven years, so you might as well get used to it."

Seven years. Seven. Bad enough that he was losing seven years of his life, but to be living them as someone else entirely . . . Tate couldn't even begin to wrap his mind around that. He hunched over, shaking his head uselessly.

"Okay." The man's voice was softer now, and Tate wondered if that was because they'd broken him enough for one day. "We're gonna give you a sedative. It will sting a little. You hearing me?"

Tate nodded, tears filling his eyes.

"We'll walk you out of here, and we'll transport you to the facility. Tomorrow you'll get your chip, and after that you'll go home with your sponsor."

Oh, back to sponsor now, not master. Back to pretending this is somehow civilized.

Tate flinched as one of the men knelt behind him, shoved his pants down, and jammed a syringe into the fleshy part of his ass.

The drug began to work immediately. Tate slumped forward, but the man caught him and hauled him to his feet. He tried to fight the effects of the drug. He didn't want to go quietly, didn't want to go peacefully. This was *wrong*.

One man on each side of him, arms under his, they walked him out of the station.

Tate stared up at the sky. Blue and free of smog. Kind of pretty, except he couldn't focus on it. Beulah was really pretty, and everyone was really nice, except for those guys . . . those guys back at the . . . back somewhere. Shadow men.

Where was he going now?

They loaded him into the back of a van, onto a mattress, and Tate sank into it.

The hum of the engine put him to sleep instantly.

CHAPTER
THREE

Tate fought them when they came for him, but it made no difference. It took four of them to manage it, but in a few minutes they had him strapped facedown to a gurney and were wheeling him into surgery.

The procedure itself was painless. He watched as a nurse slid a needle into the crook of his elbow, and he didn't remember much else after that. Some pretty colors, some weird dreams, and maybe some people talking. He didn't know if that was in his head or if he'd actually heard the surgical team talking. He couldn't remember anything they'd said, and it wasn't important. Just weird, he'd thought at the time, that he could hear anything at all. A general anesthetic wasn't all it was cracked up to be. He'd had better blackouts on alcohol. The headache after surgery was milder than after a bottle of vodka, though.

He lay awake on the narrow hospital cot and wondered if he should feel any different. Shit, there was a chip in his head. A chip. In his head. Crazy.

And maybe it wasn't working because he wasn't thinking any differently than usual. Maybe it was all bullshit. Maybe the technology just didn't work on him. Maybe he didn't have the sort of brain that could be rewritten to make him a happy slave.

He wasn't thinking any differently.

He didn't want to get on his knees for anyone. Didn't want to suck anyone's dick.

Maybe if he played along, if they thought it had worked, maybe he'd be able to get out of here.

Because it hadn't worked. There was no way in hell that he was a slave. Not now, and not fucking ever.

When he was a kid, he'd had seizures. He'd grown out of them, but they'd been frightening. He'd never known when they would come. And, for years, he'd never trusted that they'd stopped. He wasn't like the other kids in his neighborhood. Didn't think he was invincible. Never did drugs to lose control, to get out of his own head. He hated that sensation, that weird dizzy prickliness that preceded a sudden loss of consciousness. Strange electrical misfires somewhere in his brain that he'd been held ransom to. It wasn't until he hadn't had a seizure in years that he'd even started to drink alcohol.

Maybe it was what was saving him now. That brain of his that never worked exactly the way it should. Because he didn't feel any different.

Fuck Beulah, and fuck their legal system, and fuck their chip. They hadn't gotten into his head at all. He forced himself not to smile and give the game away.

"All right," said the surgeon who came to inspect the stitches in the back of his neck. "That seems to be healing well. How do you feel?"

"Fine," said Tate, keeping his voice respectful. *Happy slave, happy slave.*

"Good." The surgeon smiled. "Let's activate the chip."

Shit.

Aaron was as good as his word with the groceries, meaning that Rory woke up on the first day in his new house—he still couldn't stop the thrill of excitement that ran through him every time the realization struck that he had a *house*—to kitchen cupboards packed with enough basics to see him through the next few days. He made scrambled eggs and toast, simply because he couldn't remember the last time he'd been able to afford the luxury of eggs, or any fresh food, really. Produce was too expensive in Tophet even if his debts *hadn't* been bleeding him dry.

He ate standing at the sink, staring out into his back garden—*his* back garden—and decided that yes, he'd get chickens. He'd figure out how to build a coop to keep them out of the vegetable garden and everything.

The only dark cloud on his horizon was the . . . What had Lowell called Rory's assailant? The *rezzy*. Because sure, maybe the system worked. And sure, maybe Rory wanted to do his part to be a good citizen and help rehabilitate the guy, but to have him in his *house*? God. He didn't even know why the guy had hit him. He wasn't sure he'd ask, either, because if he'd driven the guy to violence just by standing there, imagine what talking to him might do. Rory would be afraid to wander around his own house if his assailant was sharing it with him.

Which one of them was getting the prison sentence, exactly? Because it felt as though he was being punished for something that wasn't his fault at all.

He sighed, left his dishes in the sink, and went to try to reclaim some of his prior good mood by inspecting the house again.

Last night, eating takeout, he and Aaron had poked around a little. There was the main bedroom, a spare bedroom that he decided he could use as an office, and a smaller, narrower room behind that. Aaron told him it was a storage closet, which was hard to believe since Rory had rented rooms that were smaller than that. It would be perfect for the rezzy, Aaron had said. But a narrow, windowless room? It seemed a little too much like a cell to him, but then Aaron had pointed out that the rezzy was an outsider as well. It would seem more like a palace than a prison to him. And it wasn't too small to fit a bed.

The house also had a neat and tidy laundry room with a new washing machine. No dryer though.

"Sunlight," Aaron had told him with a grin. "Why waste power on something the sun will do for free?"

Rory liked that. He liked the marriage of technology and simplicity here. He liked that it was second nature for people in Beulah to think about their impact on the environment. And a part of him even liked the idea that they thought people could be rehabilitated, educated instead of punished, even though he really didn't want to be a part of the process in his assailant's case. He liked it in the abstract at least.

Which, Rory supposed, would be the first test of whether he would embrace his new life as a citizen of Beulah or if he'd remain an outsider at heart.

So he'd do his best to help rehabilitate the man, to put aside his old prejudices. He'd do his best to trust the system that had delivered such a high standard of living to the citizens of Beulah. This place had given him a fresh start, hadn't it? He could at least try to show the same courtesy to his assailant.

A fresh start.

All it took was a couple of taps to the doctor's keyboard. This wasn't sci-fi, just an ordinary medical procedure. It was practically routine, except for the part where it was supposed to turn him into a slave. Deceptively ordinary, almost infuriatingly ordinary. To do something like this to a person . . . It should be dramatic, shocking, terrifying to see. But it wasn't. All the terror was trapped inside Tate's head.

"Almost there," said the surgeon.

It didn't . . . didn't *hurt*, but he was aware of the strangest sensation of falling, like he felt sometimes in that weird place just before sleep. Like he had to reach out desperately to hold on but there was nothing there.

And then it was done.

He was there, but he wasn't.

His consciousness, his self-awareness, the part of him that translated to a snarky voice in his head, all still there. All there but so far away.

Not . . . not at the front anymore.

"You may feel disoriented," the surgeon said.

Tate blinked at the man. There was a fog in his head.

There was a fog and . . . and closed doors. He rattled the doorknobs. The real Tate was just behind the doors, but they were locked. Locked. And receding into the fog.

Lost. He was lost and afraid.

"Kneel."

He sank to his knees.

Less frightening on the floor. Not as far to fall.

No. It was less frightening because the surgeon had told him what to do. Until then, he hadn't known. He was still lost but it was okay as long as someone told him what to do.

The distant part of his mind, the part that was still his, fought for a moment, pushed futilely against those locked doors. Couldn't get through to him.

He looked up at the surgeon.

"Good boy," the man said, turning from his keyboard. He patted Tate on the head.

Warmth spread through him.

Somewhere through the fog, he knew this was wrong. He knew this was the chip, but it didn't matter. His own consciousness had been locked away. He had to listen to *someone*; otherwise, there'd just be nothing. He couldn't let himself be nothing. He couldn't. He had to hold on to this new feeling or lose himself entirely.

"You did a bad thing," the man said, patting his head again. "But you're very sorry now."

"Yes," he agreed, relieved.

"Take your clothes off, Tate."

He froze for a second, just a second. No longer than the space of a heartbeat. Then he tugged his shirt over his head, the pull of the stitches in the back of his neck breaking him out in gooseflesh. He lifted himself up far enough to shove his loose pants down, almost tangling himself up in his hurry to get them off. Then knelt there, expectant and hopeful and so fucking pleased that he'd done the right thing.

"Now, if your head hurts, it's because you're not doing something right. You're thinking the wrong things or you're doing the wrong thing or there's something you ought to be doing that you're not. These are like hunger pains, Tate. You need to listen to what your body is telling you and learn how to avoid the pain. Do you understand?"

"Yes."

"Very good, Tate." The doctor spun his chair so he faced his computer and recorded something into a form. "You're taking to this very well. Most everyone responds positively to simple commands after the procedure, but once it escalates to things that skirt the edges of propriety, things that people find humiliating or degrading, malfunction—pushback—becomes more common. Tell me you have a small dick."

His eye twitched, but then his mouth opened. "I have a small dick." How could he feel so horrible and so relieved at the same time?

"Yes, yes. You're doing very well." More typing. The doctor's voice was cool and clinical, but there was a lizardlike quality to it too, a sort of lazy, hungry pleasure that simultaneously disgusted Tate and made him so, so happy. "All right, now I want you to crawl across the floor to that table there." He pointed at a medical tray on wheels, draped in that antiseptic blue paper.

Tate crawled.

"How did that feel? Be honest."

The words were out of his mouth before he could stop himself. "I hate it. I want more."

Tap tap tap went the keyboard. "Yes, that's normal. All to be expected. Now, if those last few actions have a four percent malfunction rate in initial tests, this next one has a twenty percent chance of malfunction. Of *failure*, Tate."

The words twisted somewhere in his gut. He didn't want to fail. He wanted to please the man. He wanted the man's praise to deaden that abortive knocking in the back of his head. To silence the part of him that was still screaming and searching for a way out.

"It's not really your fault, although you'll feel like it is. Honestly, it's just a matter of human nature that the self-preservation instinct is one of the hardest for the chip to override. Far more difficult than the need we all feel to preserve our dignity—a much more modern concern, you understand."

Tate listened avidly, but he didn't understand at all. He just wanted to do well. To be *good*.

"Stand up, Tate." The doctor smiled. "Now take the cover off and tell me what you see."

He obeyed. A scalpel gleamed on the metal tray. "A . . . a blade."

"Good. Pick it up."

The metal was cold in his fingers.

"You have two choices, Tate," the doctor said. He had the kind of voice you'd hear on those old hypnotize-yourself-at-home sound files. "A scalpel is just a tool. It serves a single purpose: to cut. Human flesh, specifically. But like any tool, it can be turned to another purpose. To harm rather than to heal. If you wanted to, you could hurt me with that."

He stared at the scalpel in his hand. His heart clenched.

"It's a tool, Tate," the doctor repeated. "You've picked it up, so now you *must* use it. Two choices."

The doctor, who'd humiliated him, who'd degraded him.

Or himself.

For a moment, rage welled inside him. He gripped the scalpel tightly and imagined what it would be like to shove it into the doctor's gut. Or to slice it across his throat in a sudden, sharp motion. But as soon as he saw it in his mind's eye—the awful spray of arterial blood arcing across the room—it sickened him beyond anything he'd ever felt before. Not only the blood but the betrayal. And what was worse, he didn't even know if it was his old self—his old self who did have morals, really, who didn't want to hurt anybody, not ever—or his new one, resistant to ever causing a master harm. God, no, he couldn't hurt this man. He needed this man.

Tate turned the blade inward.

"Just there next to your groin, if you please," the doctor said, smirking.

He pressed the blade against his inner thigh. Drew it across the skin. The pain was sharp and biting. The blood welled up dark and thin, streaking down his leg. The relief was instantaneous.

"Oh, you are a perfect little pet, aren't you? You'll do very well, Tate. Your seven years will pass in dream." The doctor smiled. Typed one last thing into Tate's file, then hit Print. The 3-D printer on the shelf whirred to life and spat out what looked like a pair of inch-thick plastic circles. Wrist cuffs, he realized, as the doctor buckled them around Tate's forearms. They locked into place, their seams solidifying into a single, continuous circle. "These let everyone know your status and can be scanned to reveal all of the information I've recorded about you here. Why you're a part of the program. Your sentence. Your scores. Who *owns* you now: the man you hit, that immigrant man. I almost wish I'd been at the station the other day. Maybe then you would have hit *me*, hmm?"

Tate flinched despite the praise. The thought of hitting the doctor—of hitting *anyone*—was abhorrent. Inhuman.

"Then I could have you all to myself. Seven years of you instead of a day. Seven years of you naked at my feet. Wouldn't that be nice? You could greet me at the door after work every evening like a good little pet . . . Ah, that would be the life." He shook his head.

Tate placed the scalpel back on the tray and dropped to his knees again. He peered up anxiously at the doctor, and the man's delighted smile warmed him.

"Ah, well, one more trick for the road, eh, pet? Wipe your hand through that blood on your leg like a good lad and jerk off your tiny cock for me. It's not strictly a part of the standardized postimplant tests, but you'll indulge an old man, won't you?"

No.

He was shocked at the vehemence of the thought. He pushed it away. He was being good, so good. His hand shook as he wiped the cut on his thigh, coating his palm in hot, dark blood.

"That's it," the doctor coaxed.

Yes, Tate liked the sound of that. Liked the pleasure coiled in the man's voice. Liked knowing *he* was satisfying the man's lizard hunger. Tate let out a sigh as he wrapped his hand around his cock and gave it a tentative stroke. The hot, tight wetness of his hand felt good, especially if he closed his eyes and blocked out the red. His cock thickened.

"That's it," the doctor said again.

His breath caught at the doctor's tone. So pleased with him, so proud. He grew harder.

"It feels good, doesn't it, to do what you're told?"

"Y-yes." He released himself for a second and swiped his hand through the blood again. Gripped his shaft and began to stroke.

"Almost a sexual pleasure, isn't it? You may notice yourself getting the occasional erection in response to following orders. You mustn't tell your new master why. You mustn't tell him anything about any of this, you understand? As far as anyone else knows, the chips are purely to ensure you don't try to escape or use violence against him. For both your safety and his, you understand? You must never tell *anyone* outside of this building the true extent of the behavior modifications we have programmed you with."

Tate didn't quite understand, but it felt good to agree. The sudden rush of pleasure made him dizzy. "Yes."

"You'll find that if you do try to talk about the chip, it will feel bad. If you try to go against the chip, it will feel bad. Very bad. And it's far better to feel good, isn't it?"

He opened his eyes, nodding quickly. "Yes. Yes, sir."

"Tell me what the chip *really* does, Tate."

He opened his mouth. Tried to push the words out but couldn't. Not pain exactly, but the edge of it, like the twinge of a strained muscle warning against further exertion. He closed his mouth again.

The doctor's smile widened. "Good. What a quick study you are, Tate. Now, you mustn't be embarrassed to tell people what you did, how you hurt a man."

Tate's rhythm faltered. God, he'd hurt someone.

"Keep going, that's a good lad." The doctor's voice was soothing. "People are very interested in knowing about such things. It is very rare for most citizens to even come into contact with someone who has committed a crime. When you are asked, you will answer in a polite, respectful tone and tell them how sorry you are and how glad you are that you are being rehabilitated. You *are* glad, aren't you, Tate?"

"Yes," he gasped. He was suddenly desperate to show the doctor how grateful he was and how good it felt. The shallow wound on his thigh was already drying, but Tate smeared what blood he could find over his palm again. Wrapped his fingers back around his cock. "Thank you!"

The doctor smiled at him. "So clever, Tate. Your master is a lucky man. Other than the broken nose, that is."

Guilt bit at Tate. "I'm sorry!"

"Of course you are," the doctor said. "You're a better person now. I am very pleased at the change in you, and your master will be pleased, as well. That feels good to know, doesn't it?"

The pleasure swept back in and drowned the guilt, carrying Tate over the edge. He came with a groan, blood and cum seeping through his fingers. He panted, holding his hand up and staring at it. He was *bleeding*?

I'm fucking bleeding.

Then the moment of horror vanished.

"Good boy," the doctor said, his voice low with pleasure.

Tate smiled with pride.

"Next time, no tears," the doctor said. "Just a little adjustment, and it won't be a problem."

Tate raised his clean hand to his face and was surprised to feel the dampness there.

When had that happened?

And why had it happened when he was happier now than he'd ever been in his life?

CHAPTER
FOUR

That afternoon, despite Jericho Lowell's insistence that he take time off from the job he hadn't even started yet, Rory walked to the train station by the university and bought a transport card. The light-rail system was another marvel of Beulah's: it was cheap, reliable, and energy efficient. In less than twenty minutes, Rory was in the center of the city, wondering how to find the Hall of Justice. He wanted to at least stop in, get his bearings, and possibly meet a few colleagues before he officially started his work.

The day was too nice to rush, though, and Rory found himself detouring through a large park. There was a lake in the middle, with rowboats and people sitting around in the shade laughing and talking as they ate their lunches. Cyclists made use of the many smooth concrete paths that cut through the landscaped greenery.

Even in the center of the city there wasn't a single building that appeared to be more than four of five levels high. Certainly none tall enough to keep the sunlight from reaching the streets. Many of the buildings had roof gardens, practical in terms of insulation and pleasing to the eye. There was no smog in the air, no haze hanging over the city. No snarling traffic, and no continuous wail of sirens in the distance. It was beautiful here.

The weather was perfect. The day was warm, and the breeze was light. A few clouds chased across the brilliant sky.

The Hall of Justice, when he found it, was an impressive building, with a domed roof and columns reminiscent of another time. The building's grandeur was softened by the sheer number of trees and shrubs lining the path from the street. Purple blossoms, not garbage, littered the ground. The doors of the building opened into a large high-ceilinged foyer. Rory was reminded of museums and old libraries. Or a church. The place seemed venerable, not like any other government building he'd ever been in, where workers jostled for office space and people waited on hard, plastic chairs to be seen.

But even justice was different in Beulah, wasn't it? It was Rory's understanding that the courts dealt mostly with civil matters—in the interpretation and application of legislation. Criminal law, in Beulah, was almost entirely unnecessary. *Almost.* His nose still hurt, after all.

He looked up at the words set high on the foyer wall, carved in the stone: *Rehabilitation through Restitution.*

"Can I help you, sir?" the older woman behind the reception desk asked.

"I'm Rory James," he said. "I'm Mr. Lowell's new assistant."

"Oh, of course," the woman said, smiling and extending her hand. "It's a pleasure to meet you. We're all so sorry about what happened! Let me take you through. You'll be needing this." She opened a drawer and pulled out a lanyard with an ID card attached. "Mr. Lowell said he thought you might come by, even though he told you not to. This is yours. You can use the card to swipe in anytime, and it also gets you a discount at the coffee shop across the street, which is much more useful in my opinion. I'm Margaret, by the way."

"Nice to meet you," he said, taking the card and slipping the lanyard around his neck. "This is a great building."

"It's very old," Margaret told him. "Many of the government properties are, which makes them terribly expensive to heat in the winter and cool in the summer, but you can't just knock down all of your history, can you?"

"No," he agreed, following her deeper into the building.

Margaret gave him a running commentary as they went: the courtrooms, public facilities, and press rooms on the ground floor, the stairs to the basement where the records were kept for twelve months before being moved out to a different facility, then up the stairs to the second level where the justices and their staff worked.

"Now, each justice runs his department a little differently," Margaret told him in a low voice. "Mr. Foster makes his staff bring in their own pens if they ask for too many! But you've been very lucky with Mr. Lowell. His staff speaks very highly of him. I've never heard a bad word."

Rory was glad to hear that. Also, he had the impression that Margaret knew absolutely everything that went on in the place. Which was a relief because Rory didn't know much at all. He'd gotten this job with only the most basic understanding of the legal system in Beulah—whatever he could pick up online mostly. But then, it wasn't like the ways of Beulah were well-known in the outside world. There was a lot of speculation that Beulah was a secretive, closed society set so far apart from everything else that it couldn't be *right* because it was so different. Rory wondered now how much of that was jealousy. What if Beulah did have all the answers? What if it really was possible to build a happy, clean, productive society? What if Tophet and the rest of the world just didn't want to admit all the ways they had fucked up?

From what Rory had seen, Beulah was genuinely perfect. He felt like he was in one of those old martial arts films where a lowly pilgrim would ascend a towering mountain, seeking the teachings of a wiser race. *Please, I've come so far from such abject beginnings. Let me walk among you and learn your ways.*

Rory had been nervous about coming here, not knowing anything much at all and half convinced that the pictures in his immigration package had been lies, and it was a relief to find that everyone had been friendly and welcoming so far. He'd been afraid he'd be treated like an outsider from the start, but that couldn't be further from the truth. Sure, everyone here recognized he was new, but that only meant they put in the extra effort to nurture and guide him.

"These are Mr. Lowell's offices," Margaret said. "Now, when you're here officially, make sure you grab a coffee with me one morning."

If it weren't for the fact that everyone in Beulah was so damn friendly, Rory might have thought she was coming on to him. "I will, thanks."

He took a breath—*fresh start, fresh start*—and pushed the door open.

Aaron was on the other side, mug of coffee in hand.

"I knew it!" he said with a laugh.

"He's here?" a male voice called from somewhere out of sight. Lowell's voice, Rory was pretty sure.

"You betcha, Mr. Lowell!" Aaron replied. He held the mug out to Rory. "We had a little office wager about whether you'd come in today."

"You did?" Rory took the mug of coffee, dumbfounded. Obviously Aaron had won that bet, since he'd made Rory a coffee and all. "Who bet against me?"

Aaron laughed, clutching at his slim waist as if he were going to burst at the seams. "Well, that's the thing. Nobody did! Mr. Lowell eventually did the honors just to round out the pool. He's buying us all lunch."

The man himself stuck his head out from around his office door. "I'm buying, Aaron, but you're going to collect it."

"Happy to, sir!"

Lowell shook his head and smiled fondly at the intern. Then at Rory. "Well, since you can't be trusted to stay at home and rest up like I told you to, what would you like for lunch?"

"I, uh," Rory stuttered. Back in the outside world, he'd liked the food truck two blocks down, where he could get tacos dirt cheap. He wasn't sure what they ate in Beulah. Did their commitment to environmentalism extend to them all being vegetarian? "I'm not sure, sir. What do you suggest?"

"I suggest you have a look in Aaron's drawer," Lowell said with a wink. "If there's a takeout place within a five-block radius and Aaron doesn't have their menu, I'll be struck down where I stand."

Aaron shrugged. "He's got me." He gestured toward a small but sturdy-looking office desk that was tucked into the corner of the room. Which, sure enough, had a top drawer packed full of takeout menus. "Go on. Just take the pile. I'll come by before lunch, and you can tell me what you want."

Arms full of flyers, Rory wandered, bewildered but blessed, into the first day of his new life.

At lunchtime, Rory went for a little curry place that had a very attractive purple flyer with gold lettering. Not vegetarian, as it turned out, but it certainly had more than a few vegetarian options. Which pleased him massively, despite the fact that he ordered lamb for himself.

"Okay," Aaron said, writing it all down. "So that's a sub from Petro's for me and a salad from Farm Fresh for Mr. Lowell. And Ruth and Zac wanted curry too, right? Do you think they'll be finished with court in time, sir?"

Lowell looked at the clock on the wall. "Oh, I should imagine so. It's only an application for development. It shouldn't take them much longer at all. But you know lawyers, Aaron, they'll never pass up the chance for a good argument."

Aaron grinned. "I'll head out now then, sir. See you soon, Rory!"

The door slammed behind him.

Lowell shook his head and laughed. "He's a force of nature, that one. Such an eager boy. He could talk under wet concrete, I'll bet."

"I got that impression," Rory smiled. "He was great helping me get to my house and with the shopping. Thank you for sending him, sir."

Lowell waved a dismissive hand. "It was the least I could do, Rory. My star hire is the victim of a freak act of violence on his very first day? I think a loan of Aaron barely scratches the surface of what I should be doing to make up for it. I'm just glad you didn't hop straight on the next train out."

"Not a chance!" Rory laughed. "My old place . . . God, it was a nightmare."

"That bad?" Lowell sighed. "You know, we get some of your news reports. It seems almost unbelievable. Tophet—along with the rest of the world—was never perfect, but even thirty or forty years ago, they were still functional at least."

Functional. It had been a long time since Rory had heard that term used to refer to the society he'd been born into. "Well, things seem very different here."

Lowell nodded. "Cooperation. Stunning what a shared vision and passion for a place can create. When people work together, miracles happen. It wasn't so long ago that Beulah was no better than anywhere else in the world. But we worked hard. We were committed to change. And, you might call me biased, but there's nowhere else I'd rather live."

"I've been here a day, and I already feel the same."

"Good! That's the spirit. That's the kind of man I need on my team. Only when you understand how special this place is can you really put in the kind of effort that it needs to function. Beulah is a wonderful place, but it takes dedication. If you'll excuse my language, you can't half ass it and still expect results like this."

"No, sir," Rory agreed.

"So, what say you and I get to work then, hmm? I desperately need some research done for a press conference I've got at the end of the week. Now, I know you don't have a background in our legal system yet, but it's a general sort of thing. There's a developer seeking approval to build a new housing estate on the south side. That's the application being submitted today, by the way. It's a good, solid application, and I have no doubt it'll be approved. I think it'll be of great benefit to Beulah and allow us to take more immigrants like yourself, so I just need you to do a bit of research on how similar projects have strengthened the economy." Lowell worried at his lower lip. "And pretty it up a bit. I'm sometimes a little too plainspoken in my press conferences. In fact, maybe you could just write up a few short talking points for me? Aaron will get you a tablet so you can set me up some cue cards."

"Of course, sir. I'd be happy to. I was top of my class in persuasive speaking."

"I know you were." Lowell winked. "You were also one of the few applicants I got from outside of Beulah, and the only applicant from Tophet. That's what this place needs, you know. Some fresh blood."

"I didn't think I had a chance," Rory admitted.

"Whyever not?"

"Well, it's not like I have any real experience."

Lowell snorted. "Experience? How does anyone get experience if nobody will give him the chance? No, it's enthusiasm I look for. Why do you think I found your application so irresistible?"

"Irresistible, sir?" Rory said with a raise of his eyebrows. "You make me sound like a big slab of cake or something."

"Well, then I suppose I'll have to gobble you up!"

Rory's face flushed. Was that . . . flirting? No, of course not, just teasing between men.

Which was commonplace here, according to the online research on Beulah he'd done before he left Tophet. Rory had hardly dared to believe it before now, but in Beulah, there was no prejudice, not based on sexuality or gender or race or any of it. All the worst of the old world, stripped away. As briefly as they'd interacted so far, Lowell did seem to be proving the research right.

It certainly would be refreshing to work with an employer who saw nothing wrong with two men teasing one another. A workplace where Rory didn't feel the need to hide who he was just because it was easier than having to defend himself. Where he didn't have to worry about labels. Not only would no one here mind that Rory thought of himself as gay, but they wouldn't even understand what "gay" was, why anyone had ever bothered to claim such a title—or have it thrust upon them—in the first place. In Beulah, people were people. Straight and gay weren't even concepts here—that was what the rumors said.

And, if Rory was honest, that had called to him a hell of a lot more than any solar panels and fresh air ever could.

Lowell laughed at his blush. "We may be a little more relaxed around the workplace here than you're used to, Rory. I like to think of my team as a family. And I don't mind if we all joke around a bit, as long as the work gets done."

"Of course, sir. I don't mind at all. Honestly, I'm just not used to seeing open affection between men." Or used to talking about it. He stammered a little. "I'm sure you understand?"

"What a shameful world you come from," Lowell said with a disappointed cluck. "I'm honored to have rescued you from that backward mess."

Rescued. An odd turn of phrase, and one that sat a little oddly with Rory. He nodded, ignoring his unease. "Well, it was a relief to get out."

"Have you any family there?"

"Not anymore." None close enough to miss him, anyway. His mother had died when he was young, and his father had dumped him on his grandmother to raise before taking off. Then his grandmother had passed away twelve months ago. He had a few uncles and aunts and cousins, but he'd lost contact with them over the past few years.

Some of them hadn't even come to his grandmother's funeral, so Rory felt no obligation to try to reestablish contact.

Lowell's face softened. "That's a shame, Rory, but I hope your time here in Beulah helps you discover that there are bonds stronger than blood."

It all looked so perfect on paper. Sounded so perfect spilling out of Lowell's mouth. The man was charming, charismatic, and enthusiastic, and Rory wanted to believe what he was saying. He didn't want to sabotage his fresh start with his own cynicism. Sure, the attack proved it wasn't all sunshine and unicorns and angelic fucking choirs. So Beulah wasn't *perfect*. So what? Nowhere was, and it was still better than Tophet. He needed to stop fixating on that punch to the face like nothing else mattered.

"We make our own bonds," Lowell continued. "We make our own families from the people we choose to share our lives with."

Rory shifted uneasily. "Like sharing my house with . . . with that man?"

"Ah." Lowell sighed. "It's difficult to comprehend, I know that. But believe me, the system does work. The rezzy wouldn't be placed with you if he didn't want this chance to be rehabilitated. Can you trust in that, Rory? Or at least wait a short while before you set yourself against it?"

Rory sighed. "It was. . . It was just one punch. And now I have to live with the guy?"

"Just one punch," Lowell said. He frowned slightly and crossed his arms over his chest. "And if you'd cracked your skull when you fell and died, would the fact that it was 'just one punch' be any excuse?"

"I guess not, sir."

Lowell nodded. "Give the system a chance, that's all I'm asking you to do. That's all I would ever ask any citizen to do."

Citizen. Not immigrant. Not outsider. Citizen. Yes, Rory wanted to live up to that name. And he would. He'd more than just give the program a chance; he'd throw himself into it wholeheartedly. He'd do his best to believe in it. A common dream—yes, that was what Beulah was built on. Miracles. The evidence was all around him, in this place that somehow thrived while the rest of the world, still caught up in centuries' old ideas about economic systems, about crime and punishment, and about societal structures, sank into decay.

Miracles like a victim and an assailant working together for a better future for them both. Making amends. Learning from each other. Maybe even becoming friends?

Rory almost snorted at that idea. Okay, so maybe not friends exactly. It's not like Rory could imagine them kicking back and drinking beers together, but maybe they could at least be respectful of one another. If the man was as serious about rehabilitation as he claimed to be, if it wasn't just some line he'd spun. And, in this place, who wouldn't be serious about it? Only the most stubborn, stupid, or delusional person would fail to see that Beulah was better than the outside. Would fail to take the chance to live well for a change. The pilgrim on the mountain again: *Please, I've come so far from such abject beginnings. Let me walk among you and learn your ways.* Because if the man was approaching his rehabilitation with even a fraction of that earnest honesty, then of course it could work. And if Rory could do the same, then it *would* work.

Miracles.

They would make a miracle together. Become one of the foundational blocks of Beulah's success, its very existence.

All Rory had to do was give himself over to the dream and hope the other man would do the same. Of course, telling himself that and actually making it happen were two very different things. He just hoped he could let go of his past long enough to trust.

Tate didn't see the doctor again, but he thought of him. Thought of how good it had felt to be praised by him. How it had filled his entire body with warmth. When the guard came and fetched him for his exit interview, Tate was nervous, but he hoped he could do well again. He *needed* to do well.

"Hello again, rezzy," the guard said with a smile. It was one of the men from the police station.

Tate was filled with sickening shame. The things he'd said to this man last time, the way he'd fought . . . He didn't deserve that smile.

"Hello, sir." Anxiety knotted in his gut.

"Anything to say to me?" the man asked as he escorted Tate down the hallway.

"I'm sorry, sir," Tate said. "I'm so sorry."

The guard's smile grew. "That's okay, rezzy. I know you are."

Tate sagged with relief.

"Now, your lawyer has come to see you." The guard stopped outside a door and paused with his hand on the knob. "Be good, Tate."

"I will, sir."

The guard opened the door.

"Ah, Mr. Patterson," Cal Mitchell said. "Sit down. How are they treating you?"

"Good, sir," Tate said. Better than he deserved. He sat at the table.

Mr. Mitchell spread his paperwork out. "Okay. Now, as soon as we're finished here, you can start your rehabilitation with your sponsor." He looked at Tate.

Tell him, the faint voice in his head urged. *Tell him.*

Tate nodded. "Yes, sir. I'm looking forward to it."

Not that!

But Mr. Mitchell seemed so pleased with Tate's answer, that he couldn't disappoint him.

"Now, tell me why you hit that man," Mr. Mitchell said.

"I'm sorry I did that," he said. "God, I'm so sorry. I thought . . ." What had he thought? He couldn't really remember now. "I wanted to get away."

To get out of Beulah. To get the debt collectors off his back. To get home to Emmy, and those fucking cops were right behind him, and . . .

Emmy.

He didn't *want* to serve. He wanted to get home to Emmy.

"T-to . . ." Tate stammered. Something weird happened in his head then. A sharp spike, like his brain suddenly jumped the tracks. "I never meant to hurt anyone. I just wanted to run, and he was in my way. I'm really sorry."

"Acknowledging your guilt is an important step, Mr. Patterson." The lawyer wrote something down. "And I must say, it's encouraging to hear you talk like this after last time, when you were so adamant about wanting to go to trial."

"I was wrong to want to go to trial. I want to do better," Tate said. "I want to be a better person."

Something snagged in his memory. A better person . . .

"You fucking kidding me, Tate? You can't look after yourself, let alone . . ."

"Fuck you, Paula. I can. I can do better, I know I can."

Then it was gone, and peace settled over him.

"Restitution can help you with both those things," Mr. Mitchell said, smiling softly, as if *touched* by Tate's earnest words. He patted the back of Tate's hand. "Seven years from now, you won't even recognize yourself."

I already don't recognize myself!

The violent, desperate thought came out of nowhere. He could hardly register it before it was gone again, smothered by that strange sensation gnawing at his stomach. The need to please.

"I want that, Mr. Mitchell," he said earnestly. He wanted to make the doctors happy, and the guards happy, and Mr. Mitchell happy, and he especially wanted to make the man from the railway station happy. Because if he could do that, then he would be happy as well. "I'm going to try my best in the program."

Mr. Mitchell nodded. "Well, I'm glad to hear that, Mr. Patterson. A positive attitude is the best thing you can take into the program."

Tate hadn't realized he'd been holding his breath until it escaped him in a relieved sigh. Yes. He'd made Mr. Mitchell glad. Mr. Mitchell was happy with him. And Mr. Mitchell had faith he would do well. Even the thought of being judged unworthy of that faith was terrifying, dizzying. A knot of fear clenched in his gut.

"I'll work hard," he said, and the knot loosened a fraction. "I will, Mr. Mitchell."

Mr. Mitchell beamed at him. "I'm certain of it."

Tell him, the voice in his head urged desperately.

Tell him what?

There was nothing to tell.

CHAPTER
FIVE

The van that pulled up was nondescript. There was no signage on it, but Rory knew exactly who it was. Shit. In that second, all his bravado from earlier in the day deserted him. Because how could this not be an absolute fucking disaster?

The man who climbed out of the van was spry, cheerful, and definitely not the guy who had punched him at the station. He strode up the front path, a sheaf of paperwork in his hand, and Rory ducked back behind the blinds so he didn't look like he was just standing there waiting, anxious *or* eager. He didn't think either impression would look good on a man about to take charge of another man's life. He waited until the third knock before he opened the front door.

And couldn't help staring over the man's shoulder at the van.

"If you'll just sign here," the man said and followed his gaze. "Ah, he's in the back. Just a few things to go through before I hand him over."

"Of course," Rory said, as though he'd done this a hundred times. Like ordering takeout, except instead of a couple of greasy styrofoam containers, the delivery was for a human life.

"Now." The man gave his clipboard a once-over. "You'll be compensated by the government of Beulah for the rezzy's living expenses. A stipend to cover electricity and water and such. He comes with his own clothes and toiletries, but if there's anything you need to buy him, you'll be reimbursed in full, just make sure to save your receipts. Do you live here alone, sir?"

Rory nodded.

"Well, in that case, it's up to you if you want to feed him yourself—again, those costs are reimbursed—or if you want his meals delivered each week. A lot of families prefer their rezzies to eat separate, that way they can help out at mealtimes, take care of the kids, that sort of thing."

Rory tried not to let his surprise show. People let criminals care for their children?

"But if it's just you . . ."

"Um," Rory said. "No, well, I don't think I need meals delivered for him. Not . . . not if he'll be cooking mine anyway."

The man smiled. "That's what I thought, sir, but I had to ask. Now, the tracker's already on, so he shouldn't give you any trouble."

"The tracker?"

The man touched a blunt finger to the back of his neck. "Rezzies get chipped as a part of the program. It's a basic GPS tracker to make sure he doesn't flee—not that we've ever had one go anywhere but the grocery store—and it also suppresses any violent urges."

"V-violent urges?"

"Oh, don't worry. You're perfectly safe, despite his history." The man shuffled his paperwork. "Which is . . . *here*. Interesting reading, but don't pay it too much mind. Once you meet him, you'll see you have nothing to worry about. He's apologetic to the point of blubbering."

That was a relief, but to be honest, for a minute there, Rory was more concerned with the fact that the man had been subjected to any form of behavior modification. He'd seen what kind of evil and abuse those chips could be used for on the outside—luckily they were crude enough there that it was easy to spot someone under their influence. But not here in Beulah, he reminded himself. Things were better here. Humane. The chip was just a precaution, no more a violation of the rezzy's life than being behind bars would be on the outside. And you gave up certain rights when you committed a crime; that was the social contract.

Yes, his conscience was clear.

"Shall I fetch him, then?" the man asked. "If you'll just sign here, and here, I'll go get him."

Rory applied what must have been his shakiest signature ever to the documents and watched nervously from the front door as the man walked back to the van and opened the rear doors.

His rezzy—Rory scanned the paperwork quickly—Tate Patterson, 21, citizen of Tophet, wasn't what he'd been expecting. He'd been imagining someone brutish, he supposed, though he hadn't gotten a decent look at the guy at the station. The man walking up the front path now was slight but tall, with softly rounded shoulders and terrible posture. His head was bowed, his face hidden by a mop of wavy black hair, and his arms were a light golden brown, without tattoos or jewelry. Just a set of wristbands that seemed huge around his small wrists. He was carrying a bag.

He looked so skittish, so utterly unthreatening, that Rory felt a moment of outrage: This guy? *This* guy had flattened him?

Had they caught the wrong guy?

No, of course not. He'd confessed.

"Tate," the delivery man said, "this is your sponsor, Mr. James." And then in a stage whisper to Rory, "It's up to you how formal you want to keep it, sir."

He didn't know if he should shake the guy's hand or introduce himself by his first name or what, so he just stood there blankly.

Tate lifted his head, and his brown eyes were huge and liquid, like a man starstruck by a celebrity. He had long black eyelashes and lots of them. "Mr. James!" he gushed.

Rory was taken aback. Okay, so he'd had a few seconds to come to terms with the fact that Tate Patterson wasn't brutish, didn't look like a criminal at all, but no time at all to prepare for the fact that he was . . . stunning. He had fine, almost delicate features, yet full lips. He looked like one of the boys in the magazines that Rory hadn't dared pack from home in case his bags were opened at customs.

"I'm very sorry for hurting you," Tate said, and then he fell to his knees. He grasped at Rory's pant leg desperately. "I'm so, so sorry. I want to make it up to you."

Rory took a startled step back.

"Told you," the delivery man said. "Tate, get up! He's just a little overwhelmed, sir. He'll settle in a day or two."

Tate, wide-eyed, climbed to his feet. "I'm sorry. I'm sorry."

"Any problems, give us a call," the delivery man said and, with a quick wave, headed back to the van.

Shit.

Rory stared at Tate, who was standing on the front step, shoulders hunched as though he were trying to disappear into the narrow space between them.

"Um, come in," he said. He reached down for Tate's bag—habit, he supposed. You had a guest, and you carried their bag—but Tate lurched forward, grabbing it first. He shuffled inside behind Rory.

And suddenly that house that had seemed so welcoming the day before felt . . . empty. A big, empty shell with nothing to fill it but awkward silence.

"Your room is through here," Rory said at last and led him to the closet-room.

Tate followed him and set his bag down between the bed and the wall. He stood there, arms by his sides, not looking Rory in the face but obviously waiting for something.

"Um," Rory said, and Tate's gaze flicked up before it dropped again. "I'll let you settle in, then."

And count down the hours until I can go to bed and not have to make awkward conversation.

But better that than wander around in a state of half-panic, wondering when the guy would attack, right? If he didn't know better, Rory would have thought he couldn't flatten a butterfly. He looked way too meek to hurt anyone.

Well, Rory knew better all right. And had the busted nose to prove it.

He sighed. "Listen, I don't know what shit you spun your lawyers, but I'm from the outside too. We're both Tophet boys, even. I know what it's like there. If you're prepared to give this an honest go, we don't need to tiptoe around each other, okay?"

Tate looked up, confusion written over his face. A tiny worried crease appeared at the top of his nose. "Please, sir, I want to do well. I want to be a better person. I want to repay my debt."

Yeah, right. That's what everyone said. After they got caught.

Wait, did Tate just call him "sir"?

He sighed. "Rory. Just call me Rory. We're living together so we might as well do it on a first-name basis."

Tate nodded quickly. "Yes, s— Rory."

"Okay, good," Rory said, and Tate visibly relaxed. "Right, well, I'm going to heat up some leftover takeout for dinner. Do you want some?"

"I'll do that," Tate said. "Please, let me."

"I'll do it myself," Rory said. "Just . . . just settle in, okay?"

Tate nodded again. "Yes, Rory."

Tate wasn't sure what he was supposed to do to "settle in." He didn't have any personal items to set up, didn't have any clothes beyond a series of plain gray scrubs that they'd given him at the induction center. At least they weren't prison uniforms. He put them in the dresser anyway and then sat on the end of the narrow bed.

He could hear his new master—Rory, the man wanted to be called Rory—muddling around in the kitchen.

Rory made him uneasy. He wasn't like the doctor, or the guards, or even his lawyer. He didn't ask questions. Didn't give orders. Didn't really show Tate his place at all. It left him unsettled, unanchored, and a little nauseated. He seemed nice enough, but nice wasn't what Tate needed right now. He needed directions and orders, and for the man to put him in his place, where he belonged. He wanted to be back with the doctor. The doctor who'd made him do such terrible, wonderful things, and then praised him for them.

Tate curled his hands into fists and squeezed his eyes shut.

His head hurt. A weird, crawling feeling at the back of his skull that he wasn't sure how to fix.

"Now, if your head hurts, it's because you're not doing something right. You're thinking the wrong things or you're doing the wrong thing or there's something you ought to be doing that you're not."

If he could *do* something, that might make it better, but he was "settling in."

He stood up again, opened the dresser, and pulled all his shirts out. He shook them, refolded them, and put them back again. For a moment, the tension in his head eased, but then it was back, as bad as before.

Guilt bit at him.

How could he have hurt that man? Rory, his *master*.

And now he was sitting here, letting the man cook for him?

He felt ill. His stomach roiled and his joints ached, and oh God, he needed to do *something*. Because the longer he stayed in this room, the longer he did nothing to appease the guilt gnawing at his gut, the more and more unsettled he felt. Chills shuddered through him until his teeth chattered. He wrapped his arms around himself and clambered to his feet. The kitchen. He could clean the kitchen.

He felt better now that he had a plan. Felt less . . . scattered, on edge. The prickling need faded, like a hunger slowly easing under the promise to feed it. The discomfort was good. It would remind him to work hard, to do the right thing. To serve and to repay.

He left his room.

In the kitchen, Rory had made a mess. Noodles and sauce were splattered all over the countertop, trailing from the now-empty takeout containers to the microwave. Rory was leaning against the counter, watching the timer.

"I can clean," Tate said nervously.

"Shit!" Rory started. Color rose in his cheeks. "Sorry, I didn't see you there."

"I can clean," he repeated.

Rory opened his mouth, then closed it again. He stared at Tate for a moment. "Look," he began at last. The timer on the microwave beeped. Rory sighed. "Just come and eat something, okay? Do you like chow mein?"

"I like . . ."

I like whatever you want me to like.

Fuck.

Help me, please.

The words were trapped inside Tate's head. He wanted to say them, wanted to push them out, but God, they'd hurt. They'd rip his head apart. He didn't want them in there at all, but speaking them wouldn't make it better. He wanted them to go away. He wanted them to have never existed in the first place. He wanted to be helpful, useful, to be happy.

"I like chow mein."

Rory took the takeout container out of the microwave. He set it on the counter while he got a couple of plates from the cupboard. Split the food evenly between both.

Tate worriedly watched him.

He doesn't like *you.*

How could he? Tate had hurt him. Busted his nose and gave him those bruises and *hurt* him. Earning his master's praise would be harder than earning the doctor's or the guards'. Tate had never injured them. They only knew how bad he was from reading his reports. They'd never seen it, never felt it.

Rory slid a plate toward him, along with a fork. "Eat." He sighed and touched the purpled bridge of his nose. "Please. And stop staring at me like that. You're freaking me out."

Oh God.

"I'm sorry!" Tate said, his voice rising in desperation. He immediately averted his eyes. "I'm so sorry. I'm so, so sorry. I didn't mean to. I won't look at you anymore."

"And stop fucking apologizing!"

Tate froze, hunching over. Nausea rose in him.

"Look. Just—" Rory made a sound of frustration. "I'm just going to come out and say it: I'm uncomfortable with this whole arrangement. Because you hit me, remember? Remember that?"

"Yes," Tate managed, fighting the urge to be sick. He blinked away hot tears. "I remember."

"I'm going to do my best to make this work, but I'm not naive." Rory's voice was calmer. "Like I said, I'm from the outside too."

The outside. Tophet. Tate could remember it . . . but he couldn't. He could picture it, but he couldn't *feel* it. As though every image he held of the place was as impersonal as if he were watching a documentary or reading a newspaper article. The slum housing he lived in. His clothes shoved in a box in the moldy cupboard. The bathroom down the hall where all the taps leaked. The water stain on the wall that grew every month. The syringes in the hallway.

"You think you can look after Emmy? Here?"

"I can do a better fucking job than you!"

He could, too. He had, when he'd needed to. When Paula was so fucked up, either high or coming down, that someone had to.

"You think you're better than me?"

He'd laughed at that. Laughed. Of course he was better than her.

But now, with those words skittering around the edges of his consciousness, Tate didn't understand it. He knew those people were in his memory, but he couldn't *feel* them. Just words, recalled at random, with no context. The only thing that mattered was here, now, the man standing right in front of him.

"I don't think you're naive," he said, softly. "I just want . . ."

I want you to give me orders. Make this pain and confusion stop.

Rory watched him sternly, but there was a little bit of softness in him too. Between his eyebrows maybe, where the angry curve smoothed into something sympathetic. "So just cut the bullshit, okay? If you do that, then maybe we can actually make this work."

"I want it to work," he said. "I do. I want to work for you. I want you to be happy with me."

No, not wanted. *Needed.* But Rory didn't understand that.

Tell him. Tell him what they fucking did.

Pain bit at him; the words wouldn't come. Tate dropped his gaze again, his heart beating fast.

"Okay," Rory said, quiet, still a little wary. "So let's eat our dinner and try to figure out how we do this, yeah?"

"Yes." Tate sighed with relief. At last, a direction he could follow.

They ate in the open-plan living room, at the small table there. Tate wasn't hungry, but he ate because Rory had told him to, and tried to remember everything he'd learned at the facility. About being on his best behavior. About being invisible until he was needed. About being quiet and neat and clean. About anticipating his master's needs. About obeying commands. And especially about how those were the only things that could make him happy.

"Can you cook?" Rory asked him.

"I . . ." He hesitated. He didn't want to lie to his master. "Some things, I can. Easy things. But I will learn the rest."

Rory wrinkled his nose. "What about gardening?"

"I've never done it," he said.

Rory almost smiled at that. "Me neither. Never thought I'd have a garden."

Tate didn't, either. Everything was pavement back in Tophet. And that was if you were lucky enough to live in a place with a yard instead of in the overcrowded apartment blocks.

Nothing green or growing. The idea of being allowed to tend a garden was intoxicating. Not just because he would be serving Rory but because a garden was a luxury, a reward all its own. An undeserved reward. "Maybe," Tate began hesitantly, "maybe there are books about how to do it?"

This time Rory did smile; the question pleased him. "I'll see what I can find on my way home from work tomorrow."

Tate sighed, hoping he'd found his footing at last. "Thank you."

They ate in silence for a while, and the strange not-hunger crept up on Tate again. He was itching to clean the mess in the kitchen. Itching to keep busy, to find a way to earn Rory's praise.

Rory stirred his fork around his bowl. "So, I'm just gonna clear the air here, and I'm only going to ask you once. Why'd you hit me?"

Tate could hardly breathe. His hands shook, his fork rattling against his bowl. His face burned, but he forced himself to meet Rory's gaze. He didn't know what to say. He wanted to fall to his knees, to beg Rory for forgiveness, except—*"And stop fucking apologizing!"*—except how could he apologize if Rory didn't want to hear it?

Pain stabbed through his skull. Nausea rose in his stomach, and Tate struggled to keep his composure, to answer. "I . . . I don't know. I wanted to get away."

Rory didn't look angry. "Well, that didn't work, did it?"

"No," he said, the sudden pain fading away again into nothing, his stomach slowly settling. "I'm glad it didn't."

Rory rolled his eyes. "Of course you are!"

I can't tell the truth. I can't tell you why I want so bad to tell you lies to make you happy. I can't tell you. I'm trapped and I'm falling to pieces and I want to tell you the truth but the truth is ugly and I want to tell you a lie because the lie is pretty but I don't want to tell you a lie because even the pretty lies don't make you happy and I need you to be happy but the truth is, the truth, the truth—

The chip.

The chip wants to make me forget the truth. Never tell you the truth. Never make you unhappy. Never break its control. I have to lie.

Help me.

Help me.

Help me.

"Help—" he choked out as stabbing, searing pain shot through his head like electricity, frying every nerve and cell until he fell forward onto the table and sobbed. "I want to . . . I want to *help*."

The sudden scrape of chair legs on the floor as Rory stood. He was pale and drawn, standing there at Tate's side, listing and lurching like he wanted to comfort him but also wanted to storm away. He was conflicted. Genuinely conflicted, not controlled, not trapped like Tate. "Are you . . . are you okay?" he finally asked.

Tate straightened. "I just want to help."

Rory shook his head. "Fine. Help, then. Clean the kitchen up, and make me a lunch to take to work tomorrow. Make sure there's coffee waiting for me in the morning. I-I'm going to bed. I have a long day tomorrow, and I've lost my appetite."

No. Please don't leave me alone with this pain.

But Rory was already gone.

Tate sucked in a deep breath and sat there resting his aching head in his hands. When the pain had eased enough, he climbed to his shaking legs and carried both unfinished bowls into the kitchen. He made Rory's lunch. He cleaned. Watched himself as though from a distance. Watched his hands, swiping the sponge over and over the counter. Stood there and did it for hours because he didn't know what else to do.

The house was quiet and dark before Tate had finished, before he was too weary to continue. He returned to his room and lay there in the darkness, consumed with misery.

CHAPTER
SIX

"Hi, Rory," Aaron said, scrubbing his fingers through his hair. Not that it helped any; he looked like a wreck, from the off-kilter tie to his bloodshot eyes. "I got hardly any sleep last night. I went out with some friends from school to catch up, and all of a sudden it was 3 a.m. Do I look that terrible?"

A little bit, yeah, but Rory didn't say so. Didn't have any room to talk, really. He hadn't slept either, but he didn't even have a fun story to fall back on.

"You look fine," he said and hoped Aaron would extend him the same courtesy.

Aaron barked out a laugh. "Thanks for lying."

Lying.

His gut lurched, thinking of last night. That awkward dinner with Tate. Tate, who was so repentant and sweet and full of *bullshit*. Rory had read his criminal record. Tate had once served time in Tophet for theft and assault, and when he'd been arrested in Beulah, they'd found him with a bag of stolen property and a fake passport. He was only repentant because he'd been caught, and that was what irked Rory the most. Tate Patterson thought he could play the system in Beulah, where they really did believe all that rubbish about society being to blame. Well, Rory had grown up in the same society Tate had, and he'd never stolen anything. He'd never hurt anyone.

"Do you want coffee?" Aaron asked. "I'm going to get coffee."

"Thanks," he said. "And then I need your help to track down some info for Mr. Lowell's speech, if you've got time."

"No problem!"

Rory watched him go and slumped down further into his seat.

He was too exhausted to even sit up straight. He'd spent last night tossing and turning because all he could think about was that there was someone sharing his house with him. Someone he didn't trust, didn't like, and who, for all Rory knew, was creeping into the kitchen to grab a knife and finish the job once and for all. Because nobody was that fucking contrite. Someone needed to tell Tate Patterson that he was overacting with his big fucking eyes and his hangdog expression.

"Lying fucking asshole," he muttered.

"Problem, Rory?"

Rory's head snapped up. *Shit.* "I'm sorry, Mr. Lowell, I, um . . ."

"Didn't see me standing right here?" Lowell smiled. He grabbed the chair from Aaron's desk, turned it around, and sat down. He rested his arms on the back. "Something wrong?"

Rory sighed. He felt bad admitting to it, but nothing about Lowell so far had suggested he'd be anything but sympathetic. "I know it will probably sound pathetic, but I'm just . . . I'm having a hard time warming up to . . . my rezzy."

"Ahh," Lowell said with a nod. "I should have known. Not that there's anything wrong with you, mind. I don't look down at you at all. But I do understand. It must be a hard adjustment for someone who hasn't grown up with our customs. If you'd been here since childhood like I have, you'd know how completely safe you are. We wouldn't place a rezzy with you if we thought there was any risk to your safety or well-being."

"It's not that," Rory said, although it sort of was. "I mean, okay, fine. The guy who dropped him off said he was chipped to suppress violent urges, and I believe that. I trust the system, I do. But he just acts so *weird*. It makes me uncomfortable."

"How so?" Lowell asked.

He sighed. "I don't even know how to explain it. The constant apologizing. When he first arrived, he got down on his *knees*."

Lowell laughed.

Rory raised his eyebrows. "Sir?"

"Well, he's playing you," Lowell said. "Playing *us*, I should say. We look like a soft touch from the outside. He probably thinks he's going to get some sponsor who'll fall for his sob story and let him off without washing the dishes or something."

Rory relaxed. "That's what I thought! But I haven't let him off anything. And I think I may be *harder* on him if he keeps trying to trick me. Eventually he'll figure out his plan is backfiring."

"That's the ticket!" Lowell said. "These are just growing pains. I promise. Soon, you two will figure out a balance, and it will feel as natural as breathing. You might even become friends." He laughed again, but this time probably at the face Rory was pulling. "Well, maybe not friends, but you'll find your footing in a day or two, and it will be smooth sailing from there."

He couldn't help but smile at the man's confidence. "I hope so."

"Have a little faith," Lowell said.

Rory's smile grew. "Well, that's the problem with faith, sir. Some of us are just more comfortable with doubt."

Lowell laughed. "Don't get too comfortable with it. The system works, you'll see!" He turned in his seat as Aaron came back into the office. "Aaron, I hope one of those coffees is for me."

Aaron grinned. "Of course, sir."

"Good lad," Lowell said. "Now, I want you to help Rory out today. No crawling off to the records room to sleep off your hangover, hmm?"

"Sir, I would never!"

Lowell laughed. "I'm just teasing you. I was an intern once upon a time myself. I know you kids have to let steam off sometimes." He sipped his coffee. "Let's just pretend your hard-ass boss isn't here, and tell us what hijinks you got up to last night."

Aaron flushed and grinned at the floor. "Well, nothing *too* bad, sir."

Lowell raised his eyebrows but didn't say anything.

"I mean, I maybe drank a little too much." Aaron's grin was caught somewhere between cheeky and sheepish. "And maybe Alexandra Holt and I kissed and made up over the whole internship squabble. Okay, maybe more than just kissed—"

"That'll be quite enough, Aaron," Lowell scolded suddenly.

Aaron's grin faltered.

What had happened to their friendly boss, the one who'd been so eager to hear the gossip?

Rory cleared his throat. "A gentleman doesn't mention a lady's name, Aaron," he said. "Or a fellow gentleman's, as the case may be," he added with a wink, hoping to ease the tension.

That seemed to work because Lowell clapped him on the shoulder. "That's right. That's good advice."

"Oh." Aaron looked a little hesitant. "Okay. Um, sorry."

"All right," Lowell said, rising to his feet. "I can't stop and chat all day. You boys get some work done, hmm?"

"Yes, sir," Rory said.

Aaron echoed him, lacking his usual enthusiasm.

Lowell returned to his office and closed the door. Aaron stared at it, a pitiful expression on his face.

"Come on," Rory said. "I'm going to need your help to find that info." He lowered his voice. "Every boss gets snappy once in a while. Don't take it personally."

"Yeah," Aaron said. "I guess. He's easygoing so much of the time, I guess I didn't realize that even he has a limit when it comes to workplace-appropriate stuff."

"Exactly. But now you know, right? And hey, you can tell *me* all about Alexandra while we work. Would be nice to get my mind off things."

"'Things?' . . . Oh, your rezzy," Aaron said, looking relieved to change the subject. "What's that like?"

"Why don't you show me where to find the records room, and I'll fill you in."

"Okay." Aaron's smile was back, and only a little dull around the edges.

By the end of the day, Rory was pretty confident about his ability to do his job. He was still overwhelmed, but at least he could find his way around the Hall of Justice now without getting lost. He had a headache, though, so he was looking forward to going home, Tate or no Tate. He used the walk from the station to his house as an opportunity to clear his head, or at least fill his lungs with fresh air.

As confident as he'd been earlier talking to Lowell, now that he was alone again, the thought of interacting with Tate was beginning to worry him. He wished Lowell could have come along for moral support, but no, this was something Rory needed to do on his own. How could Tate ever respect Rory's authority as a sponsor if he needed Lowell to hold his hand through all the rough spots?

As he turned into his street—still not familiar enough with it to be absolutely certain he was in the right one—a white, unmarked van with heavily tinted windows passed him. It looked like the one that had delivered Tate to his doorstep yesterday. And, although he couldn't be sure, it seemed as if it had only just started moving. Had it been at his house? Or was there another rezzy being delivered on the street? Of course, it could have been a laundry service for all that Rory knew.

He turned off the footpath and headed for his house. The front door opened before he could even dig his keys out of his pocket.

"Good afternoon, Rory."

"Tate." Rory frowned at him. "Have you been waiting for me, or was someone just here?"

"There was nobody here," Tate said. His gaze flicked to the road, to the direction the van had gone, and then back to Rory. "Can I take your bag?"

"I've got it." Rory entered the house, and Tate closed the door behind him. As quiet and dignified as a butler. It should have been satisfying, but instead it was just unnerving. And irritating. He didn't trust that Tate was telling the truth. God, he hated this whole situation. So much for Mr. Lowell's pep talk earlier.

"How was your day?" Tate asked.

Rory refused to look at him. "Fine. Yours?"

"I did all the chores you asked me to do. And a few you didn't. I made dinner. Hope you like steak."

"Sure," Rory said. "Who doesn't? Gonna eat alone in my room and get some work done now, though. Make sure the kitchen's clean before you go to bed."

"R-right. I will."

Rory frowned. Something was off here, and he was sure that Tate was lying about the van. "So *no one* came here today?"

"No, Rory," Tate said. His gaze flicked up, then down again. "But I did want to speak to you, if that's okay."

"What about?"

"About my behavior," Tate replied. "Yesterday. I was . . . I was *playing* you."

Rory couldn't help his small smile of triumph. "That's exactly what I thought."

Tate's voice gained strength. "And I know you don't want me to apologize, to be, um, a sycophant, so I won't say I'm sorry. But I will promise that it won't happen again."

"Fine," said Rory. He wasn't sure he trusted this new Tate any more than he trusted the old one, but Tate didn't push it, didn't turn on the histrionics like he had yesterday. He only nodded and backed away.

"Let me know when you're ready, and I'll bring your dinner."

"Thank you." Rory headed for his bedroom. He dropped his bag on the floor, closed the door, and rolled his shoulders. God. That encounter was almost *more* awkward than their first, with Tate crying on his knees. And wasn't that a depressing thought. Rory rubbed his still-aching forehead and sat down on the bed. He took his painkillers from the bedside table and swallowed two.

At least he'd managed a little alone time for tonight. If Tate would just keep himself scarce, maybe Rory could manage this whole restitution sponsorship thing. He unfastened his tie and tugged it off, then lay back on the bed with a sigh. Maybe he'd feel better after a nap. He had half a mind to head outside and demand that Tate be the one to eat in his room. After all, this was his damn house, which he'd earned, and it wasn't fair that he wasn't able to actually *live* here, and all because of some jerk who'd punched him in the face and then hadn't had the decency to get away. But he was too tired to force the issue at the moment.

He wasn't keen on confrontation, either, especially not after Tate had finally—seemingly—cut the bullshit for the first time.

Punched in the face on the first day. Hiding in his own house.

Beulah was nothing like he'd expected, and not only that—he felt damn sorry for daring to feel disappointed by it.

He sighed again and closed his eyes. He must have dozed because he didn't even realize anyone was in the room until his mattress dipped. His eyes snapped open. Tate. Tate was kneeling on the bed beside him, one shaking hand reaching out for Rory's belt.

"Jesus, what are you—" Rory froze with shock.

"You seem so stressed and high-strung. Let me help."

"Help?" Rory croaked. "I don't need . . ."

Tate tugged his zipper down, swiped his tongue across his lips, and leaned in. And—oh shit—every objection Rory wanted to make died right then and there as Tate, his face hidden by his gleaming dark hair, mouthed his cock through his underwear. Tate's hot, wet breath soaked through the cotton.

"How—" He gasped. "How did you know I'm gay?"

Tate pressed the side of his face to Rory's growing bulge and stared up at him through glassy, half-lidded eyes. "I didn't. But a hole's a hole, right? And a mouth's a mouth?"

"Oh fuck," Rory whispered. "Yeah, I guess."

He could blame this bad decision on his painkillers later.

And as for the guilt? There *would* be guilt. But knowing that wasn't enough to make Rory refuse Tate now. It had been so long, and he'd been so fucking *lonely*.

Tate hooked his cold fingers around the band of Rory's underwear and pulled it down. Kept one hand on his bunched-up underwear and trousers, holding them out of the way, and wrapped his other hand around the shaft of Rory's cock. Licked his lips again. Bent his head down.

"Help." Tate shivered suddenly, jerked his head. "Let me help."

"Shit," Rory breathed, as Tate's lips pressed against the head of his cock. Hot and wet and so soft. Plush against the hardness of Rory's erection. Then Tate's lips parted, and he took Rory's cock into his mouth. "Oh shit, shit, oh yes—"

Tate moaned. Stared at Rory through his hair, his eyes dark, his lips stretched around Rory's cock, looking every inch one of those boys from Rory's magazines. Fucking gorgeous. And he felt even better, so wet, suckling the head of Rory's cock so very gently, flicking Rory's foreskin with the tip of his tongue.

"Tate, fuck!"

Tate's eyes shone with pleasure. The corner of his mouth twitched, spasming from being stretched around Rory's girth, maybe. "Pl . . . ease," he gritted out.

"Yes," Rory replied. He lifted his hips, wanting more. God, it had been so long. "Yes, yes."

Tate bobbed his head down, too fast. He coughed and tears filled his eyes, but he didn't ease back or make any attempt to pull away. Shit, Tate didn't have much finesse, but Rory couldn't fault his enthusiasm. He gagged again but kept going, eventually faltering into a rhythm of sorts. Stuttering strokes that dragged along the shaft of Rory's cock, punctuated by choking noises.

Rory dropped his head back onto the mattress and groaned. He shouldn't be doing this. He shouldn't be letting this happen. He and Tate had no reason to want to share something this intimate. But then, maybe a blowjob wasn't intimate to a person like Tate. He was a crim, wasn't he? Maybe even an addict, on the outside. Like the guys that hung around the streets near Rory's old apartment block, the ones who'd do anything for money or drugs. Not that Rory had either, but maybe he had something else Tate wanted. Like his docile fucking cooperation. Like he could buy Rory's goodwill this way. Wrap him around his little finger while he was at it.

I was playing you, Tate had said earlier. And fuck him, he was still playing him, only using a new game.

Just like that, Rory's cock softened. Tate whined in exaggerated despair, wrapping a hand around Rory's shrunken cock and trying to stroke it back to life.

"Get off," Rory demanded. "I know what you're fucking doing. Get the fuck off and get out."

Tate leaned back, eyes wide in shock. He wiped his mouth with the back of his hand. "I don't . . . I don't understand . . ."

Rory rolled away from him, tugging his pants closed. "Get out."

"I wanted to," Tate said, climbing off the bed. He was panting. Something like panic flashed in his eyes. "I wanted to!"

"Get out!"

Tate fled.

In the sudden silence, Rory struggled to make sense of what the hell just happened. He dropped his head into his hands, groaned at his own stupidity, and wondered what the fuck he was supposed to do now.

Tate hugged the toilet bowl. He had no idea if his sudden urge to puke was because of the fact that he'd had another man's dick in his mouth or if it was the chip, punishing him for displeasing his master. Maybe both.

He was crying, and he'd never cried in his fucking life before they'd put that chip in his head. And even *thinking* about it hurt. How was that fair? Bad enough that he couldn't talk about it, but he wasn't even allowed the privacy of his own thoughts?

His head throbbed.

The man who'd come today for Tate's routine check-up had promised it would get easier. Told him not to try so hard. Told him to be less of a *sycophant*. By "easier," Tate understood that he'd stop feeling this conflicted eventually, this push and pull between what he was supposed to be and the man he had been. And he wanted that. He wanted to be at peace, even if it was terrifying at the same time. Because then he'd be gone, wouldn't he? He'd be gone, and there would be no coming back. But if he stayed like this, if he struggled to keep himself whole, never stopped fighting, he'd never be happy, never stop hurting, never, never—

Even now he could feel the chip's influence stealing him, silencing his thoughts. Smothering them.

Why hadn't Rory let him finish? Why hadn't Rory let him . . . make him happy? Why couldn't he see or sense what was happening inside Tate's head? What was he doing wrong?

Tate lifted his head as he heard footsteps. Rory on his way to get his dinner probably. Another thing Tate had fucked up. Should have taken his dinner in like he'd said and not tried for anything else. But he'd seen Rory lying there, his forehead creased with tension, and all of a sudden he'd remembered the men at the police station. They'd said he'd do it, said he'd suck dick, even though Tate had never done anything like it in his life. Never wanted to. But all of that was different now. Now he just wanted to please Rory, and what man didn't like to get his dick sucked? So he'd done it. Fought against all the screaming in his head, even the bits that had escaped his mouth, and done it, but Rory hadn't been happy.

Tate moaned and knocked his head against the toilet. Why couldn't he get this right? He was trying, but it just wasn't working. Damn, they should give Rory a chip to make him easier to please.

Just the thought made him puke all over again, retching his empty stomach out over the bowl.

No. He wouldn't wish this hell on anybody.

Especially not his awkward, unassuming master, who hadn't asked for this any more than Tate had.

God, he wished he could just tell the man what was happening to him. Maybe then he'd—

What, let you suck his cock just to alleviate your pain . . . after you punched him in the face for no reason?

No. Shit. What was even wrong with him? He didn't deserve Rory's pity. He didn't deserve his compassion. He didn't even deserve his fucking cooperation. He didn't deserve *anything*.

CHAPTER
SEVEN

D ays passed, and Rory was relieved that for the most part, Tate made himself scarce. When he woke up in the morning, his slippers were next to the bed, and his breakfast and packed lunch were ready in the kitchen. When he got home at the end of the day, every room in the house was spotless, his bed made and his laundry washed, and there was a hot supper waiting for him on the table.

Tate didn't join him for meals. Didn't come out when Rory got the chance to laze around and watch TV in the evenings. Didn't speak to him, except the occasional, "Do you need anything?" to which Rory always mutely shook his head.

It was a small house, so yeah, Rory saw him, but it was only ever brief glimpses as he hurried from one room to the next, moving like a shadow. The guy seemed to look paler and more withdrawn every time Rory saw him, but at least things between them were peaceful, all boundaries respected, and no lying whatsoever. And that was fine. It was *working*.

Except one night when Rory had woken and, heading for the bathroom, heard a strange sound coming from behind Tate's door. A kind of snuffling and a strangled whimpering. He'd stood there in the darkness, shocked.

Tate had been crying.

He couldn't help but feel guilty for that. Was it because he'd rebuffed Tate so soundly? Shit, had Tate maybe *not* been playing him, not been working some angle? Rory had been too ashamed, too afraid, to knock on the door and ask. But the next morning he'd made sure to seek Tate out to thank him for breakfast, and his smile seemed so genuine, so entirely without artifice, that Rory had felt guilty for most of the day.

Maybe Tate really did want to do a good job. Maybe his apology and his promise had been just as genuine as his smile. And if that was the case, was the blowjob genuine too? You couldn't fake that kind of enthusiasm, could you? Well, not unless you were a practiced whore, he supposed. But practiced whores didn't cry over being rejected, did they? Which meant . . .

Rory kicking Tate out of his bed like that had been a cruel and unnecessary rejection of a man who had genuinely wanted him. Hard to believe, maybe, but it was the only thing that made sense.

No wonder Tate had been so upset.

"Do you need anything else?" Tate asked the next morning after serving Rory his coffee, already half turning away because Rory never did.

"Actually . . ."

Tate spun back, expectant. His eyes had lit up, and there was even a smile tugging at the corners of his soft, pouty mouth.

Rory, unable to face that expression any longer, averted his eyes and just blurted it out. "So, Mr. Lowell has his speech today, the one I wrote for him." He wrinkled his nose. "There's no way he isn't going to knock it out of the park, so he thinks we should do something to celebrate all our hard work and . . . well, he's kind of invited himself here. In a nice way, I mean. He's also invited Aaron and Zac and Ruth." He looked worriedly at Tate.

Tate's smile grew, his pretty face lighting up. "What do you want me to do, Rory?"

"We could get takeout," he suggested.

"Let me make something," Tate said. "Let me try, please. You can't feed your boss takeout. Not if he's coming for dinner."

"O-okay," he said, a little taken aback by Tate's enthusiasm. "Like to cook, do you? What do you suggest?"

"It makes me feel useful," Tate replied, which wasn't exactly an answer to Rory's question, but oh well. "I've been learning. Practicing. I think if I can pull off a nice roast; it would make a good impression for you."

"I don't know . . ." Rory shrugged. "I mean, are you sure you know what you're doing?"

Tate nodded. "I'd like the chance to prove myself."

Something about the stubborn tilt of Tate's chin impressed Rory. "Okay. I'll leave it in your capable hands, then. So tonight, six o'clock?"

"Six o'clock," Tate said. Then his stubbornness vanished, his expression softened, and he bit his lip almost shyly. He stepped forward. "Thank you, Rory."

Rory flushed, drawing back from him slightly. "Don't thank *me*, you're the one doing all the work."

Tate nodded and smiled. He dropped his gaze. "Still. Thank you for giving me a chance. I won't disappoint you again."

Again? Rory's face burned. The aborted blowjob. As though he needed another reminder of that. It was bad enough looking at Tate's face and seeing those lips stretched around his cock every single time. "I'm not, um, I'm not keeping score or anything, you know. And you haven't disappointed me."

Confused the shit out of me, maybe.

Tate seemed pleased.

"Okay, so I'll see you tonight." Rory grabbed his bag and left before he felt the urge to say something else and probably ruin both their good moods.

It felt wonderful to work hard for Rory. Tate cleaned the entire house, paying special attention to the dining room and the bathroom. He didn't want Rory's guests to think that he wasn't doing a good job. He especially didn't want them to think that Rory was doing a bad job managing his rezzy. After cleaning, Tate went to the grocery store. The staff there still glanced at his wristbands curiously, but Tate had told them solemnly on his first visit that he'd punched a man and he was very sorry, and now they treated him kindly enough.

Even though he'd been there numerous times now, he still stared at the shelves with a mix of wonder and horror. Wonder because he'd never seen such plenty, and horror because he didn't know what to choose when there were so many options. Not the fault of the chip, he knew, but because he was an outsider. There had been no stores like this in Tate's old neighborhood. Just a twenty-four-hour convenience store with half-empty shelves. And the soup kitchen line, of course, but that was before Tophet's government had cut Tate's benefits as a part of the No Handouts for Crims bill.

No fresh food. No *choice*. Tate hadn't even known there were so many different kinds of milk. He'd only ever seen the powdered stuff before Beulah. Tate was so very lucky to be here.

So lucky.

So grateful.

So happy.

"Well," Lowell said as he arrived, "something smells divine!"

"That would be me," Ruth told him with a laugh, and Zac snorted.

Ruth and Zac. The lawyers Lowell had handpicked for his department, and after working with them for the week, Rory knew why. They were both dedicated, ambitious, whip smart and, most importantly, untainted by professional jealousy. They worked well together, a brilliant team.

"And you must be Tate," Lowell said, holding out his hand.

Tate shook it. "Pleased to meet you, sir."

"You'll be joining us for dinner, I hope." Lowell smiled at him. "If Rory agrees, of course."

"Of course," Rory said, gratified. He'd been worried there might be some awkwardness with Tate. If Rory hadn't yet figured out how he fit into his life, then how would the others react? He was glad to see them taking their lead from Lowell and shaking Tate's hand.

"You still don't have any pictures up," Aaron commented, stepping inside. "It looks like you only moved in today!"

"I haven't had time to take any yet," Rory told him.

"You should go to the North Lakes on the weekend. If you like ducks." Aaron straightened his tie. "The sunsets are really beautiful there. They'd make a nice picture."

"Let the man decorate in his own time, Aaron," Lowell chided him.

"It's a good idea," Rory said. "I'd love to see more of Beulah. I don't have a decent camera, though."

"You can borrow mine," Aaron said. "Wow, dinner *does* smell nice! I hope it tastes half as good!"

"Tate's learning to cook." Rory cast him a proud look. It really did smell amazing.

Lowell clapped Rory on the back. "See? Already his restitution duties are fostering a new skill set."

Tate smiled, his face lighting up with pleasure. "Would anyone care for some wine?"

Rory relaxed. No, there was no need for awkwardness at all. He should have known that. His colleagues were good people, open and friendly, and not prejudiced. Nobody here thought that Tate was less of a man because he'd committed a crime. No, that had just been Rory, bringing his outside prejudices in.

Tate had already proven to everyone else that he was taking his restitution seriously, that he wanted to get better and earn people's trust. And like the good and honest people they were, the citizens of Beulah were welcoming him with open arms. Now all Rory needed to do was follow suit.

And it was hard not to be impressed with Tate. He'd chosen a good wine to go with dinner, and dinner itself was great. Hell, Rory had never tasted anything so delicious. The roast was perfect, not too dry, and Tate had made some sort of sauce, as well, although Rory didn't know what it was. He'd even baked fresh bread. Rory felt more than ever like Beulah truly was paradise. He could never have imagined that one day he'd be eating a meal like this, surrounded by friends like these. They talked and laughed and joked, and even Tate was smiling and looking relaxed.

"That was perfection," Lowell announced. "Marvelous. I really ought to invite myself to dinner more often, Rory, if Tate will cook every time!"

Tate flushed at the praise, his smile widening.

"You need to get married, sir," Aaron grinned. "And stop eating takeout."

Lowell raised his eyebrows. "Are you offering, Aaron?"

Aaron blushed all the way to his ears. "Um . . . no, sir!"

Rory was pleased to see that Lowell was teasing Aaron again. Ever since he'd been brusque with him the other day, Aaron hadn't been himself. It was obvious that he worshipped Lowell and he'd been upset that Lowell had been short with him. And whatever had been bothering Lowell enough to take it out on his eager intern, it seemed to have passed, as well.

"I made dessert too," Tate volunteered.

"Ah, then let's have at it!" Lowell patted his slight paunch. "And is that another bottle of red I see on the counter?"

Tate stood up. "Let me get it for you, sir."

"Nonsense. You get the dessert, Aaron will get the wine." Lowell raised his eyebrows. "Aaron?"

"I'm on it, sir," Aaron said, giving the man a mock salute.

Rory laughed.

"Oh, he is the best intern ever," Ruth said under her breath as Aaron headed for the kitchen. "Nothing's too much trouble."

Zac rolled his eyes. "Except sitting still in court. He's like a puppy."

"Hush now," Lowell said. "Enthusiasm's no bad thing."

"No, but if his tongue starts hanging out, you're going to have some explaining to do."

Lowell roared with laughter.

"What?" Aaron asked, setting the wine on the table. "What did I miss?"

Lowell reached out and tugged Aaron down onto his lap. "Nothing at all, my boy."

"Um." Aaron smiled awkwardly, his face flushed. "Okay. I think, um, I'm going to have to stand up to pour the wine, though."

He squirmed a little, trying to pull himself up, but Lowell just tightened his grip. "Nonsense. That's what Tate's here for. You've run yourself ragged today; you deserve a little fun time."

Rory glanced at Ruth and Zac to find that they were suddenly looking somewhere else. Shit. So Lowell got a little handsy when he was drunk. A little too handsy. At the moment, one of his hands was tucked into Aaron's jeans. And Aaron looked petrified.

"Aaron, I think Tate needs a hand in the kitchen," Rory said, his gaze fixed on Lowell. *Please don't make this a big thing.*

Lowell laughed and let Aaron go. Maybe he hadn't realized he was being inappropriate, and all it took was a gentle reminder. He was still a good man, Rory told himself. Good men were allowed to have faults, especially when they were gracious about having them pointed out.

Aaron headed for the kitchen, face bright red.

Nobody scolded Lowell for what he'd done. Nobody even commented on it.

"I won't stay for dessert," Ruth said, standing. "I've got an early deposition tomorrow. Thanks for having me, Rory. Thanks, Tate!"

"I'll give you a lift," Zac said.

"Thanks for coming," Rory said, seeing them to the door.

Aaron was still hiding in the kitchen when he returned to the table. Lowell poured himself a generous glass of wine.

"So tell me," Lowell said, leveling his twinkling gaze on Rory. "Have you availed yourself of Tate's *other* services yet?"

"O-other services, sir?"

"Two healthy young men living in close quarters, and one of them so very, very enthusiastic about his placement?" He shrugged and leaned back into his chair with a chuckle. "Ah well, I suppose the two of you have seven years to give in to your baser desires, don't you? All good things in time."

Oh God, he thinks I'm going to have sex with Tate. Have had sex. Am having sex. Rory flushed hot. "Isn't that a little unethical, sir? What with me being in a position of authority?"

"Of course not! Not if he's willing. Not if he approaches you, especially. It's not like he stands to gain or lose anything by it, after all. His position here is safe and secure regardless." He took a slow sip of his wine. "All I'm saying is, if that's something you do want, there's no need to threaten him for it or make yourself feel guilty over it. Make yourself available and I think you'll find him only too happy to play along."

"He, uh—" Rory flushed, wondering if he should really admit it, considering Lowell's earlier behavior. On the other hand, it would be nice to have someone as respectable and educated as Lowell soothe his conscience on the whole thing. "He actually already *has*, sir. Sort of."

Lowell slapped his palm against the surface of the table with a roaring laugh. "That's what I like to hear! And you enjoyed it?"

"I actually, um, I actually put a stop to it. I didn't think it was appropriate at the time, especially since, well, I couldn't be sure he wasn't playing me."

"Oh, Rory. You need to be more trusting. Tate's a good man. He likes you. You're attractive and fit and pleasant. Of course he'd want to explore that option with you. Really, isn't seven years with a lover so much better than seven years with a stuffy, by-the-books sponsor?"

That was true.

"My advice is, enjoy his company. Cut yourself some slack and stop worrying and just *trust the system*. Tate obviously does. He wants to enjoy himself and take advantage of this opportunity."

"But . . ." Rory rubbed his hand over his forehead. Could it really be that simple? "But what if I met someone? Someone else."

Lowell swallowed another mouthful of wine. "You're a strange bunch, you outsiders. Why deny yourself a bit of fun and friendship now, just on the off chance you'll meet someone in the future? Relax, Rory, and worry about crossing that bridge when you get to it."

Well, shit. Maybe it really was that simple after all.

Or maybe it was the wine talking.

"God, I don't know," he groaned. "I think I've had way too much to drink to be thinking logically right now."

Lowell laughed. "How's that dessert coming, boys?"

Rory couldn't help noticing that Aaron walked the other way around the table this time.

"I'm sorry that Ruth and Zac couldn't stay," Tate said. "If there's enough left over, maybe you could take some into work tomorrow, Rory?"

"I will, thanks," Rory said. He blushed when he saw Tate's answering smile.

"Don't count on leftovers," Lowell warned him. "Tate, you're a marvel!"

"All this time I had a hidden talent!" Tate agreed.

"And just think, Rory, if not for the restitution program, he'd have never discovered this side of himself. Isn't it amazing, the wonderful things we are capable of awakening in a man?"

"Y-yeah," Rory said, looking at Tate with new eyes.

Tate looked *happy*. The smile curving his generous lips was genuine, and his eyes were bright. He didn't look at all like the kind of guy who could attack a stranger . . . Rory killed the thought. No. He was the only one still judging Tate by that. And if he kept doing it, he'd be the one who undermined Tate's chances at rehabilitation. All Rory had to do was trust and believe.

Not such a hard thing as he watched Tate smiling and gathering up armloads of plates, laughing at Lowell's jokes. Rory's own prejudices were more dangerous than Tate's history.

Well, not anymore.

"Let me drive you home, sir," Aaron said. "You're in no condition to walk. It's no trouble." He tried to smile, but the kid was still a little bit shaken. He was trying nobly to push through it, though. Tate admired him for that.

Aaron carried a plate over into the kitchen, and Rory followed him.

"Are you sure?" Rory asked, his voice pitched low with concern.

Tate began to fill the sink.

"Yeah." Aaron smiled. "He's just a bit tipsy, that's all. I can handle him."

"Okay," Rory said.

Tate liked—*loved*—that about Rory. He worried about people. It was nice. It was nice to know that there were people like that in the world, and Tate was honored to have one as his master. He didn't deserve Rory, but he could spend the next seven years trying to be worthy of him. And he wanted it, more than he'd ever wanted anything in his life.

"Goodnight, Tate!" Lowell called from the dining room.

"Goodnight, sir." Tate smiled at the sight of Aaron trying to help the man into his coat.

"See you tomorrow, Rory," Aaron said from somewhere under Lowell's arm. "Bye, Tate."

Soon, they were gone, and Tate was left to clean up the imposing stack of dishes they'd left.

A sign of a successful meal. Tate was proud of that. It would probably take all night to get through this stack, but he'd do it, and he'd be happy. He'd made Rory happy, and that was all that mattered now. He settled the first of the plates in the sink and began to wash them.

He jolted when a warm, firm shoulder nudged his own. Rory, having shed his buttoned shirt in favor of a soft white undershirt, was standing next to him, drying and stacking plates.

"Oh no!" Tate protested. "Oh no no no no no, you don't need to do that, please. Please, go relax. I'll take care of things here."

"No way. You slaved away"—something in Tate twinged—"all day in here and made me and my boss an amazing meal. Least I can do is dry some plates. It's no trouble, really." He knocked their hips together. "And anyway, I was thinking . . . I was thinking maybe we could talk. Get to know each other."

"R-really?"

"Yeah. Look, I'm sorry for the way I've been acting around you. I'm just not used to all this, you know? You've taken to it so well and here I am, ten steps behind." He laughed self-consciously. "But I see that you're trying really hard to make it work, and I want to try too."

His praise warmed Tate. "I *am* trying, Rory. But you haven't done anything wrong. I mean, it's—" *The chip. It's the chip.* His skull pounded. "—it's different here."

Rory smiled, crinkles appearing at the corners of his eyes. "God, you can say that again!"

A joke. Rory was joking with him. Tate laughed, and it felt so good to laugh. Tonight had been perfect, more than he could ever have hoped for. Rory *liked* him.

"I never cooked before I got here," Tate volunteered. "I mean, there was no kitchen in my place. Just a hot plate I heated cans on."

"I had a microwave," Rory said.

"Oh! A *rich* man!"

Rory burst out laughing, and warmth spread through Tate.

When the last plate had been cleaned, dried, and stacked away, Rory stretched. "Want to watch a movie?"

"Yes," Tate said eagerly. So many nights going to bed alone, lying awake on that narrow mattress and listening to Rory watch television or make himself coffee, wishing he could go out and talk to him, have some company, *beg him for help*, just get to know him. And now it was finally happening. "Please."

He was surprised and gratified when they went into the living room and Rory made space for him on the couch. He'd never sat on it before, not even during the day when Rory was at work. It seemed presumptuous. If he was done with his chores and wanted to sit, he either found a place on the floor or he went to his room and sat on his bed. The furniture was Rory's.

Tate sat perfectly still, perfectly upright, with his hands folded in his lap. He stared at the TV screen but didn't see it. He was too aware of Rory sitting beside him, and of the heat where their thighs touched. He wanted desperately to lean toward Rory, to relax against him, but he didn't dare.

The movie was dumb. A dumb comedy, but Tate found himself smiling a little, and once he even snorted and Rory laughed. When Tate turned to look at him, embarrassed, Rory's face softened. "You did really well tonight."

"Thank you." The praise was electric. He turned toward Rory, leaning into him, unable to articulate what he wanted but needing to get closer. He wanted Rory. He wanted Rory to want him. Tate swiped his tongue over his bottom lip.

Rory sighed and slipped an arm around his waist. "Are you sure, Tate?"

Tate turned toward him. He'd never been so sure. "Yes," he whispered.

Rory's face was drawn with worry. "Because I don't want to, like, pressure you, or—"

Tate kissed him. Kissed a man. His master.

A sudden flare of pain in his skull. *What the fuck are you* doing? *You don't even like men. You shouldn't be making out, you should be trying to get the hell out of here.*

But God, Rory tasted so good. Like dessert. The dessert he'd made but hadn't eaten because it wasn't for him. He didn't deserve nice things like that, and anyway, he needed to keep himself slim and fit and attractive. Needed to be everything Rory wanted.

He shivered as Rory's tongue pressed against the seam of his lips and opened it. His entire body was alight, pleasure building on itself over and over again. Not the kiss, not just the kiss, but the sheer wondrous delight of being Rory's. Of giving himself to Rory, and

Rory taking him. Tate was being so *good*. He hadn't felt this much pleasure since the doctor's office.

Would Rory like that? Would Rory like to see his blood? His cock? Would Rory like to see him crawl?

He'd do anything.

And if Rory just wanted this—soft, gentle kisses—then Tate wanted it, as well. He sank back into the couch, letting Rory climb on top of him, letting Rory deepen the kiss with low, eager moans and a possessive sweep of his tongue.

Possessive, yes. That was what Tate wanted, to be possessed.

This time, he'd let Rory dictate the pace. He'd let Rory take control. The blowjob had been a mess, had gone all wrong because Tate had tried to take the lead and go somewhere Rory wasn't ready to go yet. Tate knew better now.

Rory slid a hand up underneath Tate's shirt. He kissed along his jaw for a moment. "Do you want to . . .?"

Tate arched toward him. "Yes!"

Anything. Yes.

Rory pulled back and stared into Tate's eyes. "Are you sure?"

Tate nodded. "I'm sure."

Rory rubbed his abdomen. "Okay. But this couch isn't very comfortable. Come to my room?"

"Yes," Tate said, his stomach twisting. That voice locked away in the back of his head was suddenly *screaming*. Screaming a thousand things. Fear. Anger. Disgust. Hatred. But none of them could even translate into a sound. Tate only had one word for Rory. One, single, heartfelt word. "Yes."

CHAPTER
EIGHT

Tate's hands shook as he undid his zipper. He kept his back to Rory, just for the moment. Because he wanted this, he wanted it more than anything, but the fear was there too, creeping into his mind. Bringing that voice with it.

Run. Just run.

Or tell him. Tell him about the chip.

His head felt like it was splitting open.

Or just let him fuck you. Let him fuck you, and you'll be so happy.

Yes. There was the voice it didn't hurt to hear. The one he actually wanted to listen to.

He slipped his pants and underwear down and immediately felt hands cupping his hips, a still-clothed groin pressing against his exposed ass. Rory groaned. "God, you're gorgeous."

His praise chased Tate's fear away, for just a moment.

"Please," Tate whispered. *Please keep saying nice things. Please make it stop. Please make me happy.*

"God. Turn around so I can look at you."

Tate did. Didn't even cover himself, even though some part of him insisted that he should. His cock curved upward, begging for a stroke. His chest heaved. Rory rubbed his shoulders, nudging their mouths together for another gentle kiss.

"You seem nervous," Rory said.

Terrified, actually. Tearing myself apart.

"Let me help."

Help. Fucking help! Yes, help me!

Tate nodded, gave him another little kiss on the chin followed by a playful nip.

Another kiss. This one took the edge off his rising panic, and then Tate couldn't even say why he was scared. This was Rory; Rory wanted it, and whatever Rory wanted was for the best. He *knew* that. He knew that with absolute certainty.

And then Rory lowered himself to his knees—*his* knees!—and pressed an open-mouthed kiss right to the tip of Tate's cock.

No man had *ever* touched him that way before. Revulsion and desire rose up in him side by side. It felt good, but it also felt *wrong*. Wrong because Rory was a man, and wrong because it should have been Tate on his knees. Because Rory shouldn't do the dishes or share the couch or suck Tate's cock.

Tate put his hands on Rory's shoulders and tried to push him away. "Let's just . . . just . . . Fuck me, please. Just fuck me."

Rory looked up at him, his dark eyes huge and his black eyebrows furrowed. "You don't like it?" he asked and sat back on his heels. He kept his hand wrapped around the base of Tate's cock, and Tate couldn't help but thrust into it, and what was more, he didn't know if that urge was because of the chip or because of his own need.

"No! I do, I do, of course I do. I . . . *love* . . . everything you want to do to me." *That's a lie, oh God, it's all a lie. Help me. Don't touch me, help me.*

Rory's eyes twinkled. "Now how could you possibly know that? You have no idea what I want. What if I want something twisted, huh?"

I would want that too. No matter what. If you wanted to piss on me or fuck me with your fist or dress me up as a girl, whatever twisted thing you could dream up, I would want it. I want all of it. The chip makes me want it.

"I want . . . I want . . ." He slammed a hand to his forehead as white pain sliced through his skull. "Rory, I want you to fuck me now."

"O-okay." Rory rose to his feet. He held Tate by the hips and walked him backward to the bed. "So eager!"

Tate's knees hit the mattress, and he sprawled back onto the bed. "Yes."

"How long has it been?" Rory asked, pulling his shirt off.

Tate stared at his muscles. He was broad. Stockier than Tate. "Wh-what?"

Rory fumbled with his belt. "How long has it been? Since you made love? How much prep do you need?"

"I've . . ." He couldn't tell the truth. Couldn't. Whether it was because he knew Rory expected him to be experienced, and he didn't want to disappoint him or because of some defense mechanism built into the chip, he couldn't admit this was his first time. Couldn't admit that he was scared and that a part of him was still screaming that he didn't want this. He needed to be what Rory wanted him to be, so he compromised. "It's been a while."

"Okay," Rory said. "We'll take it nice and slow."

Tate curled his fingers into Rory's sheets and nodded. "Yes, please, Rory."

Rory stripped. He'd always been a little self-conscious about . . . not his body, but the required level of intimacy it took to display it in front of a relative stranger. Tate had been nervous as well, but he'd turned around when Rory had asked, so he felt he had no right to be modest when it was his turn. Of course, there was the added pressure that Tate was so beautiful. The lean, golden lines of him, laid out on the bed. He was like something out of a fantasy, or at least out of one of Rory's favorite skin mags.

Rory, by comparison, was broader and less defined, with paler skin that wasn't nearly as rich and luminous a brown.

He crossed to his dresser and pulled open the top drawer. Found the lube he'd brought from the outside, half a tube left even though he'd had it for ages. For much longer than he wanted to admit. He found a box of condoms as well and had to check the expiration date.

"I'm clean," Tate said. "I'm clean, Rory."

Rory hesitated. "They checked you?"

Tate nodded. "It's in my records."

Sure. It probably was. Rory hadn't been able to bring himself to look at the entire file he'd been sent, not after reading the clinical details of his own assault. But how did Tate know that Rory was clean? He was, of course; they'd tested him as a part of his immigration requirements. But *he* didn't have a file, or at least not one Tate could access. It seemed an awful lot to take on trust.

"Me too," he said and put the condoms back. "So, um, it's okay?"

"Yes." There was a note of longing in Tate's voice. "Whatever you want."

Rory closed the drawer and returned to the bed. He hesitated, and then saw that Tate was shivering. He climbed onto the bed beside him and put an arm around Tate. Drew him close for a gentle kiss and felt his breath shuddering against his lips. "If you're uncomfortable, we can still use the condom. Or we don't have to do it at all. We can just kiss some more, or we can go back and just watch the movie—"

"No! I want this. Please." Tate wriggled against him. He got a hand between their bodies and slid it down. Curled it around Rory's cock. "Put it in me."

Jesus. Nobody had ever spoken to him that way before.

"Please, please." Tate was *begging*. He rolled onto his back, spreading his thighs and tilting his pelvis up. "Please!"

"Just . . . just wait," Rory gasped.

Tate bit his lip. "On my stomach instead? On my hands and knees?"

Rory straddled Tate's hips and held his fluttering hands down. "No, this is good. But just wait. We're taking it slow, remember?"

"I can't, I can't. I can't wait, I—" But then Tate nodded, his eyes owlishly wide. He seemed to subside a little, to relax into the mattress.

Rory stroked his face. "That's it. Deep breath. You'll get what you want from me."

Tate's breath hitched, and he jerked his head before lying still again. "Yes."

Rory moved back, kneeling in the space that had opened up between Tate's thighs. He fumbled in the sheets for the lube, and opened it. He spread the gel over his fingers, warming it.

God, Tate was lovely. That smooth skin, that hard cock that curved upward, not a lot of hair. And the way he opened himself to Rory's touch . . . He flinched a little as Rory ran a slick finger behind his balls, searching for his hole.

"Cold?" Rory asked.

"Wh—" Tate swallowed. "No."

Rory pressed his finger inside slightly, and Tate's shoulders lifted off the mattress. He stifled a whimper. Rory tried rubbing gentling circles on Tate's lower abdomen, drawing his fingertip out until it was just barely penetrating. Tate was tight. He hadn't been exaggerating when he said it had been a while. Rory waited until he relaxed again, and pushed his finger back inside. He went deeper this time, twisting, searching . . . and smiled when Tate's hiss told him he'd found the right spot.

"I'm ready," Tate gasped.

"You aren't," Rory told him firmly. He wanted to open him properly first, to hear him beg again before he even tried to fuck him. He withdrew his finger, got more lube, and this time returned two fingers to Tate's entrance. He pushed them in.

Tate made a strangled noise and squeezed his eyes shut. When he opened them again, they were bright with tears. "Feels . . . feels g-*good*."

Rory felt overwhelmed as well. He'd almost forgotten what it was like to do this, to share this with someone. Too many lonely, solitary nights when he'd desperately wanted someone to hold, to touch. To make fall apart, like Tate was falling apart now.

Tate rocked his hips slightly, finding the start of a faltering rhythm. "More. Please, more."

Rory scissored his fingers, and Tate cried out. His cock was leaking now, shiny with pre-cum. Rory took his free hand from Tate's abdomen and stroked his cock. Tate whimpered with pleasure, thrusting up into Rory's hand.

"Please, Rory, now. Please, now!"

He'd never met or experienced someone so hungry for pleasure, so greedy, so willing to let his desperation show. Tate didn't hide anything. It made Rory feel powerful, to be the one to bring him there, to be the only one capable of satisfying that bone-deep need. He withdrew his fingers and pushed Tate's thighs wider apart. He lifted them and pushed them back, so that Tate's spine curled a little, and then shuffled forward so he was in position. "This might hurt," he said. "Impatient boy."

"I like it when it hurts," Tate said, his eyes dark.

Rory lined the head of his cock up against Tate's hole. He'd never done this without a condom before. Strange, how different it felt. How much more heated. Or maybe that feeling was because it was with *Tate*, condom or no. He pressed in.

Shit. So tight.

Tate's body arched, as tight as a bowstring. He cried out, clutching at the sheets, his eyes wide. "Hurts, hurts. *Hurts*."

Rory faltered.

Tate reached up to grip his arms. "More!"

The urge to conquer, to fill him, to make Tate *take it*, was strong. It took everything he had not to pin Tate to the bed and shove in hard enough to shut his begging up. Rory didn't know how much of it was just the sex going to his head or how much was leftover anger toward Tate. Either way, it was hardly the gentle, considerate lovemaking he'd planned for Tate. "I don't know . . ."

Because he didn't want to hurt him, not like this.

Tate lifted one hand to Rory's face, carding his fingers through Rory's hair. His eyes were wide, desperate. "More!"

"Okay!" Rory leaned down to capture Tate's mouth in a kiss, and Tate moaned. Squirmed underneath him as though he didn't know what the hell he wanted. Rory pushed further inside him, and Tate's breathing grew ragged. He dropped his head down onto the mattress, squeezing his eyes shut. A tear escaped the corner of his eye.

It was intense. Tate was intense. Rory kissed him again, gently, and Tate sucked in a deep breath. Opened his eyes and stared up at him again.

"You don't have to do this," Rory said.

Tate's brow furrowed, and his mouth twisted in a grimace. "But I do! I do! You don't understand, you don't—" He tossed his head, as if in pain. "I need this. Please, I need it."

God. Something wasn't right here, but Rory pushed it to the back of his mind. Tate wanted him, was begging for him, and he wrapped his legs around Rory to draw him further in. So what if Tate was hurting? He said he liked to hurt. So what if it wasn't sweet and gentle like Rory had wanted? Tate was hot and tight and whimpering eagerly as Rory thrust forward.

Rory leaned back for better leverage and pumped his hips.

Tate's fingers scrabbled in the sheets again, the bands on his wrists shifting as he writhed.

"All the way in," Rory said, rubbing Tate's lower abdomen again. His cock was soft against his belly, its head still wet with pre-cum. Tate's muscles clung to him, spasming as they adjusted to his girth and length. "You're so tight."

Tate bit his lip, panting.

Rory withdrew slightly, then thrust back inside. Tate arched up off the mattress.

"That's it," Rory moaned. "You're good, aren't you? You're so good to me. So good at taking my dick. Can you see? Look and see."

Tate's eyes popped open, and he frantically lifted his head, trying to see the spot where their bodies joined. Where Rory's hips were pressed flush to Tate's ass.

"Oh . . . oh God." His voice hitched. He shook his head. "Oh fuck." He stared up into Rory's face. "Is it good? Are you happy?"

Weird thing to ask, but balls-deep inside Tate? Rory was fucking ecstatic. "It's so good, Tate. You like it?"

Tate clenched his fists. "Y-yes!"

Rory began to move, making smooth, strong thrusts, each one bringing a strangled gasp from Tate's open mouth. Rory couldn't look at his face—to watch him would be to come too soon. He leaned over Tate, bracing his weight on his arms, driving into him again and again. Tate was hard now, his cock sandwiched between them, in the close, slippery heat of their bodies. His heels dug into Rory's ass, urging him forward every time. Wanting it faster, harder. Even though it hurt him. Even though he had no reason to want this from Rory. No reason except convenience, probably.

No. He couldn't think like that or he wouldn't be able to keep up the pace. Keep his erection, period. Tate wanted him. Tate wanted him. Tate wanted him. The noises he was making, small and desperate, *needy*, proved that.

"Tate," Rory ground out, "I'm gonna come!"

Tate moaned. "Do it. Come in me!"

Come. Come. Come in him. His brain shorted out thinking of that, thinking of owning Tate that way, filling him with cum, no barriers. The thought of it—his cum in Tate's ass—was enough to push him over the edge. His hips jerked as he came, hard. He reached down and gripped Tate's cock as he rode it out, his nerves on fire.

"Come on," he groaned. "Come on, Tate."

"M-m—" Tate rolled his head back and forth on the mattress.

More, Rory thought. *More.*

But that wasn't the word Tate cried out as he came, hot and sticky in Rory's hand. His eyes wide, his body shaking, Tate opened his mouth, fixed his burning gaze on Rory, and screamed, "*Master*!"

Clean.

He wouldn't be clean again.

Tate winced as he ran the washcloth over his ass.

Never be clean.

"Tate?" Rory was knocking on the bathroom door. Still. "Tate?"

He should have been happy, but if he was happy, why was he crying? The shower washed his tears away, but they kept coming. Why wasn't he happy? Hadn't the doctor told him? Hadn't the doctor told him next time no tears?

And yet they just kept coming.

A gush of Rory's cum escaped him, drizzling down his inner thighs, and the tears got worse. He hiccuped. Sobbed.

Rory's knocking got stronger. "Are you okay in there? Are you hurt? Did I hurt you?"

Tate crouched, trying to smother the sound, trying to ease the deep pain inside him.

The chip. The fucking chip. If he had to have it, couldn't it work *properly*? Couldn't it make him happy? Happy to let a man fuck him, hurt him, come deep inside him and claim him.

"Tate, I'm coming in!"

Tate stood quickly. Shit, it hurt, too. He winced and braced himself against the shower wall. He didn't want Rory to see that he was hurt. Rory wouldn't like that. Rory didn't deserve that. Tate was the one at fault here, the one broken, the one with the thing in his head that wasn't working the way it should. He drew a deep breath, the water running off the end of his nose, and tried to calm himself. He needed Rory to be happy with him now more than ever. He didn't think he could handle another setback. Another gut-twisting failure. Another visit with the men in the van, who'd come that first day when Rory was away at work and made Tate swear not to tell.

They'd destroy what was left of him.

But wouldn't that be better? Wouldn't it be *easier*? Maybe they could make it stop hurting for good.

"Tate?" Rory pulled aside the shower curtain, letting the steam escape. His face was bright red. "Are you okay? I didn't want to intrude, but . . ."

But he was worried. He was a good man.

A ball of frustration formed in Tate's stomach. He didn't need a good man; he needed a master.

"I'm okay," he said, his voice even. He couldn't tell if he was still crying or not. He willed the chip to make this right, to make him calm. "I think . . . I think I just pushed myself too fast, too hard."

Rory tsked. "I knew I should have gone easier on you. I'm sorry. Are you sore?" And then, without warning, he climbed into the shower alongside Tate, drawing the curtain behind him. His gentle hands closed around Tate's shoulders, rubbing them in small circles.

"A little."

Rory kissed his back, right between his shoulder blades where the hot water sluiced down the indent over his spine. "I'm—" another kiss, this time lower "—sorry." Another. "So—" another "—sorry."

Tate warmed with pleasure. With guilt, too. "Don't say that. Please, don't say that."

It wasn't right that Rory should apologize for hurting him, or for anything. Rory was supposed to take what he wanted, to *demand* it, and it was supposed to make Tate feel good. So why didn't he feel good?

Rory had lowered himself to his knees. Hands on Tate's hips now, and he turned Tate's body until they were facing each other. He pressed his kisses to Tate's thighs. Gently scrubbed his hands over them, over Tate's groin and back, softly down the cleft of his ass, which was still so tender and puffy but somehow soothed by Rory's touch. Then squinted up at him through the shower spray. "What you said . . . master. Where did that come from?"

"I . . ." From the chip. From the core of his being. Tate didn't fucking know. He couldn't think, either, not with Rory's lips making trails across his sensitive flesh again. "I don't know."

Rory looked disappointed now. The kisses stopped. He picked up Tate's discarded washcloth and began to sweep it over Tate's skin, perfunctory. "You don't know? Really? Because you say that, but your expression says different."

Lying. He's accusing you of lying to him.

"It felt . . . it felt right," Tate managed.

"I don't want you to think of me like that," Rory said. "That's not what this program is about, and . . . and I want us to be friends. Can we do that?"

I hit you. You fucked me. How can we be friends?

"I think," Tate began tentatively, "I mean, in my head . . ." No. Dangerous. It would hurt. He pushed his thoughts away from the chip and back to safer ground. "I want that too."

He's touching you like he owns *you.*

He fucked you and came inside you and fucking bred you like he owns you.

Hit him. Hit him again. Do it fucking properly this time, so he never gets up.

Thoughts of blood. Of pain.

Blood on his hands. His hard cock. Jerking off for the doctor with his own blood, soaked in blood and abject humiliation.

No. No no no.

Tate dropped down onto his knees. Cupped Rory's chin in his hands.

I don't want to hurt you. Not ever. You are *my master. You* do *own me. That's okay. You'll take care of me. You'll help. You'll help me get better. You'll help me serve you. You'll help. Me.*

"Help . . . me."

White pain pierced Tate's skull. His vision blurred, his chest tightened, and he crashed forward into Rory's arms.

Gone.

CHAPTER
NINE

ory hadn't known what to do, or who to contact, when Tate had collapsed. He'd called Lowell, hoping he could recommend a doctor or tell him where the closest hospital was—anything. But ten minutes later, Lowell had been knocking on the front door. He'd been drunk only a few hours ago at their dinner, but it was obvious his concern for Tate had sobered him right up.

"I think he had some kind of fit or something," Rory said, looking down at Tate's sleeping form, covered in a sheet. His small bed was so narrow and uncomfortable that Rory had laid Tate down in his own instead. "I think he was hurting. He asked me to help him, and then he just collapsed."

Lowell made a worried face.

"It couldn't be his chip, could it? I mean, he had a full health checkup, right? He was healthy? No epilepsy or anything?" *No STIs. I fucked him without a condom. He let me do that.* "But if he's fainting, it must be in his head. Are those chips safe?"

"Of course they are," Lowell replied. "The technology here is so much better than what you've encountered in the outside world. And the modifications are really so tiny there's almost no risk that it would cause any kind of side effects."

Rory nodded, still worried.

"It might be something as simple as stress," Lowell said. He moved forward and put his hand on Tate's forehead. "I'll bet he worked himself ragged preparing dinner tonight, didn't he? But I've called the medical team from the restitution program just in case, and they're sending someone over."

Rory glanced at the clock. "It's three in the morning!"

"Don't worry about that." Lowell smiled. "Tate's health and safety is their priority twenty-four hours a day. If a rezzy gets so much as a splinter, they'll come and check it out."

Rory drew a deep breath. That was a little reassuring. So now if Tate would only wake up . . . "I'll, um, have to get that number. Put it on the fridge or something."

"Stop hovering like a worried wet nurse," Lowell said, his tone indulgent. "He's breathing, he's comfortable, and he'll be just fine."

Except how could Lowell know that? What if Tate had an aneurysm or if he was bleeding internally for some reason? What if it looked like he was sleeping but he was actually dying? Rory couldn't tell the difference, and he was pretty sure Lowell couldn't, either.

Rory pinched the bridge of his nose and flinched—still tender. Okay, so Lowell was just trying to stop him from worrying or, worse, panicking. Even if Tate had had an aneurysm, what would Rory's worry do for it that Lowell's calmness wouldn't?

"Does your nose still hurt?"

"A little."

Lowell nodded to the painkillers sitting on the bedside table. "Take your meds, Rory. It does me no good to watch you suffer needlessly."

Rory sighed and picked up the small bottle. "They make me drowsy."

"They're supposed to," Lowell said. "When you rest, your body repairs itself. Which is what Tate's is doing now, I'm sure. Sit down beside him and hold his hand. It will do him good, I'm sure, to know you're here."

Rory swallowed two of the pills and sat. Then he laced his fingers through Tate's and wiped his damp hair back from his forehead with his free hand. Tate sighed and shifted. He opened his eyes.

"Wh-what happened?" His confused gaze shifted from Rory to Lowell.

"You fainted," Lowell told him. "Don't worry, the medical team is on the way."

Tate's eyes widened. His mouth moved soundlessly, like he was trying to say something but couldn't find the words. At last, he managed, "Fainted?"

Lowell patted his arm. "You worked hard today, Tate, didn't you?"

Tate glanced quickly at Rory and then back again. "Yes, sir."

"See?" Lowell said. "He's just overextended. I suppose your former life of petty crime didn't much prepare you for the rigors of preparing a four-course dinner party, did it?"

"No, sir." Tate's voice was curiously flat. "I'm sorry if I caused any trouble, sir."

This wasn't right. This wasn't Tate. This wasn't the Tate who'd been so happy earlier this evening. Not even the Tate who'd been so intense in bed with Rory an hour ago. Rory squeezed his hand. "What happened, Tate? Was it your head?"

"My . . ." Tate glanced at Lowell again.

"You were just dizzy, I expect," Lowell offered.

"Yes." Tate blinked up at Rory. "I was dizzy."

Rory frowned. "When the medical team arrives, you need to tell them exactly what you felt, do you understand?"

"I was dizzy," Tate said, "and then I fainted." The words ended on an upward lilt, as though he was asking a question. As though he wasn't sure what had happened. Or he didn't want to say.

"There, you see?" Lowell stepped back. "He'll be as right as rain come morning. You should get some rest, Rory. I'll stay here, and watch out for Tate until the medical team arrives."

"Tate?" Rory asked, looking to him. He stifled a yawn. "Do you want me to wait up with you?"

Again Tate looked to Lowell. "No, that's all right, Rory. I'll stay with Mr. Lowell. He'll take good care of me."

"I don't know. I'd feel better if I waited with you." Tate was his responsibility, wasn't he? More so now, given what had happened between them tonight. It was normal to feel a little possessive of Tate, surely. Rory wanted to be the one who took care of Tate. He wanted Tate to need him too.

"I'll be fine," Tate told him with a smile.

Rory nodded, sweeping a hand over Tate's curly hair. "I'll get your clothes."

"Yes," Lowell said. "You do that, and I'll go fix us some tea. Does that sound nice, Tate?"

"Thank you, sir," Tate said, smiling slightly. The color was slowly coming back into his cheeks again, and he seemed more alert. "But I should make the tea."

"Nonsense," Lowell replied, already heading toward the door. "I know my way around a kitchen. You get dressed, make sure Rory goes to bed and gets to sleep, and then meet me out there when he is. The tea will be waiting when you do."

"Are you sure?" Rory asked Tate in a low voice once Lowell had gone. "I can stay up. It's no problem." He wasn't sure it was true though. The painkillers were already making him drowsy.

"I'll be fine, Rory," Tate said. "I feel better already. And Mr. Lowell is right. You need rest, and you can't be late to work tomorrow. Especially not on my account."

"Okay." Rory released his hand at last, almost unwillingly. "I'll get your clothes."

Tate smiled at him.

"Let me make it, sir," Tate said, moving around Lowell in the kitchen.

"Rory's asleep?" Lowell took a seat.

Seeing the man seated, taking on the natural role of service, filled Tate with immediate relief. "Yes, sir. As soon as he lay down, nearly. The pills make him tired, but it must have been a long day for him."

"And for you too," Lowell said. "You shouldn't be up and walking around after your little episode, should you now?"

Tate paused, his hand hovering over the kettle.

"You should be over here," Lowell said. "On your knees."

Tate's gut lurched, but then a calmness spread over him. It felt good to be told what to do. It felt safe. Lowell's strong, certain voice was so much more comforting than Rory's waffling. Tate took the kettle, poured a mugful of hot water over a tea bag, and brought Lowell his cup of tea. And then, finally, he knelt.

He sighed with pleasure. Wonderful. So wonderful, as warm and fortifying as any cup of tea.

Lowell leaned back in the chair and spread his legs.

Yes. This was what Lowell wanted. Tate too. He inched forward on his knees and reached for Lowell's belt buckle.

deep, deep, and Tate choked loud and hard enough that his entire body convulsed.

"You'd beg to stay with me," Lowell said. He suddenly pulled Tate's head back again.

Tate blinked up at him, confused.

"That was the door, boy," Lowell said. "Go and answer it before they wake Rory."

Naked? Some small part of him asked. Yes, naked. And then the men at the door would know immediately that he was a rezzy, ready and willing to be mastered and used. That was what Tate wanted. Yes.

He went to the door. Through the glass, he could see two shadowy shapes. He remembered them, but this time, he didn't feel fear, not like before. Because Lowell was here with him, and he was naked, and all he had to do was serve. He opened the door and immediately knelt.

"Hello, Tate," one of the guards said. "Are you causing problems for your sponsor again?"

Lowell had risen and was standing behind him. In direct opposition to Tate's simple nakedness, Lowell had done up his trousers again and was standing fully clothed. "There's nothing wrong with his chip at all. The problem is with his sponsor. What happened, Tate?"

Tate flushed with shame. "He wanted to be my friend, sir. Asked me what I wanted."

The men at the door snorted and shook their heads. "Friends! With a rezzy! What does he think this is, a playdate?" said one.

"Well," said the other, "we'd best run you through your paces just in case. The doc's getting his bag from the van."

"Not here," Lowell said quietly. "His sponsor's asleep."

"There's room in the back of the van," the first man said. "Come on, Tate. Let's go see the doc."

Tate nodded and stood, padding out behind them through the cool, midnight air. Lowell followed as well, and all of them piled into the van.

Tate remembered this. Remembered the mobile treatment unit with its blindingly bright lights and narrow bed with restraints. The guards in their uniforms and—

It was a different doctor than the last time he'd been in this van. But Tate still recognized him: the doctor who'd first activated the chip. The one who'd made him cut himself and then use the blood as lubrication on his cock. The doctor with the lizard smile.

With a little shudder of fear, he knelt.

"Justice Lowell," the doctor said, a smile curling his thin mouth. "Are you taking a personal interest in every rezzy you send me?"

Lowell smiled back. "Just one or two. This one belongs to my assistant, so of course I want to make sure he's performing at peak capacity."

"You certainly do look out for your employees! If only we could all be so lucky."

The doctor turned to Tate now, taking out a little light and flashing it into Tate's eyes. Tate flinched but didn't turn away. Didn't complain. *Obey.* He had to obey.

"Yes," said the doctor. "I was worried you might be some trouble, rezzy. Your scans did indicate some damage to your brain. Seizures, I believe, as a child? Nothing the chip couldn't work around, I assumed."

"The sponsor may be more to blame than the chip," Lowell reiterated. He looked at Tate expectantly.

"He wanted to be my friend," Tate told the doctor. "He wanted to know what *I* wanted."

"An outsider, remember," Lowell said.

The doctor shook his head. "Screen them all you like, outsiders just don't understand our ways."

"He'll learn. He just needs time, and some guidance. We have to let outsiders in, after all, or else we'd wind up with a bunch of incestuous offspring, wouldn't we?"

"Thus why my allies and I in the scientific and medical communities think it would be best to institute a controlled breeding program. Import sperm. Import eggs. Import genetic material and breeding stock but leave the outsiders—and their lack of understanding of our values—where they belong."

"You can import all the genetic material you want," Lowell said, "but it's not just bloodlines that stagnate; it's ideas. It's civilization. The boy has a good mind. Once he acclimates, he'll be a wonderful asset. And helping him acclimate is why I'm here, and why I want you to make sure his rezzy is absolutely perfect. Isn't that right, Tate? You want to help, don't you?" He ruffled Tate's wet hair.

It had been ages since the shower. Why was he so sweaty? Why was his heart pounding so hard? He didn't need to be afraid. He was serving. He never needed to be afraid so long as he was obedient to his masters.

The doctor clicked his tongue as he ran a scanner over Tate's wristbands. "Well, the chip's functioning well. No error reports. A spike, earlier tonight, but nothing to be alarmed about."

Lowell's brow furrowed. "Apparently, he cried out 'Help me' before he collapsed."

"Oh. Oh, now that's a little disconcerting." The doctor wheeled his chair over to Tate and took his chin in his hand. "Why were you asking for help, boy?"

Because . . . because . . . Tate didn't remember. Couldn't grasp that feeling, not now that he was draped in the blanket of certainty Lowell cast over him. "I . . . I don't know. Because he asked me what I wanted. I wanted . . . I wanted . . ."

"Enough," the doctor said. He smoothed Tate's hair and glanced at Lowell. "Yes, this is a problem with the sponsor, not the chip. He's not providing a stable home environment for Tate. If this happens again, we may have to transfer him somewhere there won't be such a . . . fertile breeding ground for these kinds of insecurities." Now, he looked to Tate. "Boy, you must help your sponsor to be a better master for you. That's why we call them sponsors; they're an important part of the process. They contribute, just as much as the chip does. You feel calm when you're around me and Justice Lowell, don't you?"

"Oh, yes, sir," Tate said, even though his body was trembling. His body didn't count here, only his mind.

"That's because we're ideal sponsors. We take control. We give you boundaries. We satisfy your need to serve, so that your brain doesn't go haywire struggling to make that connection. It's true it's a born attribute to be a master, but Justice Lowell is confident it can be taught so we'll do things his way . . . for now." He gave Lowell a hard look over Tate's head.

"The boy will learn," Lowell said, his voice tempered with a smile. "Both of them will."

"You know my opinion on immigrants," the doctor said. "An unknown quality and an unnecessary risk." He turned his attention back to Tate. "From now on, you must help guide your sponsor into being who he needs to be. You must teach him how much you love and crave service. You must show him how happy serving him makes you. When he asks you what you want, you must tell him you want to serve him. Maybe if he sees how happy you are, he'll become more comfortable with his role. So here's what you must do. If ever you feel that . . . uncertainty you felt earlier tonight, you must push yourself into service immediately. You must not express that confusion, and in doing so, encourage his uncertainty. Rezzy and sponsor feed off one another. The better you service him, the more confident he becomes in his place as your master."

Tate nodded, frowning. "I . . . I will *try*, sir."

The doctor sighed. "And if he's making it difficult for you, Tate, then you only need to remember that to serve is your purpose. If he won't give you any instructions at all, then find a way to serve. Seduce him. Polish his shoes. Whatever makes him happy. And take comfort in the knowledge that you *are* good, and that I know it and Justice Lowell knows it and so do the guards. Do you think you can do that?"

"Yes, sir," he said, his voice more firm.

The doctor's gaze flicked to Lowell and then back to Tate. "Good. You'll prove it for me now, won't you?"

"Please, sir. I want to prove it."

"Has he fucked you?" the doctor asked.

"Yes, sir."

"Did you like it?"

Tate hesitated. He didn't want to lie. He *couldn't* lie. "I liked it when he used me. I liked it when he came inside me. But it hurt. And he was upset that it hurt."

Lowell, silently standing aside, reached down and gave his groin a conspicuous rub.

"Well, you possibly need to loosen up a little," the doctor said. "Or at the very least, you need to learn to keep that hurt to yourself, especially if it displeases your sponsor and makes him think you don't enjoy service, even when you do. I think I've just the thing to help you."

The doctor reached into his bag. Tate's eyes widened.

No.

It was too big. He wanted to serve, but the thing the doctor held was too big to fit inside him.

No.

Tate wavered, afraid that his visceral reaction would cause that tearing pain in his skull to return. He drew a deep breath and remembered what the doctor had told him: *"If ever you feel the uncertainty you felt earlier tonight, you must push yourself into service immediately."*

He squared his shoulders.

"That's right. Don't show fear."

The dildo had a suction cup on the bottom, and the doctor stuck it to the floor.

"You may begin," the doctor said.

Tate crawled forward, forcing himself to breathe deep and even. He could do this. He could do this. He opened his mouth and lapped at the simulated head, thicker even at its narrowest point than the entirety of Rory's cock. Wet. He had to make it wet.

"Gentlemen. Give the boy some help."

Hands closed around Tate's biceps, pulling him upward until he was squatting.

"This will hurt you, boy, but it's all for the best. Remember, your sponsor is displeased by the sight of your pain. It makes him squeamish. Unable to master you."

Yes. This was for the best. He would serve, he would, and Rory would learn to be the master he needed, just so long as he could hide the pain, squash the fear, silence the voice that cried out, *Help me.*

The guards' fingers dug into his arms. Forced—no, *guided*—him down, spearing him on that massive, barely slicked implement.

When he cried and gritted his teeth, the burn *destroying* him, Lowell and the doctor both solemnly shook their heads. Tate almost sobbed in despair as much as pain. The men at his sides didn't let up; they surely knew that mercy wouldn't help him in the end. Tate knew that too. Knew it, but it didn't make the pain hurt any less. There was no point even trying to ride this out. Tate could only hope to disguise the spasms as shudders of pleasure.

Lowell stepped toward him, unzipping his fly. "Time to finish what we started, Tate."

Yes. Please, yes. Something to distract him from the pain. Serve instead of begging for help or mercy or reprieve. Just serve. And yes, his mind was at peace with that; his mind was, even if his body wasn't. Even if his body was being torn apart.

Tate blinked away his tears. Tried to pitch his voice more toward need than the ragged end of pain. "Yes, please let me serve you!"

The grips on his arms shifted as he finally seated himself on the dildo. Keeping him upright now. Lowell took Tate by the back of the head. Tate closed his eyes and opened his mouth.

This was the way to happiness.

CHAPTER

TEN

Something wet and warm flicked between Rory's legs, behind his balls. Layers of dreams—of vines and tentacles and unfurling flowers—fell away, leaving . . . a tongue. Someone was licking him. Playful, affectionate licks that sent tingling warmth through his skin. He bucked his hips and stretched lazily, not wanting to open his eyes and ruin this wonderful feeling. This feeling of being just on the edge of sleep, trapped between two perfect, shifting pleasures. Not even aware of where he was or who—

Tate. Tate was licking him. Tate was in his bed, under his covers, lapping at his balls and aching-hard shaft.

Rory moaned his encouragement and reached down with both hands, gently brushing his fingertips through Tate's soft curls. "Tate. You're feeling better today?"

"Mmm." Tate didn't even try to speak, which Rory couldn't fault. He nuzzled against Rory's balls, warm breath and wet kisses.

He must be better, to be waking Rory up like this. He closed his eyes and let his head sink back into his pillow. Imagined that he could wake up to this every day, here in paradise. Just him and Tate in this perfect little house. Cooking together, getting to know each other better, making love.

To think that on the outside, Tate would be in a prison and Rory would go the rest of his life hating and fearing him and missing out on all of this. No perpetrators and victims here, no defined roles to fall into and be bound by. Just two people, learning to forgive and start again.

Starting here, with this. Sharing a bed. Rory cupped Tate's face, tilting it upward. "C'mere. I want to kiss you."

Tate beamed at him from under his veil of Rory's blankets. He slid, lithe and naked, up Rory's body, kissing his skin as he went. His smile became impish, teasing. Holding Rory's hooded gaze, he dipped his head and laved his tongue against Rory's nipple. Then bit.

"Fuck!" Rory arched off the mattress. "Tate!"

Tate licked his lips. He widened his eyes. "Yes, Rory?"

He reached down and gripped Tate's hair. "Don't play innocent!"

Tate laughed and squirmed closer. He kissed Rory on the cheek. "And are you feeling better too, Rory?"

"I am now." Rory slid his hands down Tate's body and held him by the hips. They fit together well like this, their erections rubbing together. "What did the doctor say?"

"That I was tired and I fainted." Tate turned his face away and hid it against Rory's neck. Found a place to lick and nip. "But I feel good now."

"I can see that," Rory growled, thrusting against his cock for emphasis.

Tate moaned into his throat. "Feels good. I feel good."

"Are you sore from last night?"

Tate stiffened suddenly, then his breath shuddered out of him. "No. It was good. F-felt good. It made me happy." He raised his head and met Rory's gaze. "You made me happy."

Rory smiled, sweeping a bouncy ringlet of hair out of Tate's eyes. "Will I make you happy again?"

"Please," Tate whispered. He jerked his hips. "Will you? Do you want to?"

"Of course I want to." Rory held Tate tightly and rolled them over. "I want to do this again and again and again . . ."

Tate smiled at him, so beautiful and trusting. He shifted, parting his legs and drawing them up. "That's what I want too."

He knelt between Tate's legs. He closed his hand around Tate's cock, loving the way it made him shudder with pleasure. Tate's chest rose and fell rapidly, and he bit his lip. His fingers were clenched into fists, as though he was desperately trying to hold on to something that wasn't there. His composure. His control. He was already on edge, and Rory couldn't wait to push him over and watch him come apart.

And then he slipped a hand between Tate's legs, seeking out his entrance, and Tate hissed in pain.

Rory's brow furrowed. "Are you sure I didn't hurt you?" he asked, sitting back on his heels and withdrawing his hand. He rubbed Tate's thigh instead. "It's okay to admit it, Tate."

"You . . ." Tate shook his head. "It's a little sore, but I want it anyway. I want *you* anyway."

It was obvious Tate was ashamed, putting on a brave face, so Rory made sure to keep his voice light. Push down his feelings of concern, of apology for ever causing Tate pain. "Don't think for a second I don't want you too. But how about we give you a couple days to bounce back, huh? I can think of other things we can do together."

Tate looked guardedly hopeful. "Like what?"

Shit. He really wasn't very experienced at all. There was an innocence to him, and an eagerness, that made Rory think he hadn't done much at all in the past. Although Rory wasn't surprised. Being openly gay in the outside world just painted another fucking target on your back. Rory rubbed his thumb across Tate's balls, and Tate jerked and gasped. "Like I can touch you and kiss you and even make you come in my mouth."

Tate's eyes widened. "God, Rory."

Rory just smiled. Ducked down and took the pretty head of Tate's cock into his mouth. Gave him a gentle, teasing suck. Just a second or so before he pulled off with a kiss. Tate shivered, squirmed. Rocked his hips upward.

"Rory," he whispered. "God."

He looked so astonished, so worshipful, that Rory almost laughed. "Have you forgotten how to say anything else?"

"Um." Tate gasped. "Fuck."

Rory did laugh that time and dipped his head to lick Tate's cock, laving his tongue over the slit. "Do you like that?"

Tate whined. "Y-yes!"

"Hmm," Rory said. He licked again. "Maybe I can do this every morning."

"Wh-whatever you like." Tate's body twisted, the sheets bunching up underneath him as he did.

"Whatever *you* like," Rory corrected.

"I like this," Tate said. "God, I like this."

Rory laughed again and licked him again. Yes, this was how he wanted all his mornings from now on. Him and Tate, and sex and laughter. Tasting Tate, making him moan and squirm. Giving and receiving pleasure both. Learning the things Tate liked, the things that drove him wild. To wake up to this every day would be paradise.

Except . . . Rory quickly glanced at the bedside clock. Except he had to wrap this up or he was going to be late for work. He didn't have time to tease Tate for ages, to take him to the edge and hold him there until he was begging. But he'd make time, next time.

"I have to go to work," he murmured.

Tate's eyes widened with disappointment.

"But, before I do . . ." Rory curled his fingers around Tate's shaft and took the head in his mouth again. He sucked on it, hard, and Tate moaned. *That's it, that's it.* He slurped and bobbed, rapidly working his hand over Tate's cock, wringing the orgasm out of him.

"Th-thank you!" Tate cried, just before his cum flooded Rory's mouth.

Paradise.

Tate stayed naked all day, fantasizing that maybe one day Rory would master him the way he needed. It felt good to be naked. It felt proper. To know, that if his master was there, he only needed to nod, and Tate would be on his hands and knees for him, ready and eager to serve. Except Rory wasn't here. Rory was at work. But one day, one day he would master Tate properly, like Lowell had the night before. And then Tate would be truly happy.

He swept and mopped the floors. His back ached by the time he was finished, but it was a good ache. It was an ache born of hard work and proud service. He had never been more proud of anything in his life than serving Rory.

Emmy.

Emmy . . .

The name cut through the static in his head, and he froze, the mop in his hand.

No. That name belonged in his old life, not inside the walls of this house. He hadn't been good before. He hadn't been happy. He had been angry and cruel and sometimes he had been violent. He had lied and he had stolen and he had hit the man who would become his master. He had not been a good man. He had not been deserving of redemption.

Here, he was better.

Here, things made sense.

He closed his eyes, drew a deep breath, and continued to work.

The beds were next, and then the laundry. Tate bundled up the sheets, inhaling their scent before putting them in the machine. They smelled of Rory, of Tate, and of cum and sweat. His face burned as he thought back to the morning, to when Rory had blown him and Tate had done nothing in return. It had been an uneven exchange, strange but wonderful. Was it possible he could serve Rory best by allowing Rory to serve him?

No.

That was wrong.

He just had to try harder. Maybe today. He could greet Rory on his knees, naked at the door. Show him how good following their roles could feel. Suck *him* off. Swallow *his* cum. Things that he had never imagined doing before but wanted to do now. Needed to do now, for his penance. To make himself a better person.

But more than that too. Because with everything he did, Rory proved himself a good man. A kind man. And Tate burned to repay him for that. He would worship him, if only Rory would allow it. Until that day, he could only serve in other ways.

Like preparing dinner, for instance. He could start on that now.

He worked carefully in the kitchen, pausing every now and then to refocus as his cock grew hard. The doctor had warned him that could happen. His body was finding pleasure in his service, even in service as mundane as chopping vegetables. But, of course, no service was mundane, was it? There was nothing beneath Tate, and nothing that he wouldn't do if it pleased Rory. His body knew it, even if his mind still stumbled sometimes.

Tate still hurt from the night before, but the pain was useful to him. He tested its limits as he moved, clenched his muscles and tried to make it hurt more so that he could overcome it by the time Rory came home. So that when Rory fucked him, he would only show his pleasure.

As the afternoon drew to a close, Tate anxiously watched the clock. He lingered in the kitchen, still naked, still half-hard, and worried that any minute Rory would be home. Worried that he should put clothes on because Rory might not be comfortable with him naked. Worried that he should kneel instead of stand, that if he was naked, he should at least present himself *properly*.

Thinking about it was awful. Tate couldn't make a decision. In the end, he let instinct choose for him. He heard Rory's key in the lock and still could have made it to his bedroom in time to grab his clothes, but he didn't. He hurried to the door instead and dropped down onto his knees.

Heard the doctor's voice in his head: *"Seduce him."*

He understood in that moment that Rory would not be seduced by submission. Rory wasn't a master. Not yet. So, when the door swung open to reveal Rory standing there, gaping at the sight of Tate naked on his knees, Tate didn't bow his head, didn't drop his gaze, and didn't throw himself at Rory's feet. Instead he smiled, and swiped his tongue over his lower lip. "Hey Rory. I think I owe you for this morning. Want me to pay up?"

"Jesus," Rory exclaimed and quickly shut the door behind him. His eyes shifted back and forth nervously. And then his gaze fell onto Tate again and all that furtive fear left him. Rory's expression darkened. His lips twitched into a hungry smile. "Not giving me much of a chance to say no, are you?"

He shook his head and licked his lips again.

"Well, that's just unfair," Rory said. "Something smells delicious, and I have to choose between my stomach and . . . and you."

Tate bit his lip and looked up at Rory hopefully.

"And I missed lunch today," Rory said with a rueful laugh.

"Really?"

"Aaron called in sick or something. I hope it's nothing to do with last night, you know, when Mr. Lowell got a little handsy? He might be embarrassed or something. I'll call him tomorrow if he's not in." Rory dropped his bag on the floor. "Anyway, I had to find all the files

I needed myself. I spent the whole afternoon just dreaming of getting home and eating something." He shrugged. "And suddenly I'm not even hungry."

Tate reached up and rubbed a hand along Rory's abdomen, drawing Rory's heated gaze. "I'll feed you after, I promise."

"And I'll feed you first?" Rory asked with a smirk, hands reaching for the fly of his smartly pressed slacks.

Rory fully dressed in a suit, standing. Tate on his knees, naked and sucking Rory's dick.

He couldn't think of anything better. He shuffled forward. "God, yes. Feed me."

Rory's smile vanished. He stared down at Tate, his eyes narrow with desire. He fumbled at his fly. The rasp of the zipper caused Tate to shiver. Rory must have noticed because he chuckled, thrusting the fingers of one hand into Tate's hair and drawing him close. "You like sucking dick, huh?"

"If it's yours." His face pressed to the bulge showing through Rory's fly, he breathed deep. That tangy, masculine smell. He never thought he'd like it so much—he'd never even dreamed of doing this to a guy—but here he was. So close to happiness. He reached up and tugged at Rory's trousers, pulling them down to his ankles. He rubbed a hand along the fine hairs on Rory's thighs, watching them prickle under his touch and loving that he was able to give Rory such pleasure. Then, impatient for more, he curled his fingers around the elastic of Rory's briefs, and peeled them down, exposing Rory's cock. Hard, and already wet, and so, so ready for him. He sighed and sucked the head into his mouth.

Froze for a second—just a second—and then began to work his tongue and bob his head, trying to find a rhythm.

"T-Tate—" Rory fell back, slamming into the door with a whine and a groan as his knees buckled. "Oh, Tate . . ."

Rory's pleasure was Tate's pleasure. His head swam with it. If he hadn't been on his knees already, he might have fallen. He dug his fingers into Rory's hips and took him further into his mouth. His throat was still sore from last night, but he didn't let that stop him. More. He needed to give Rory more. He needed to give Rory everything. He sucked harder, his cheeks hollowing, and Rory gasped his name again. Rory's fingers twisted in his hair, and Tate moaned.

Yes, use me.

This was what he wanted, what he needed. Tate's cock was hard as well, but he resisted the urge to touch himself. He kept his hands on Rory's hips. He gagged, and Rory pulled his head back gently.

"Take it easy, Tate," Rory panted.

"Want you," he said, his voice rasping. Rory didn't understand. Tate didn't have experience, or anything approaching finesse. He could only offer *this*. This willingness. He pushed forward, taking Rory's cock into his mouth, into his throat. Gagged again but didn't let Rory pull him away this time. Whimpered his displeasure when Rory tugged at his hair.

Didn't stop. Wouldn't stop.

"Tate," Rory groaned. "Oh fuck, Tate!"

Yes. This was right. This hard rhythm. This ache in his jaw. This fight to breathe around his master's cock. Tate moaned.

More. More. More.

Rory tensed and cried out, and Tate's mouth was suddenly flooded with hot cum. He swallowed eagerly, coughed, and laid his head against Rory's thigh, panting.

"Fuck," Rory gasped, his fingers loosening in Tate's hair. "Are you . . . are you okay?"

"Yes," Tate murmured. He sat back on his heels and wiped his mouth with his hand. "Are you still hungry?"

Rory stared down at him, looking a little shell-shocked.

Tate rose to his feet, his erect cock bobbing. "Go put your feet up, Rory, and let me get you dinner."

Rory, wide-eyed, only nodded.

Later, Tate curled on the couch beside Rory. They watched a movie together, sharing a blanket that they pulled up to their chins. Rory dozed, and Tate tried not to become too anxious with their newfound familiarity. If this was what Rory needed, then it was enough. He would learn how to be a master to Tate soon. Tate would show him. Once Tate was properly on his knees, once he was properly serving him, Rory would see that it was right.

Until then, it was comforting to cuddle with Rory. To close his eyes as Rory carded his fingers through his curls.

"Is it really this easy?" Rory murmured.

Tate shifted. "Is what this easy?"

Rory smiled at him, flushing. "Is it really this easy to be happy?"

"Yes," said Tate.

Rory's mouth quirked. "Really?"

"Yes." Tate curled his fingers through Rory's. "If you want to be happy, then you are happy."

"I don't think it's that simple." Rory sighed. "Is it?"

"Why can't it be?"

Seduce him.

Tate lifted his face and brushed his lips against Rory's jaw. "Why can't it be?" he asked again.

Rory smiled at him and drew him closer, and Tate was filled with warmth.

They exchanged soft kisses awhile, until finally Tate slipped completely under the blankets.

He missed the end of the movie.

CHAPTER
ELEVEN

The next day at work, there was a girl standing by Rory's desk looking a little out of place.

"Hi," Rory said. "Can I help you with something?"

The girl hesitated for a moment, then thrust out her hand. "I'm Alexandra. Alexandra Holt." Then, before Rory could remember where he'd heard the name, she added, "I'm the new intern."

"The new intern?" Rory shook her hand and looked around the office. Zac was in court. Ruth was working at her desk. She seemed engrossed in her work, too engrossed, and Rory wondered why she was avoiding his gaze. "Where's Aaron?"

Alexandra smoothed her skirt down and fiddled with the thin bracelet on her wrist.

"Where's Aaron?" Rory asked again.

Lowell stepped out of his office, face grave. "Rory, can I have a word, please?"

"Sure." Rory trailed into his office. "What's going on?"

Lowell sighed heavily, shut the door behind them, and leaned against his desk. "Aaron's gone."

"Where?" Rory frowned. "He didn't mention anything the other night."

Lowell drew a hand over his forehead. "God, I don't even know how to say it, so I'll just come right out with it. The other night, when I had a little too much to drink at your place, Aaron saw me home. Then, what with the upset with Tate, I was running late the next morning. Well, when it came to pay for my coffee at the station, I thought I'd maybe misplaced my card somewhere." Lowell shook his head, and for a moment his eyes swam with tears. "Aaron had taken it. Used it. I mean, if he'd needed money, he should have come to me."

Rory felt sick. "What . . . what happened?"

"I had no choice," Lowell said, his voice cracking. "I called the police."

"But why . . . why would he do that?" Rory shook his head. "Why would he steal from you?"

God. Aaron worshipped Lowell. And Rory was sure Aaron didn't have a criminal bone in his body. Stupid fucking kid.

Lowell shrugged. "I wish I knew."

"Okay." Rory frowned. "Um . . . How does this work with you being a justice? Is this office prosecuting him? Or can you give him a character reference or something? Will this be a conflict of interest at trial?"

"Not necessary. His case isn't going to trial on account of the fact that he's . . . confessed. He took the plea bargain."

"Shit," Rory said. "Sorry, I just . . . I'm just finding it hard to believe."

Lowell clapped a hand on Rory's shoulder, face drawn. "Me too, Rory, me too."

"God." He felt a stab of sympathy for Aaron. He was just a kid, whatever stupid thing he'd done. And Rory liked him—all that crazy energy and enthusiasm. "Where is he?"

"He's in the induction program," Lowell said.

Rehabilitation through Restitution. Rory had passed underneath the words carved high into the foyer wall of the Hall of Justice only ten minutes ago. A high ideal that seemed suddenly hollow.

"Oh, don't look so upset. Think of Tate. He's not unhappy, is he? He's getting another chance with you. Aaron will get the same." Lowell squared his shoulders and smiled. "In fact, it's almost for the best, really. Now whatever he needs, I can provide for him as a sponsor. He should have just asked me for help before, but now, at least he'll be taken care of all the same. Isn't that good?"

Good? Good that Aaron had thrown his freedom away over what had to be a stupid mistake? Rory couldn't manage a smile. "Um, I suppose. I think I'll need a while to process all this."

His belief in Beulah wasn't as unshakable as Lowell's. Rory couldn't fling himself on it and expect it not to break. Not yet.

Yeah, Aaron would be cared for. Yeah, the rehabilitation program was a hundred shades better than jail. But freedom still mattered, didn't it? Freedom was still the most important thing.

And what about Tate's freedom? the cynical, doubting voice inside him taunted.

Well, Tate was different. Of course he was. He was a lifelong criminal, and for him, restitution really was a blessing, giving him opportunities and stability he'd never had before. Aaron, though, had had everything going for him. Every opportunity in the world. To throw all that away over something as stupid as a credit card . . . Rory needed to mourn Aaron's loss of freedom before he rejoiced in the fact that he'd been given a second chance.

It didn't make sense. Didn't Beulah provide for its citizens? What could Aaron possibly need money for that badly? Did he do drugs? Owe some kind of debt?

"Rory," Lowell said. His eyes shone. "I'll look after him. You know that. I'll look after him the same way you look after Tate."

Rory's gut clenched.

Yeah, just like he looked after Tate. Fucking him, taking advantage of his generosity, sitting around while Tate cooked him meals and cleaned his house? And all the while, Tate wasn't free to come or go as he pleased.

He's my prisoner.

Because he committed a crime. Just like Aaron did.

It's better than jail.

Besides, Tate was happy to do those things for him.

And Aaron? Would Aaron be happy to do them for Lowell?

"Would you like to see him?" Lowell asked, gently. "Would it reassure you to come to my house after he arrives? See for yourself how he's settling in, that he's being fed and well taken care of and happy?"

"Could I?"

Lowell smiled. "Of course. Just because he'll be a rezzy doesn't mean he's not still your friend, or mine. He's no less of a person because he made a mistake. There's no shame in restitution. It's empowering. You've seen that in Tate. If a rezzy makes the choice to take pride in themselves, and in the program, they can turn their lives around. It's about taking responsibility, not about handing down blame."

"I know that," Rory said. He swallowed, unable to get rid of the knot of unease in his gut. He couldn't reconcile it. This was *Aaron*. "I just don't understand why Aaron would *steal* from you."

"That's a question I want to ask him myself." Lowell sighed. He stared at the wall for a moment and then appeared to shake himself awake. "But in the meantime, I've got a meeting with an environmental committee."

"Of course." Rory drew a deep breath and tried to remember his professionalism. "Your speech is in your folder. Hannah Graves is the chair, and she's bound to bring up the wetlands, but the latest study from the university says they won't be affected. You'll find the bullet points of the study underneath your speech."

Lowell brightened. "Perfect."

"I'll um . . . I'll get back to work then," he said.

Lowell gave him a warm smile.

Back in the main office, Rory found that Ruth had also left. Alexandra was sitting at Aaron's desk with her hands folded in her lap.

"Hasn't anyone given you any work yet?" he asked.

"Not yet."

He studied her. She was a pretty girl, with square-framed glasses that made her appear almost severe. Her long dark hair was pulled back and twisted into a tight bun. She looked a little like a kid trying very hard to be a grown-up. "Um, you're in Aaron's class at the university, right?"

"Yes." She stared at her desk.

And then he remembered. Alexandra Holt was the girl that Aaron had . . . hooked up with? He'd never told the whole story. She didn't look like his type at all. Aaron had wild hair and a goofy grin. Alexandra looked serious and studious, which might have been the glasses.

"You would have heard about Aaron," he said, not sure how to phrase it as a question.

"Yes. I heard." She pursed her lips.

"Um, and . . . and why do you think—"

"It's none of my business," she said, too quickly. She stood. "Can I get you a coffee?"

He should have taken that for a sign. He should have taken her at her word.

But he didn't. "Well, I'm just going to come right out and say it. He stole Mr. Lowell's credit card and made some purchases with it. He confessed to the crime." He said it clearly, without flinching, eyes focused on her expression, looking for . . . something. He wasn't even sure what.

Maybe he just wanted to see his own shock reflected in her eyes, to not feel like he was the only one wrestling with disbelief. Lowell at least had his rhetoric to fall back on. Rory had nothing.

And there it was. Alexandra's eyes widened slightly, showing the full roundness of her pupils. Genuine surprise. And then they narrowed again in unmistakable suspicion.

He leaned forward, cupping her shoulder, pressing his lips to her ear. "Doesn't sound like him to you, either, does it?"

He shouldn't be thinking like this. Hadn't he promised to accept things here? Hadn't he just heard Mr. Lowell's personal assurances?

And yet, he couldn't stop himself. Couldn't stop thinking, analyzing, *doubting*.

Was that really wrong? Justice, real justice, should hold up to scrutiny. Mr. Lowell would understand that. He wouldn't fault Rory for wanting to make sure. It wasn't like he had anything to hide.

Alexandra solemnly shook her head.

Well, that settled it. He'd talk to Aaron, get to the bottom of it. He knew from the outside that a confession didn't actually mean guilt. He'd thought Beulah was above all that but . . . Doubt crept in still. Hopefully seeing Aaron would settle this pit of unease, because otherwise . . . Shit, Rory couldn't even contemplate the otherwise. No system was perfect and every process had its flaws, but he'd tried so hard to believe that Beulah was better than that. That miscarriages of justice didn't happen here.

But Aaron had taken the plea bargain.

Fuck. Rory wanted to shake him by the shoulders and ask him what the hell he'd been thinking.

Alexandra stepped away from him. Her face was shuttered as she repeated, "Can I get you a coffee, Rory?"

He sighed, then he nodded curtly. "Sure, coffee sounds great."

He sat back down at his desk and turned on his computer. There was no point stewing in worry all day. There was no point speculating, either, until he spoke to Aaron. Until then, he still had work to do.

The following evening, Rory found himself outside Lowell's house.

From the street, the house didn't look any different than Rory's. It was small and neat and modest, and not the sort of place Rory had imagined a chief justice would live. In the outside world, men of influence liked to parade it. But in Beulah, everything was different. Everything was simpler and more complicated at the same time. His stomach was in knots as he approached the modest front door, a bottle of wine in hand. Because what the hell was the appropriate gift to bring the first time you visited your boss at home to meet his new rezzy?

Aaron. A rezzy.

It still didn't make sense.

Maybe once he saw Aaron for himself, it would.

The door opened before Rory had a chance to knock, and there Aaron was. The minute they made eye contact, Aaron's whole face lit up in a smile.

Rory couldn't help it; he pulled Aaron into a tight, bone-crushing hug.

As Aaron moved to pull away again, though, Rory just drew him closer. He had a job to do here. He wouldn't let this opportunity pass. "Is it true?" he whispered into Aaron's ear. "Did you really—"

Aaron pulled back, gracefully extricating the wine bottle from Rory's anxious, clenching hands. "It's all true," he said, calm and even, like he'd rehearsed it. "But I'm sorry. And I'm glad to be here getting a second chance."

Rory searched his face. "But did you really—"

"Rory!" Lowell called from farther inside. "He's admitted it, and we're moving on. We're not wallowing in guilt, are we, Aaron? We're going forward."

Aaron smiled, relief spreading across his face. "Yes, sir, Mr. Lowell. We're going forward."

"But your studies," Rory said. "All the things you were going to do."

Aaron's gaze went blank for a moment. "I gave those things up when I chose to break the law. I'm lucky to be getting a second chance."

Rory's shoulders slumped.

"Come on," Aaron said with a crooked smile, and slapped his shoulder. "I'm still me, okay? And I'm learning to cook! Come see."

"Don't steal my guests, Aaron!" Lowell called out, appearing at last in shirtsleeves and bare feet. He shot a smile at Aaron. "Go on. Go show Rory what you've been doing, and then we'll eat in the garden. This weather's too nice to waste."

Rory tried to smile at Aaron's enthusiasm as he grabbed his hand and pulled him through to the kitchen. He tried to imagine that this was just the same as Aaron driving him through Beulah after the hospital, pointing out all the landmarks. Or showing him the records room and the window in the attic space of the Hall of Justice that led out onto the roof. Or the best and cheapest lunch place in town. Was it only his own prejudice that refused to let him be satisfied that Aaron was happy? Did he still really believe that crime went hand in hand with guilt? That Aaron should be weeping and wailing over his ruined future, not so pleased about *going forward*. Adjusting so easily to his new life ... it was *admirable*, but it wasn't normal.

Except Aaron was smiling and joking the way he always did, his eyes shining.

"Guess who our new intern is?" Rory asked as Aaron pulled a tray out of the oven.

"Who?"

"Alexandra Holt."

Aaron hissed as he fumbled the hot tray. It clattered onto the countertop, and then Aaron stuck his fingers under the tap in the sink. "Oh. Well, she was top of our class." His voice was flat. "Does she ... does she ..."

"Does she what?" Rory asked in an undertone. "Does she know?"

Aaron jerked his head in a nod.

"She knows," Rory said softly. *And she didn't believe it, either.* "Maybe you could ask Lowell to see her."

Aaron's eyes widened with horror. "No. Oh no, oh no, no, no. No, I don't think so. No."

Was he ashamed of himself? Or—

Lowell swept into the room. "Are you all right, Aaron? I heard you—" Spotting Aaron's fingers under the tap, he rushed forward, clasping Aaron's hand between both of his own. "Oh dear! Are you hurt, son?"

"Burned," Aaron said, his eyes wide.

"Oh dear, oh dear," Lowell murmured and raised Aaron's hand to his lips. He pressed an open-mouthed kiss to the red burn mark. "Let me help with that, hmm?"

The uncomfortable feeling sitting at the base of Rory's stomach threatened to overflow. They hadn't even opened the wine yet and already Lowell was putting the moves on Aaron? Rory remembered, with dread, how awkward their dinner party had turned.

But then Aaron smiled, eyelids low, and let out a soft moan, taking Rory aback.

"It's nothing, Mr. Lowell," he protested gently but went on letting Lowell kiss his skin, his whole body seeming to reach out for Lowell's.

Rory coughed and cleared his throat.

Lowell startled with a laugh. "Oh, I'm so sorry, Rory. I suppose we got carried away, didn't we? We've been a little like a pair of lovebirds these last two days."

Lovebirds?

Lowell smiled tenderly at Aaron. "Do you want to tell him?"

"Yes," Aaron whispered, his gaze locked on Lowell's.

"Go on," Lowell urged, gentle and fatherly.

Aaron turned to face Rory. He took a deep breath and rolled his eyes toward the ceiling, as if trying to summon up the words. "It wasn't a mistake, Rory."

"What wasn't?" he asked, his throat dry.

Aaron shivered. "It wasn't a mistake, and I didn't need money, either. I-I took Mr. Lowell's card because I wanted to come here. I wanted to live here. And be with him. It wouldn't have been appropriate otherwise, with me working for him. But me being his rezzy? Well, you must have realized by now it's totally normal—expected, even— for a citizen and his rezzy to have a sexual or romantic relationship."

"Wh-what?" Rory blubbered, face flushing hot from his throat to his forehead.

He remembered Aaron's hero worship the first time they'd met at the hospital. The one-man Jericho Lowell cheer squad. *"I'm gushing, aren't I?"* And then he remembered the look on Aaron's face when

Lowell had pulled him into his lap at Rory's house the night of the dinner party. He'd looked mortified. Terrified. Rory searched his face now. Aaron was a little flushed—embarrassed by his confession maybe—and his eyes were wide and sincere.

"Aaron," Rory said, his voice catching. "Why would you do something so, so stupid?"

Aaron rested his cheek against Lowell's chest. He swallowed. "Haven't you ever done something stupid for love?"

No. But Rory had never been in love, had he?

Lowell stroked Aaron's dark hair. "When he told me, I was furious, of course, but the damage, as it were, was already done. Foolish, reckless boy, but we're making the best of it, aren't we?"

"Yes, sir," Aaron murmured. His gaze was fixed on some point in the distance, unseeing. And then his eyes fell on Rory, intense and clear. "I've gotten everything I ever wanted."

Rory wondered if he'd ever even known Aaron at all.

"Good," Lowell said, rubbing Aaron's back. "Good boy."

Aaron continued to stare at Rory, opening his mouth and then closing it again. He flinched suddenly and sniffed, then lifted a hand to his nose a fraction of a second before Rory saw the blood.

"Shit, Aaron, your nose is bleeding." Rory reached for a roll of paper towels on the countertop and tore a few pieces off.

Lowell stepped away from him. "Aaron?"

Aaron pulled his hand away from his nose and blinked at the blood. A few drops fell onto the pristine kitchen floor, and he made a small noise of distress.

Rory bunched up the paper towel and held it under his nose. "Take it. Hold it there."

"He gets nosebleeds," Lowell said in a low voice.

"I get them," Aaron agreed through the wad of paper. "Messy. Sorry."

"Don't fuss," Lowell said. "Hold the towel there." He stroked Aaron's hair tenderly.

Aaron. God.

Rory stepped back, still searching Aaron's eyes, still looking for something that wasn't here. Something that would explain why the hairs were standing up on the back of his neck.

But there was no doubt in Aaron's eyes, and there was no way he was any good at lying.

Which meant . . .

He was telling the truth about everything.

Tate woke up to hear Rory opening and closing the cupboard doors in the living room. Tate hauled himself out of bed quickly, squinting at the tiny clock beside his narrow bed. It was just past midnight. He tugged his pants low on his hips—Rory was still not comfortable with his nudity but that didn't mean Tate couldn't tease him with the hint of it—and shuffled out to the living room.

He stifled a yawn. "Rory? What are you doing?"

Rory turned. "Sorry. Did I wake you?"

"No." A lie was only bad if it hurt his master. "I was waiting for you. What are you looking for?"

"Your paperwork."

A bolt of anxiety shot through Tate. "Why?"

Rory sighed. He shut the cupboard. "I saw Aaron tonight."

Poor kid. Except to think that was . . . was wrong. Because if Tate was happy now, then so was Aaron. And at least Aaron had a master who knew how to treat him right. Keep him on his knees. Make him beg. Make him worship his master. Tate's cock hardened just thinking about it. All sense of wrongness vanished. "He looked happy?" he asked, refusing to acknowledge there was even an alternative. Because there wasn't.

Rory's shoulders slumped. "Yeah."

"Well, then, that's good. How about I take you to bed?" He stepped close, pressing his half-formed erection against the back of Rory's hip. He rubbed the muscles at the base of Rory's neck. "Hmm?"

"No!" Rory shrugged him off, then spun, grabbing him hard by the shoulders. "It's not right, Tate. Something's not right. He says he stole from Lowell so they could *be together*!"

"He's a kid," he said. "Kids do dumb things. It's kind of . . . kind of romantic. Like a movie. That big gesture right at the end, just before the kiss."

"It's not *romantic*. It's his freedom!" Rory shook his head. "I don't know. There was something off about him. They put a chip in you, right? Was it really just to keep you from getting violent?"

No. No. Tate couldn't talk about this. He might as well stab a kitchen knife into his temple. Even thinking about it caused a blast of static in his head that whited out his vision for a second. It *hurt*.

"Of course," Tate said smoothly and licked his lips. Canted his hips too. "Now come to bed. You're being paranoid. I know a way to relax you."

"God damn it, Tate!" Rory shouted. "I'm your master, aren't I? You have to fucking answer me truthfully, right? So fucking answer me! There's something going on here, isn't there?"

Master. To hear Rory say the word was intoxicating. Terrifying.

"You're my master," Tate echoed. His whole body tingled with desire. "That's right. You're my master. And I—" God, what had they been talking about, even? "I am being truthful, Master. Please, let me serve you. Let me take your mind off things." He lowered himself to his knees, catching the waistband of Rory's wrinkled trousers and pulling them down with him as he went. Rory's cock was flaccid but no less delicious looking for it. Tate could fix all that, anyway. He gave the head a kiss. "Mmm, Master." He moaned, arching, his erection rubbing against the rough insides of his plain scrub pants. "Oh, thank you, Master."

"Tate," Rory said. He pushed Tate's shoulders ineffectually. "Don't."

"Come to bed, Master. Come to bed and lie down, and I'll ride you. You won't have to work at all. I'll do everything—*anything* for you. I missed you. My little hole missed your cock. Come to bed."

"Fuck," Rory said, his jaw dropping. "I wasn't . . . I didn't mean . . . Is this a game or something? All this 'Master' shit?"

If you need it to be a game, it's a game.

Tate grinned. "Want to play?"

Rory sighed.

Tate rubbed his thigh. "Rory," he said, "it's nice that you're worried about Aaron, but you said he's happy. So you don't need to worry. Let me take care of you, please?"

"Something's not right here," Rory murmured, frowning.

Don't.

Don't ask about the chip. Don't ask about the induction center. Don't ask about the things I did there. Don't ask about before.

Before.

Tophet.

Outside.

I wasn't happy there. I didn't know what happiness was. There was nothing, until here, until you. Nothing that compared.

Not even the curl of tiny fingers around my thumb.

A white flash of pain in his skull.

Serve him. Worship *him.*

"Let me take care of you," Tate repeated, his voice low with sincerity.

This time, when he took Rory's cock into his mouth, Rory didn't protest.

CHAPTER
TWELVE

"Hmm," Lowell said, peering into his briefcase. "Aaron means well, but this sandwich looks inedible. Maybe I ought to borrow Tate to give him some lessons." He laughed. "Although I'm sure there are things Aaron could teach Tate, as well."

Rory forced a smile and checked his watch. "Six minutes until the broadcast, sir."

Lowell snapped his briefcase shut again and smiled for the girl who approached. "Ah, you've come to make me look beautiful? You'll need a bigger makeup case."

The girl laughed.

Rory moved out of the way and checked his watch again.

Lowell raised his chin for her makeup sponge but went on talking to Rory as if nobody had interrupted. "How have you and Tate been getting on, by the way? Two virile young men like you, you must have a rather vigorous sex life." He chuckled. "If Tate is even half as eager as Aaron, you must be going at it like rabbits! Me, I'm too old to keep up with Aaron. Can barely satisfy the boy, even in as good a shape as I am. But you and Tate must be pretty well matched in that area. I'm surprised you ever get out of bed at all!"

The makeup girl giggled, not the least bit put off. But then, people in Beulah were so much less repressed than those on the outside.

Still, Rory's face burned. He opened his folder and went through the notes he'd made, eager for a distraction. Stared at the words but couldn't make any sense of them. He was finally getting the hang of his job at the Hall of Justice. He was learning the quickest way to get things done, either by playing office politics with other departments or by avoiding them altogether. He could put together a press release in half an hour, now that he knew where to find the records he needed, and was even learning his way around the court briefs that Ruth and Zac dealt with. Finally he was where he wanted to be in his job, so why the hell did it feel like he was losing his grip on everything else?

He'd tried too hard to just go with the flow in Beulah, and now he was feeling like he'd been swept too far from the shore to ever find his way back.

"Is it really this easy to be happy?" he'd asked Tate the other night. It didn't feel real.

Either Rory was wrong or everyone else was.

Shit. What the hell was his problem? He had a great job, a wonderful house, and a beautiful man to come home to. A beautiful man who liked to fuck. Was Rory really such a pessimist that he could have all of those things and not trust them? And why? Because they'd come too easy? They hadn't. Rory had worked for years to get to where he was. He'd made sacrifices. He'd *earned* this, hadn't he?

"Oh dear," Lowell said when Rory didn't reply automatically. "You're still holding on to all your outsider morals and restrictions, aren't you?" He clucked and shook his head. "We're going to have to break you of those. Well, desperate times call for desperate measures. Why don't you and Tate come to my place tonight, and we'll put these worries of yours to bed?" His eyes twinkled, his eyebrows rising. "Among other things."

"I, uh." Rory squirmed. "Oh! I think I left my day planner in the office."

Was Lowell propositioning him? Rory wasn't sure. And he wasn't sure if he should be offended or not. Lowell was a good-looking man, confident and charming. Part of Rory was flattered. Another part of him whispered that he had Tate now.

"Well, head on back," Lowell said. "I think I've got everything covered here. But when you find it, make sure you write in that we're doing dinner tonight. Seven. My place." He smiled, then crinkled his nose in the direction of his briefcase and the sandwich Aaron had made him. "We'll order in, I think."

"Okay," Rory said, flustered. "Good luck with the interview."

"I don't need luck," Lowell said. "I've got the best assistant in town."

Rory returned to the Hall of Justice. It was early afternoon. Zac was in court, Ruth was at a meeting, and Alexandra had been sent on a research assignment. The office should have been empty.

It wasn't.

There was someone inside Lowell's office. He could see their shadow through the frosted glass in Lowell's door. Rooting around in Lowell's desk, by the looks of things.

Shit. Should he call security, or . . .

Body pounding with adrenaline, he burst through the door expecting a burglar.

Alexandra gasped, her hands flying to her throat. In one of them, she held a nail file.

"What are you doing?" Rory asked, looking from her to the open drawer of Lowell's desk.

"I was . . . I was looking for something," Alexandra said, her voice shaking.

"For what?" Rory asked.

She didn't answer.

Rory held her gaze. "He said he wanted it, you know. Aaron. He said he did it so he could go and live with Mr. Lowell. He said it's love."

Her hand tightened around the nail file.

"Was he serious? With you?"

"We fooled around," Alexandra said. She lifted her chin defiantly, but her gaze flickered. "It was nothing."

Liar.

Rory looked down at the drawer again. "The envelopes are kept in the cupboard outside. That's what you were looking for, right? An envelope?"

Alexandra nodded warily. "Yes. I was."

Not just a liar but the worst liar in the world.

"I'm going to see him tonight," Rory said. "Is there anything you want me to tell him?"

"No," Alexandra said, bitterness creeping into her tone. "He's happy. They're *always* happy."

And before Rory could ask her what she meant, she charged past him and fled the office.

Despite his reservations, Rory couldn't get out of dinner with Lowell. And Tate was eager to go. Rory realized, guiltily, that Tate only really left the house to walk as far as the grocery store and back. He didn't socialize or have friends. He'd seen less of Beulah than Rory had. And okay, maybe he hadn't come here as a tourist or a legal immigrant, but that didn't mean it was right to confine him to the house alone. Tate was beaming as they walked down the road together, heading for Lowell's house.

"It's nice here," he said. "So green. Sometimes, when you're at work, I just stand in the yard so I can feel the grass under my feet. Never had that on the outside. Never."

Rory smiled at him. "It's perfect."

"Perfect," Tate echoed.

At Lowell's house, Aaron pressed a glass of wine into Rory's hand the moment the door was open. "Mr. Lowell is in the study. He said you should go in. Tate can help me set the table for dinner."

Rory looked to Tate, almost for permission, and Tate smiled back. "Go ahead," he said. "Aaron and I can keep each other company."

He headed off to find Lowell. The study door was open, and Lowell was seated at his desk reading a newspaper. He looked up and smiled when Rory appeared, and folded the newspaper up. "Damn opinion polls. I don't know why they even run them. Politics isn't about popularity, it's about the ability to govern."

"A bad result?" Rory asked, sitting down. He sipped his wine.

"Not at all," Lowell said. "It just irritates me when the focus is on me personally, rather than what I'm trying to achieve here. The cult of personality is a dangerous one. History has taught us that."

Lowell was a rare man indeed. A popular politician who didn't care about popularity. Didn't get pumped up on his own ego.

"There's no place for this sort of populist nonsense in government," Lowell said. "Or in the home, either. It's all about a common goal, Rory, and a common good. Political leaders too often forget who is really in charge."

"And who's that?"

"The people," Lowell said. "I'm a leader, but I also have a million employers. If I lead, I also serve. In many respects, I'm not so different than Aaron." He picked up the bottle of wine from his desk and topped up Rory's glass. "You know, in ancient times, it was seen as something admirable to serve the public. Then, somehow, it got all mixed up with money, and the rot set in. But I like to think of myself as a bit of a rezzy myself. I owe Beulah a debt as well. A debt of gratitude. And I try to repay it a little every day."

"That's an admirable philosophy," he said. "Most politicians don't share it."

"Maybe not on the outside," Lowell smiled. "But things are different here. We know how lucky we are. We know that it's an honor and a privilege to serve. Outside, people have lost any sense of community."

That was certainly true. Rory drank.

"Which brings me to Tate," Lowell said.

"Tate?"

"Tate wants to serve, as well," Lowell said. "He's been on the other side, and so have you. You both know what it's like out there. And Tate is working hard to show that he's grateful, to show that he's better than his past. He needs you to acknowledge that. He needs you to set goals for him, and boundaries. Do you do that?"

"I don't know." He frowned. "I mean, he does chores around the house. And I thank him for it."

Lowell's smile grew. "How do you thank him for it?"

"I tell him," Rory said. "How else am I supposed to thank him?"

Lowell laughed. "He's not your boyfriend. He's not your housewife either. He's a *rezzy*. And you're his master."

"Sponsor," Rory said, remembering the unadulterated pleasure on Tate's face when Rory had called himself his master. "I'm his sponsor."

"Semantics." Lowell waved his hand. "Look, I'm not going to get into a discussion about criminality with you, but I think you'd agree that, in most cases, it's a lack of boundaries that leads to lawbreaking in the first place. You need to give him boundaries so that he feels safe. So that he won't be tempted to stray. And you need to discipline him when he oversteps those boundaries."

"I don't know what you mean," Rory said. His wineglass was full again. "I don't know what you mean, in practical terms."

"Practically?" Lowell leaned back in his chair. "Well, take Aaron, for example. If the house isn't spotless when I get home from work, I give him five swats with my belt. And if it is spotless, well . . ." He chuckled. "If it is spotless, I bend him over the couch and fuck him until he screams."

Rory's jaw dropped.

"He loves it, too, the little slut," Lowell said, his voice warm with affection. "You need a similar system with Tate. Punishments and rewards. You're the one in charge, Rory. You're the master."

Sponsor, Rory thought, but something about the word *master* made his breath catch.

Lowell's smile faded. "The system *works*, but only if you're prepared to commit to it, just like Tate has. He needs a master, and that's your job. Teach him the value of discipline. Teach him to work hard for a reward. Teach him to be a better man than the one who broke your nose the first time you met. Don't waste your seven years. That violent criminal from the station? Don't put him back on the streets."

Rory's head swam, as much as from Lowell's words as the wine. "But this can't be . . . can't be *legal*." Then he remembered he was sitting across the desk from a justice. "Well, moral then."

"What's more moral than teaching a man how to serve others?" Lowell asked. "To serve you first, and then his community?"

"I really don't . . ."

Lowell snorted. "Because you don't *see*, Rory. It's right in front of your eyes, but you don't see. You don't see how much Tate needs it and how much it validates him." He poured more wine into Rory's glass. "Drink up, and then I'll show you."

"Show me what?" he asked anxiously.

"I'll show you how to train a rezzy," Lowell said, his eyes gleaming.

"Happy," Aaron murmured to himself, his hands on his knees.

Tate knelt beside him on the floor, clothes discarded, thighs spread. "Happy," he agreed.

Aaron turned his head toward him, smiling, as though he was delighted to have found confirmation there. "Yes!"

Tate looked at the pink line on Aaron's inner thigh and remembered the doctor who had given him the knife. Aaron had passed the test, as well. He wondered if Aaron was proud of that. He should have been very proud. Tate wondered if the doctor had made Aaron jerk himself off with his own blood.

Tate moaned at the memory.

Strange that it had ever disturbed or upset him before, when now it just filled him with overpowering pleasure. Obeying. Being so good. He wanted to be that more, do that more. He wanted Rory to take him there.

And soon, he would. Aaron had said if they waited here, just like this, then Mr. Lowell would help Rory learn what he needed to do. And help them both be the men that they needed to be.

Rory had drunk too much. He knew that the second he tried to stand up. Then, following Lowell back out into the living room, he even stumbled a little. He thought about making an excuse to leave, thought about admitting that he wasn't ready to learn whatever lesson Lowell wanted to teach him, thought about just coming out and saying that the whole rezzy thing left him with a bad taste in his mouth. He liked Tate—wasn't that enough? He didn't want to master him. Didn't want to master anyone, and he was damn sure that Tate didn't want to be mastered.

And then he saw him.

"Oh shit," he whispered. Tate was kneeling on the floor, naked, his hands resting on his spread thighs. His cock was hard. And he stared at Rory with such blatant longing that Rory didn't know what he believed anymore.

Lowell slung an arm around Rory's shoulders. "There," he said. "Beautiful, aren't they?"

Rory's hands clenched into fists, then released again. Tate and Aaron knelt in front of him, both of them in matching poses, both with matching erections and matching adoring smiles.

Yes, they were beautiful. Both of them, so beautiful. Rory's head felt fuzzy just looking at them. But there was a difference, wasn't there, between wanting and taking? There had to be a difference. Except right now, fuddled with wine, he couldn't spot it. All he could see was his own want reflected in Tate's dark eyes.

"Tell him what you want," Lowell said, his voice low.

"I don't . . . I don't know." He couldn't break his gaze. Couldn't help seeing the disappointment flash across Tate's face.

Lowell sighed and released him. "You *do* know." He crossed to the couch and sat down, legs spread wide. A playful smile lit up his face. "Hello, Aaron."

Aaron arched toward him. "Hello, sir."

Lowell patted his thigh. "Why don't you come over here and show Rory what a good boy you are?"

Aaron scrambled eagerly across the floor. He pushed into the space between Lowell's legs and pressed his face into the man's crotch. He moaned, and his body shuddered.

"Shit," Rory murmured. His *boss*. His boss and his friend. Rory didn't care how open people in Beulah were; that was not the sort of thing he wanted to see. Except . . . except he couldn't look away.

Lowell chuckled and curled his fingers in Aaron's hair. He tugged his head up gently. "Now, have I ever done anything to you that you didn't want?"

"No, sir!" Aaron's voice rose, as though offended at the very suggestion. Then, staring up at Lowell, he began to rock on his knees. "Sir. Please, sir. Please. Please."

"Not yet," Lowell chided. "Rory and I haven't eaten yet. Go and get us something, then maybe you and Tate can play while we eat."

Play? Rory's mouth was dry. He sat down on the couch opposite Lowell's. Exactly how much had he had to drink? A moment later, there was a fresh glass pressed into his hand, and a plate of store-bought snacks beside him.

"See how eager Aaron is?" Lowell said, smiling as Aaron delivered him his food. "That's what rules and boundaries and instructions do." Aaron had settled to his knees again, but he was bouncing impatiently, like he couldn't wait to hop to his feet. Lowell laughed generously. "Oh, all right. Go and teach Tate a few new tricks."

Tricks, now? Were they people or pets? Rory's head swam. He set down the wine, pushed aside the food, sank deeper into the back of the couch. And in front of him, on the floor, Aaron and Tate faced each other, still on their knees, but now they were kneeling upright, chests pressed together, kissing deeply, their cocks rubbing between their taut bellies.

Rory wanted them to stop. Couldn't stand watching them, watching Tate moan and twist. And the sounds were different from the ones he made for Rory, maybe because now he knew this was a performance. Or maybe because Aaron was better at pleasuring him than Rory was; he certainly was a great deal louder now on Lowell's floor than he'd ever been in their bed. A knot formed in his stomach. He couldn't untangle it. It was made up of lust and shame and jealousy all at once. He didn't want to watch Tate and Aaron perform like trained animals. He wanted to touch. He wanted to keep Tate for himself. He wanted sex to be special and sweet and secret, not this obscene show.

But he didn't speak up. His tongue felt fat and confused. Aaron had ducked his head, now, and was softly suckling one of Tate's perfect brown nipples as he cupped and kneaded the other with his hand. Tate was moaning, his eyes glassy, staring straight at Rory but somehow not seeing him.

"What should we make them do?" Lowell asked, eyes twinkling as he popped a cube of cheese in his mouth. "Suck each other? Wrestle? We could have Tate fuck Aaron on the floor. Or . . . use my belt on him."

"No," Rory said, the word forcing its way through his disoriented mouth. "No belts. I don't want it to hurt."

"Aha!" Lowell grinned. "So you *do* have a preference. Well, go on."

Tate looked to him, swollen lips parted, chin tilted upward as Aaron kissed and nipped at his throat. *Go on, then*, his drunken gaze echoed.

Rory was way past understanding what was happening here. Way past ignoring his lust. He crooked a finger at Tate. "Come here."

"That's it," Lowell said as Tate disentangled himself from Aaron and crawled across the floor. "You need to be able to master a rezzy, Rory. You need to be able to tell him, without any guilt, exactly what you want. And he needs to be able to serve you. We want more outsiders in Beulah, but only if they can prove themselves good citizens. You need to fit in, Rory. So does he. This is the way we do things here. Isn't it so much better?"

Was it? Rory couldn't think.

"On the outside, he'd be in a stinking prison and you'd be forgotten by a system that doesn't advocate for the rights of victims. But here, you can both benefit. You can both be happy." Lowell caught Rory's startled gaze. "You are *owed* this."

Tate had made his way between Rory's legs. Had undone Rory's fly. Behind him, Aaron had followed him over and was busy lowering himself so that he could get his mouth and tongue between Tate's legs and into the cleft of his ass.

"I want to give you this, Master, please," Tate mumbled, and his voice was broken, as if he was truly begging, begging on the verge of tears. He kissed Rory's cock through the fabric of his briefs. "Please be my master. Please let me serve you."

"Yes," Rory said, his eyes falling closed.

Couldn't look. Couldn't watch as Aaron—*Aaron!* The same kid who'd bounded into the office every day with an eager smile and a tray of coffees—lapped at Tate's ass. While their boss watched. This was some weird twilight world where all the rules had been thrown out the window. Rory kept his eyes closed as Tate's hot mouth closed around the head of his cock.

"F-fuck," Rory gritted out, biting his lip, fingers scrabbling across the fabric of the sofa for a grip. Tate was getting *good* at this. So much better than he'd been at first. So much more *precise*. The point of his tongue jabbed into the tiny slit at the end of Rory's cock, and Rory almost arched off the couch.

"You should keep him plugged," Lowell suggested. "Like I do with Aaron. Keeps them focused. Keeps their head in the game. There's nothing this boy won't do for me when he's had a plug teasing him all day, is there, Aaron?"

Rory opened his eyes as Aaron lifted his head to answer. "No, sir. Nothing."

"Back to me, now," Lowell said. "You can sniff around Tate's ass like a pup later."

Wrong. Shit. So wrong to hear Lowell talk to Aaron like that, when the other day it had all been about how they were lovebirds. It was wrong even if Aaron liked it. Maybe because he liked it. It didn't seem like love to Rory. Rory threaded his fingers through Tate's curls and watched as Aaron unzipped Lowell's fly, freed his erect dick, and straddled him. Lowell's fingers dug into Aaron's hips as Aaron lowered himself down. He whimpered as Lowell's cock pushed into him, inch by inch. Rory forced his gaze away with difficulty.

He pulled Tate's head back. "Is that what you want? Do you want that too?"

"Yes," Tate said without even looking. Like it didn't even matter what he was agreeing to. "Yes, please."

Rory pulled Tate onto his lap. Helped him settled his knees on either side of him. Guided his cock into that tight, hot hole, wet with Aaron's spit.

"When they're plugged you can use them whenever you like. They're always ready for you, nice and wet and stretched and desperate to come." Lowell grunted. Aaron had finished his slow descent, impaling himself on Lowell's dick. Lowell spanked one ass cheek. "All right, boy, look lively for our guest. In fact, why don't you turn around so he can watch your pretty dick bounce?"

"Mmm." Aaron scrabbled awkwardly to rearrange himself. His face was red with the effort of taking Lowell. The flush extended down his chest. His thigh muscles flexed. The head of his cock bobbed up and down. Lowell's hands cupped his chest, pinched and twisted his nipples until he cried out.

Rory couldn't take his eyes off him. Even with Tate nuzzling at his throat, rocking back and forth on his cock, it was Aaron Rory stared at. So athletic, so small and slim and fucking himself hard on his master's length. The expression on his face reminded Rory of pictures of saints and martyrs: pain and rapture at the same time. Whatever it was, it didn't look very much like love. Maybe love looked different in Beulah than it did on the outside.

He noticed a scar on Aaron's upper thigh, nearly hidden in the crease of his groin. Tate had a scar there too. Odd.

Rory traced it with his fingers, drawing out a shudder in Tate. Tate arched his back, gasped, and rocked harder on Rory's cock. His hands held tight on Rory's shoulders, his cock slapping his abdomen as he moved. Hard and fast, so hard it must have hurt.

But Tate liked it to hurt. That was what he'd said.

"Slut," Lowell said to Aaron. Rory couldn't tell if it was affectionate or not. It didn't seem affectionate, but Aaron moaned high and needy like it was. "Little tease."

Aaron's eyes flashed wide for an instant. "I'm sorry, Master," he cried, his words jostled by the movement of his body. "I'm so sorry for ever teasing you."

Lowell laughed and raked his fingers along Aaron's chest, leaving red marks behind. "Come on, lazy boy. Faster."

"Master," Tate whispered in Rory's ear. "Please, Master."

Rory pulled his gaze away from Aaron and Lowell. Kissed Tate instead. Tasting him and teasing him and making him moan. All the affection Lowell denied Aaron with his mean words and rough touches.

Lowell said he loved Aaron.

Maybe . . . maybe Rory felt the same way about Tate.

His hands slipped to Tate's waist, gentling him, slowing his pace. "That's it," he coaxed as Tate followed his guidance, his hips rolling smooth and gentle as waves in a tide pool. Could he be Tate's master and his lover? His master and his boyfriend? His master and his friend?

Aaron was howling and screaming now, not in enjoyment, but in pain; Lowell was pinching the head of his cock and deflating his erection.

Rory's stomach clenched. He gripped Tate by the shoulders and tried to push him away. He needed to help Aaron.

"No," Tate whispered. "No, he likes it. Watch. He likes it rough. Mr. Lowell knows what he needs." He kissed Rory behind the ear. "I like it rough too. You could use me that way."

Rory stared over his shoulder at Aaron. Tears streaked down his face now. His nose was bleeding again as he said, over and over, "Yes, please, more." He licked his lips, tongue swiping through the blood. Lowell didn't seem to notice or care.

Lowell's words: *You need to fit in. You need to be more like us.*

And Aaron's: *I've gotten everything I've ever wanted.*

Who was Rory to judge that? Rory was an outsider. Tate was one too, but Tate was at least willing to try. Wasn't he? Doing all this, being exactly the thing Beulah wanted him to be. Why couldn't Rory keep up? He wanted to. He wanted this to be home. He wanted this to feel right. Beulah was supposed to be perfect. Rory wanted to be perfect too.

Tate's breath was ragged in his ear. "Come in me, Master. Come in me."

His desperate plea tripped something in Rory. He came, shuddering and gasping, as Tate clenched tightly around him.

"Thank you. Thank you. Thank you." Tate kissed him over and over again.

Over his shoulder, Aaron fell forward out of Lowell's lap with a groan, landing face-first and ass-up on the floor.

Lowell, leaning back, dabbed at the sweat on his forehead, reaching out with one toe to nudge Aaron's upraised ass. "Should we let them come, Rory? Have they done well enough?"

Rory nodded wordlessly, and Tate kissed him again, slipping gracefully to the floor with Aaron.

"W-wait!"

"Come now, Rory," Lowell said. "Let the boys have their fun. This is no place for jealousy."

Jealousy. Rory's face burned. He wanted to protest—too late—that it wasn't about jealousy at all. It was about preserving Tate's dignity, and Aaron's. It was about the realization that this had already gone too far. But it would have been a lie. It was all jealousy. He didn't want another man to touch Tate.

Lowell gave a knowing smile.

Aaron didn't move, so Tate went to him, rolled him onto his back, kissed him, and gently fondled his soft, bruised cock until it began to harden. Climbed atop him, giving Rory a view of Tate gently dipping his own cock against Aaron's lips, over and over again until Aaron opened up and received him. The pair of them sucked each other, Tate fucking Aaron's face and bobbing his head.

Lowell watched with sated pleasure. Took a sip of ice water. "Play with each other's holes," he directed, waving them on lazily with one hand.

Tate's fingers dove into Aaron's ass, three of them at once, scooping out gobs of Lowell's cum. Aaron moaned. Tate was making noise, as well. High pitched whimpers. His poor ass must be raw, and to have Aaron poking and prodding at him in the same way . . .

"I like this," Lowell said. "The boy gets his reward, but I get to rest. Best of both worlds, don't you agree?"

No. "Oh . . . yes," Rory replied. He couldn't stop looking at Tate's puffy hole, Aaron's curling and thrusting fingers. The dribbles of cum running down Aaron's hand and the back of Tate's balls.

"We could have them lick each other's asses up too. They won't even need dinner then, because their bellies will be full of cum. Ours. Each other's. Hell, have them kiss with their mouths full and then they can eat some of their own too."

A part of him wanted to see that. A part of him wanted to revel in his own power, to see how far he could push them. To see if they'd really do it, and if they did, if they'd love it and thank him for the chance.

Another part of him just wanted to go back to his own house, put Tate in a hot bath, and never go outside again. Keep him safe from this horrible, twisted place.

"Isn't it so much better?"

For the first time, Rory wasn't so sure.

In the end, Lowell had them come in each other's mouths and eat each other's asses before they exchanged a long—*gratuitously* long—sloppy kiss that covered both their chins in cum. Rory had to finish his glass of wine just to get through it. His stomach churned as he watched. Not because of the act itself but because of the exhibitionism. The exploitation. And Aaron's face, still shining with tears and snot and blood.

But when they pulled away from one another, when Lowell beamed and clapped his hands, they both smiled and flushed and laughed with pride, and Rory felt, again, that he was the only one still stuck on the outside. The only one who didn't understand how good this was, how right, how happy everyone was.

They're always *happy*, Alexandra had said.

She'd spat the words like an accusation instead of an endorsement. Like a curse, instead of a blessing.

CHAPTER THIRTEEN

Rory woke up once during the night to find Tate sleeping beside him.

He was nauseated. He'd drunk way too much at Lowell's house. He rolled over and reached for the glass of water on his nightstand. Took a mouthful of that and then a painkiller, as well.

God. What a night.

What a crazy, fucked-up night.

What the hell was he going to say to Lowell in the morning? How was he supposed to look the man in the eye when he'd watched him fuck Aaron like that? Or worse, when Lowell had been like the fucking ringmaster or something, directing his little trained monkeys to dance?

The sudden wave of nausea that threatened him had nothing to do with the wine.

He lay back down, and Tate, still asleep, snuggled closer.

He carded his fingers through Tate's curls, until he found that tiny knot of scar tissue below Tate's hairline on the back of his neck.

The chip.

The chip that tracked Tate if he ran.

The chip that stopped him from being violent.

"They're always happy."

Oh God.

It was the chip.

Rory slept in the next day. Tate wasn't surprised. He'd had a *lot* to drink the night before and had only made it home because Tate had loaned him his shoulder to lean on.

Even though Tate hadn't drunk a drop, last night was a haze for him too. It lurked at the back of his mind as he bustled naked through the kitchen, putting on a pot of strong coffee and getting together ingredients for a big, greasy omelet for Rory.

Rory, his master. He sighed with pleasure and ignored the prickle of unease at the base of his skull. What had happened last night wasn't dirty, wasn't filthy or wrong. It was right because Rory and Lowell had commanded it. It was right because serving them felt good. Just because the very idea of it would have made him sick once, just because there was a part of him still screaming silently behind the locked doors in his head, that didn't make it wrong. Just because the same fingers that had brushed Emmy's soft, downy hair back from her forehead had last night been inside Aaron's hole, every twist of them pulling pained noises out of him . . .

Tate froze, the knife poised above the cutting board.

No. He pushed the thought away before it hurt him. Before it tore through him like lightning. He needed to hold those thoughts at bay, to protect himself from the pain and the misery and the doubt.

It would all be better once Rory woke up. As long as Rory remembered his place as Tate's master, then it would be so easy for Tate to remember his place on his knees. Rory would center him. Keep him sane. Make everything make sense.

Just as a master should.

With that thought to buoy him, he returned to his tasks, plating up the omelet and pouring the coffee and washing the dishes, whistling all the while with a half-filled erection bobbing between his legs. He was *happy*. He was happy, and Rory was happy, and—

Rory stood in the doorway of the kitchen, not smiling. There were dark bags under his eyes.

"You startled me," Tate said. He smiled. "Good morning."

Rory stared at him, eyes widening, as though he wasn't sure what he was seeing. He opened his mouth and then closed it again. Grimaced as though he was in pain.

"I've made coffee," Tate told him. "And maybe you should take a pain pill for your head."

"I was drunk," Rory said in a monotone.

"Yes," Tate said. "I'll get you a pill, and you'll feel better."

"No, I don't care about that." Rory frowned. "What the fuck happened last night?"

No.

Don't you backslide now. I need you to be my master.

Tate swallowed. "I liked it. I liked it when you told me what to do. I liked it when you fucked me. I liked it when you watched me and Aaron on the floor." There was a buzzing sound in his head, but he pressed on. "I liked it when I swallowed his cum. I pretended it was yours."

Rory reeled away suddenly.

"Don't," Tate whispered. "Please!"

He followed Rory down the hallway, only to have the bathroom door slammed in his face. He leaned against it, his stomach twisting, as he listened to the sound of Rory retching in the toilet. Just like Tate himself had done that first time. But Tate was better now, wasn't he? Wasn't he?

He hadn't gotten sick last night, even with a belly full of cum. He'd lain down in his bed and closed his eyes and slept peacefully.

"Master," he whimpered through the door, knocking gently. "Please, it's all right. Please come out. I made you breakfast. Once you eat, you'll feel better." No reply. "Please, I want to make you feel better. I *need* to make you feel better!"

Silence.

And then the door cracked open. Rory poked his head out, eyes narrowed, face sickly pale. "What did you say? What did you just say?" His teeth were gritted, his hand on the door quaking, knuckles white. "What do you mean, you need it? Why do you need it, Tate? Did you need . . . did you need what happened last night?"

"I need . . ." He pushed the heel of his hand against his temple. "I need to serve you."

"Why?" Rory demanded, his voice low.

"To fulfill my conditions," he said. "T-to be rehabilitated. To be a better person."

Rory opened the door. "But what if you're not?"

"N-not what?"

"Not a better person." There was a strange light in Rory's eyes. "What if you're a bad person?"

Tate flinched with pain.

"What if I don't like you?" Rory said, stepping forward. Tate couldn't read the look on his face. "What if I don't praise you? What if I *hate* you?"

"Don't," Tate whined, a white flash of pain blinding him. He clutched his head. "Please, please, Master, don't!"

"I *hate* you," Rory said, his voice catching. "You're worthless. You're a criminal. You're a waste of oxygen. You've *failed*."

Tate's knees gave out. He didn't even feel it as he hit the floor. He was screaming, maybe. It felt like he was, but he couldn't hear anything. He tasted blood. His heart was racing, his gut clenched, and every muscle tensed. He couldn't breathe.

Then Rory's hand was on his back. "Tate."

He whimpered.

"You're good," Rory said, his voice shaky. "You're so good, okay? I'm sorry. I'm sorry! Nothing I said was true."

The pain eased. He blinked through his tears at the floor. He was shaking and couldn't seem to stop.

"The chip," Rory said. "Tell me about the chip."

"Can't," he managed. That taste of blood was back. "Please, can't." He spat, and a mouthful of stringy red saliva hit the floor. He needed to clean that up.

"Okay," Rory said. "It's okay. You're *good*, Tate." He rubbed Tate's back in slow circles, even though Tate could sense he was just as upset and shaky as Tate was.

He pulled the hem of his shirt down to try to wipe the floor.

"Leave it," Rory said, voice strained. "It's okay. Just leave it." He forcibly drew Tate back, and they ended up sitting together on the floor, backs against the wall and legs drawn up. Rory rubbed Tate's hand, comforting him and keeping him from lunging for the stain at the same time. "I didn't mean to make you hurt."

"I know."

"I just . . ." Rory shook his head. "Alexandra said that rezzies are *always* happy. When I saw Aaron, I should have seen it wasn't right, it wasn't *him*." He laughed bitterly. "Aaron loved Lowell, but not like that. The night of the party he was trying to shake the guy off. Maybe he's not even attracted to men."

Tate stared at the blood on the floor and ached to wipe it clean.

"Oh fuck." Rory flinched suddenly. "Tate?"

The buzzing in Tate's skull was back.

Rory's face was paler than before. His voice shook when he spoke. "Are you gay, Tate?"

"I serve you," he whispered.

"Oh God," Rory moaned. "Oh God, oh God, oh God. You're not gay. You're not gay."

"I'm what you want, Master," he said. He reached out for Rory's hand and gasped when Rory pulled away.

Tate's fault. His fault, somehow, for causing this. For, despite what he said, not being what Rory wanted. For not being able to serve him properly. For causing his master pain. For fucking everything up, just like always. *Worthless. Waste of oxygen.*

Rory stared at him, wide-eyed. He was shaking his head.

"Please, Master," he begged. "Please let me make you feel good!" He lunged down into Rory's lap, tugging desperately at the waistband of his pajama pants. "Please," he moaned, pressing his face into Rory's groin and finding no erection. "Please, please." He rubbed his cheek back and forth, breathed deep, fondled, all the things that Rory usually liked.

"Get off me!" Rory pushed him away.

Tate cried out, the rejection hurting as much as a blow. He lay sprawled on the floor, panting for breath. "Please, please, please. It *hurts*." His head was searing, the backs of his eyes burning.

Rory hitched up his pants, then laid his trembling hands on Tate's back. He rubbed gently. "I like you." His voice was a monotone. "You're good, but I don't want that. Okay? I don't want that."

Tate didn't understand. Of course Rory wanted it. He always had. He wanted it, and Tate needed it. He cried into his hands, right there on the floor.

"Tate," Rory said. "Tate, I need to get ready for work now. I need to . . . I need to go in today. Will you be okay?"

Tate wasn't sure if he'd ever be okay again, let alone happy. He'd had it, for one brief shining moment last night, but it had all gone to hell again.

Rory drew in a shuddering breath. Closed his eyes and blew it out again. "I want you to clean the house, okay? I would be very pleased with you if you cleaned the house."

Tate looked up cautiously, the beginnings of hope unfurling in his chest. "Yes, Master, I will clean the house."

"Good." Rory looked almost frightened, but he forced an uneasy smile. He cupped Tate's cheek and gave it a gentle pat. "That's good. You're good." He kept repeating the words, his gaze sliding from Tate's face to the wall behind him. "You're good, Tate. You're good."

Tate relaxed. He smiled at last, all his pain and misery washed away by his master's words of praise. Washed clean.

Rory wanted to be sick. He didn't even know how he'd finally managed to get dressed and get to work. He'd stared at his reflection in the window of the train as it had buzzed toward the city center. *A monster. You're a monster. You* raped *him.* And now, sitting at his desk as he stared at the blank screen in front of him, he could hardly breathe.

Alexandra moved quietly through the office.

Lowell was in court. Good, because Rory didn't know what to say to him. Lowell, with all his talk about justice and responsibility and leadership . . . Did he *know*? He couldn't know. Except Rory couldn't shake the horrible idea that maybe he did. That maybe he didn't care if Aaron really wanted it or not, just that Aaron said he did and acted like he did.

Hell. Tate wanted it too. But the idea that his want came from the chip . . .

You raped him.

Rory heard Lowell's booming laugh from somewhere out in the hall. He shook off his stupor.

"Rory." Lowell appeared in the doorway. "I'm having an early lunch with Justice Gordon. Do you want to join us?"

"I've got a lot of work," Rory managed.

"Maybe next time." Lowell smiled. "How did you wake up this morning?"

"I'm hungover," Rory said, hoping that would explain away his pallor.

"Ah," Lowell said. "Still, we must do it again sometime. Get the boys together and have some fun." He talked about it like it was so innocent. So normal. Nothing you couldn't discuss at work. Like getting together for a night of cards.

Instead of a night of depraved . . . rape.

Rory was conscious of Alexandra moving around in his periphery. "Okay."

Shit. Did he *know*? An honest politician, Rory had thought. A good man. Handsome, and friendly and charismatic. Always perfectly presented. Maybe what you saw was what you got, or maybe there was something frightening underneath. Just like Beulah itself.

Rory had no idea what to think.

The best of him. Assume the best of him.

Which meant Lowell needed to know. If he was a good man and he didn't know, then he *needed* to know.

"How about you, Alex?" Lowell asked. "Fancy an early lunch?"

"I have to run these depositions down to court," Alexandra said, blinking rapidly. "Sorry, sir."

"All work and no play." Lowell gave a little shake of his head. "Oh well, I suppose I'll have to listen to Gordon talk about his grandkids on my own."

Rory drew a deep breath. "When you get back, can I see you in private?"

Lowell looked concerned. "Anything urgent? I'll cancel lunch."

"No." Tate was safe for now, and so was Aaron. Safe from their own unwitting captors. "It can wait." He needed to figure out how to broach the subject, anyway. How did you say to a man, *"Hey, just a heads-up, but I think we may be raping our rezzies."*

"All right," Lowell said. "We'll talk then."

He left.

Rory watched Alexandra as she took a seat at her desk—Aaron's old desk—and began to work on something. *"They're* always *happy."*

"I think that . . ." he began, and she looked up as though surprised to find he was talking to her in the first place. Rory swallowed down his fear and his guilt. "Do you know something about the chips, Alexandra? The ones they put in rezzies?"

Her eyes widened. Her warm brown skin seemed to turn ashen. "Of course. They're to prevent violent tendencies." She drummed her pen against the desk rapidly.

Rory fought the crazy urge to laugh. She might have been the top of her class, but she would make a terrible lawyer if she couldn't lie. "That's not all, is it? That's not all they do."

"Why are you asking me this?"

"Because you know," Rory said, keeping his voice low. "What were you looking for in Lowell's office yesterday?"

"Nothing," she said and jutted out her chin. "A report."

"What report?" Rory asked and then guessed before she even answered. "Aaron's arrest report. Was it there?"

She shook her head.

"What do you know about the chip?"

"Nothing!" she hissed, looking toward the door anxiously. "Nobody does. And even if I did, why would I tell you? You're a *sponsor*."

It was the first time Rory had heard the word used as an insult. His stomach twisted. "Alexandra, please, I need to know if there's anyone who can take it out, or turn it off, or something."

"But he's *happy*," she said, her eyes flashing. "A happy little slave. They're *always* happy. Why would you ever want to change him back? I'll bet your rezzy does all your housework and cooks your meals and—and *plays* with Aaron too." Her voice cracked. "Isn't that what Mr. Lowell meant? About getting the boys together?"

"Yes." Bile rose in Rory's throat. "I didn't know. Not until this morning. I didn't realize."

Alexandra lifted her glasses to wipe at her eyes. "There was this guy, in our first year. His sister got mixed up in some stuff and stole a car. She became a rezzy. And she was different. She was *wrong*. There's this group . . ." She stopped and shook her head.

"What group? Do they help the rezzies?"

"Fuck," Alexandra said. Rory had never heard her swear before. "It's illegal. I don't even know how to contact them anyway. Nobody knows who they are. It's too dangerous."

Too many denials and refusals, too fast. She was a terrible liar.

"They'd never help you anyway," Alexandra told him. "Or Aaron. You're too high profile. If your rezzy or Aaron go missing, people would notice."

"What about Mr. Lowell?" Rory asked. "Can't he help?"

"I don't know," Alexandra said. She frowned. "With what happened to Aaron . . . It's suspicious, is all I'm saying. He's suspicious. Aaron said it was getting a bit weird. Like Mr. Lowell was coming on to him all the time. And suddenly he's Mr. Lowell's rezzy? I'm supposed to believe he stole the man's credit card?"

Rory's heart raced.

"It wasn't a mistake," Aaron had said. *"And I didn't need money, either. I-I took Mr. Lowell's card because I wanted to come here. I wanted to live here. And be with him."*

But if that were true, then why would Aaron complain to Alexandra about Lowell's flirting?

Because it wasn't true. Aaron hadn't taken the card. Not for money and not to be with Lowell, either. That whole story . . . that hadn't been Aaron talking at all. That had been the chip.

Rory hadn't known he was a rapist, but Lowell *had*. And worst of all, he wasn't just an opportunist raping a criminal. He'd framed an innocent man with the express purpose of raping him.

"Oh God." Everything that had happened last night flashed before Rory's eyes. Aaron and Tate and Lowell's smile. All that talk of whippings and plugs and pain. The sounds Aaron made when Lowell's thick cock entered him. His vacant eyes and his bleeding nose.

Lowell calling him a tease.

He remembered Tate in the shower, the first night they'd fucked. Remembered him trying to talk. Remembered him begging for help just before he'd passed out.

How many times had he pushed through the chip's programming? How many times had he tried to tell Rory what was happening to him? And Rory had never noticed. He had gone on telling him to make dinner and fucking him. Raping him. He'd *begged for help*, and Rory had called in Lowell and sealed his fate.

"Please help me," Rory said. "Please help me help Tate."

"I can't." But her voice wavered, and her eyes softened.

Another lie but it was enough. She'd help him, Rory knew. Eventually she would, even though it was dangerous and illegal. Because it was the right thing to do.

For once, Rory didn't feel like he was alone.

There was Alexandra and there were others, as well. Somewhere out there, beyond the reach of the tainted law.

They'd help him. They'd help Tate.

Rory would make sure of it.

There was nothing he could do to make up for what he'd done to Tate, but he could at least give him back his free will.

And then take whatever consequences the newly freed Tate would deal him.

Even if it meant Tate *hated* him.

In the end, Rory had managed to bluff his way through his private chat with Lowell.

"The press release?" Lowell had asked quizzically. "I thought you had something else on your mind. Maybe something about last night?"

"Not at all." Rory had hoped his face wasn't burning. "Last night was fun. You're right. We need to do it again soon."

Lowell's smile had been a shade too knowing for Rory's comfort. He'd babbled on a bit more about the press release and then had escaped Lowell's presence as soon as he could.

Now, sitting on the train again, he closed his eyes.

He needed to get home, to make things right with Tate somehow. To find a way to live with the man until he could fix the damage Beulah had done to him. And then they'd leave. Rory didn't care about his future here anymore—not when it had all been built on a lie.

He needed to get back to the outside world where, for all its faults, at least Rory understood the rules. Where at least the idea of freedom meant something. Beulah may have looked perfect and safe and without crime from the outside, but if the price of perfection was the rape and slavery of people like Tate and Aaron, then Rory would rather live with imperfection and crime.

He needed to go home. He needed to get Tate there too.

CHAPTER
FOURTEEN

The street was quiet. The dusk was softening slowly into darkness as Rory arrived home. He couldn't help staring at the row of small, neat houses and wondering what horrors they hid behind their pretty façades. Like his did.

Walking up the path to the front door, he was filled with dread. He could hardly reconcile this feeling with the way he'd felt on that first day, when Aaron had brought him here. He'd been almost overwhelmed with joy. And now . . . he could never be happy in this house again, not after the things he'd done here. Shit, he could probably never be happy in his own skin again.

He turned his key in the door. He paused, remembering with a flash of sickening guilt the day that Tate had been waiting there, on his knees. Naked and wanton and wicked. All a lie. Rory had only seen what he'd wanted to see. Sighing, he pushed the door open.

The house was dark and quiet. No dinner cooking in the kitchen. No welcoming lights turned on. There was a mop leaning against the wall. Rory hadn't even known he owned a mop. Usually Tate had everything cleaned up and put away before he got home.

Like a good little housewife.

Rory flipped on the lights.

"Tate?" he called, dropping his bag on the floor. Silence. "Tate?"

"In here!" a voice called cheerfully, and Rory's blood ran cold.

Lowell. Lowell was in his house. In his fucking *house*.

He ran for the living room, not caring what he'd find, not fearing anything, only wanting to see Tate safe.

What he saw instead was Tate on his knees, hands tied behind his back with the deep wine-colored silk of Lowell's tie. Naked. With . . .

With the neck of a heavy, half-full wine bottle shoved up his ass.

And he was slurping, head bobbing, Lowell's hand fisted in his black curls.

"I hope you don't mind," Lowell said, "I let myself in. Made myself at home. Sorry about your wine, but he said you didn't have a proper plug—and you know how I like my boys plugged—so we had to improvise."

"Don't," Rory said over the sudden roar of blood in his skull. "Don't do that to him."

"He likes it," Lowell said. He pulled Tate's head back and gave his hair a yank so that Rory could see his face in profile. "Tell your master that you like it."

"I like it, Master," Tate moaned. The words were slurred, his lips swollen.

Rory couldn't look at him, not like this. He forced himself to stare into Lowell's handsome monster's face instead. "You know that's not him. You know it's the chip. You know it!"

Lowell sighed, bringing Tate's face back to his lap. The sucking and slurping sounds resumed, making Rory's gut roil. "I'd hoped you'd fit in here, Rory. I suppose I couldn't keep you in the dark forever. Maybe I shouldn't have tried, eh? But isn't it too late to rebel against our ways now? You've done all this with him. You're as much a part of this as I am."

"I'm not. I'm fucking not." Rory said it, but he didn't believe it, not really. His heart hammered.

"Oh, you don't believe that. Didn't you have him ride you the other night? Didn't you watch him eat Aaron's ass and swallow all that cum? Didn't you like it when he called you *master*?" He tugged Tate's hair. "Didn't you like it when the pretty little straight boy begged for your cock?"

"Because I thought he wanted it!"

"He does," Lowell said. "Listen to him."

Tate moaned with pleasure.

"It's not him," Rory said again.

Lowell snorted. "Who cares? He was just some worthless piece-of-shit criminal out of Tophet. At least this way he's some use."

"He's not worthless. You don't know that he doesn't have any use. You . . . you took everything about him and you replaced it with something else. You don't know anything about him."

"Neither do you."

"I know he deserves better than this!"

Lowell sighed and rolled his shoulders. "Listen, Rory, I'm going to make this very simple for you. I want you to fit in. I want you to do well here. You were supposed to be my protégé, and you have so much promise. I'm not going to let this little hiccup ruin all that. So you can accept that this is the way things are here, and you can stand by my side so I can give you a life of comfort and wealth and power and all the sucking this pretty straight mouth is capable of. Or you can reject this life, and you can take your place on your knees as a rezzy. With him, and that little tease Aaron."

"No," Rory said. "Let me go home. I'll take Tate and—"

"Take Tate?" Lowell laughed. "Tate's not going anywhere. Tate has his sentence to serve."

For a moment, Rory wondered if he should just run. Try to get out of Beulah on his own and leave Tate behind. Leave him to serve his seven years with Lowell and forget about him. But he couldn't. He knew he couldn't.

"Do you know what I did after our little chat about the press release?" Lowell asked. His breath shuddered out of him, and he tugged Tate's head back again. "Ease off a bit, boy." He collected himself. "I had a quick look back over the office budgetary records, and it seems someone has been skimming from the accounts."

Rory took a step back. "I wouldn't even know how!"

"The records say otherwise." Lowell stroked Tate's cheek. "It's very simple, Rory. You're either with me or you're against me. And if you're against me, you don't get to win. So be sensible. Come here and let Tate give you a nice suck, remind you of how good you have it here in Beulah."

Yes, the voice in Rory's head told him. *Do it, and bide your time until you can save Tate. Until you can get ahold of that resistance group Alexandra mentioned.*

And then, another voice, whispering, *Yes, do it. Just give in and do it. He's happy. You can be happy too. You can stay here and be happy.*

God. Why the hell had Tate punched him and started all this? He could have lived in blissful ignorance, except for that.

"Yes," he said, his chest aching. "Tate, come here."

Lowell smiled.

Tate crawled across the floor, the bottle of wine falling loose from his body and soaking the floor in blood red. Rory couldn't tell if the look on Tate's face as he came to kneel at Rory's feet was from pain or from bliss or from some strange mix of both.

"Master," he whispered. His tone was reverent. His eyes were . . . blank.

Rory stared down at him and wondered who the hell he was. This naked man, kneeling on his floor, who would offer up any part of his body for his master's amusement but whose mind was locked away somewhere. Unreachable.

"I—" Rory choked on whatever command he'd been going to give.

"Oh, Rory," Lowell said, his voice full of glee. "What a terrible, terrible master you make. Tate, go call the police."

Tate whipped his head around quickly. "Master?"

Lowell's smile vanished. "Go and call the police and tell them Justice Lowell needs to report a fraud."

Just like with Aaron.

Rory sank down onto the sofa. What was the point of running? Tate had tried that, hadn't he? He wondered if Aaron had bothered.

"Rory," Tate whispered, his eyes large. "I don't . . . I don't *want* to." He winced and lifted his hands to his head.

Lowell's nostrils flared. "I don't really care if you want to, boy. I am a free citizen of Beulah, and I am telling you to *go call the police.*"

Rory closed his eyes, setting his jaw even as his lip trembled. "Do what he says, Tate. Don't risk yourself on my behalf. I'm not worth it. It's over." Lowell's hand clasped his shoulder, massaging it, and even that once-innocent touch felt so sexual Rory had to fight off a shudder. "At least . . . at least this way I can atone for what I did to you. It's only seven years, right?"

"Seven years of happiness," Lowell said. He smiled. "Here's an interesting point of law. Do I inherit the rezzy of the man who becomes *my* rezzy?"

Rory's skin crawled.

Tate didn't like this at all and couldn't understand why.

Lowell was a good master. Lowell forced him to prove himself and praised him for it.

And Rory . . . Rory was too full of contradictions to make Tate truly happy.

He lingered anxiously in the kitchen when the police arrived, and then they took Rory away.

No, he didn't like that at all. Rory hadn't done anything wrong. Rory didn't need to learn to become a better person because he already was one. Tate had never been a good person.

He'd tried, a little bit, when he was a kid. Then he'd started hanging out with one of the neighborhood gangs when he was a teenager, and it hadn't seemed important anymore. He'd stolen stuff. He'd vandalized stuff. He had gotten into drugs—not as much as Paula had though. Paula was a mess back then. Too much of a mess even for Tate to handle. He'd been going to dump her, until—

"I'm pregnant, you asshole! I'm fucking pregnant!"

Even then, Tate hadn't cared much. He'd yelled at her to stop using but hadn't really been bothered when she didn't. Because it didn't feel real. It hadn't felt real until the day Emmy was born, all strange and red and wrinkled, and she curled her tiny hand around Tate's finger and it had suddenly hit him: there was a person here, existing where none had existed before. A tiny, miraculous *person.*

From that moment on, he'd tried to be good. Tried to be better.

He'd failed, but he'd tried.

Tate's eyes stung when the police took Rory away, and his head pounded.

No tears, the doctor at the induction center had told him, but Tate could feel them sliding down his cheeks.

"There now," Lowell said, coming up to slip his arms around Tate's waist. "Won't it be nice to be with a master who knows what you need?"

"Yes, Master," he said but couldn't stop staring in the direction of the front door. Couldn't stop seeing Rory's pale, frightened face.

Because he didn't do anything wrong.

And if Rory hadn't deserved his punishment . . . did Tate? Sure, Tate had actually committed a crime, unlike Rory, but that didn't mean the punishment was fair.

His head ached.

His punishment made him happy. Didn't it? Wasn't this happiness?

It was getting so hard to tell.

Lowell released him. "Go get dressed, Tate. I can hardly have you walking home naked, can I? You might frighten the neighbors."

Home.

Wasn't this his home?

It had felt like it, for a little while. This was where he belonged, serving his master. But not all his happiness had come from that. Not all of it. Curled up with Rory watching movies, he'd been happy in a different way.

It hurt to think about it.

Tate headed into his tiny bedroom and dressed quickly. When he came back outside, Lowell was waiting by the front door.

"Come on, Tate," he smiled.

Warmth spread through Tate at that smile, but it couldn't prevent the shiver that ran down his spine. "Yes, Master."

The night was cool and quiet. The air smelled of orange blossoms. He could see the stars. He'd never seen the stars in Tophet. The buildings were too tall. There was too much light pollution. Not to mention the smog.

And yet, he remembered sitting on the fire escape off of his apartment with Emmy in his arms, watching her. Singing the few lines of the lullabies he could remember as she slowly drifted off to sleep. Emmy was worth more than stars.

He couldn't stop thinking about her, even though it ached like being stabbed through the eye socket. Couldn't stop thinking about Rory, either. Of lying on the couch with him, no demands, no orders, no desperate urge to please and serve. When he'd been less a master than a friend.

Lowell had said Tate would be happy here. So had Rory. He himself had said he would be happy. But was this happiness? Even if it was . . . did it really matter, in the face of those better, bigger feelings?

Maybe . . . maybe they were even worth the pain they caused.

They were. He was almost certain of it. He didn't want to lose those feelings or those memories. He didn't want to lose himself.

The pain was a tool. The pain trained him not to look for his memories, not to go knocking on those doors in his mind that the chip had created. And Tate had tried so hard for so long to do what the chip wanted. But now he wanted more.

He flinched as the chip reacted, and pain tore through his skull.

Forced himself to back away from that rebellious thought but not to lose sight of it. To hide it and keep it safe until he was strong enough to take hold of it again.

"Tate?" Lowell asked in a low voice. "Are you all right?"

"Yes, Master."

The walk to Lowell's house was short. Aaron must have been watching from inside because he opened the door before they reached it, and light spilled outside.

Tate's breath caught. Aaron's nipples were pierced, and a chain ran between them. There was a weight hanging off the chain. Tate's cock hardened as he wondered how that must feel. Pain and pleasure at the same time. A master's firm touch even when the master was gone.

Lowell ushered Tate inside and closed the door.

Tate stripped off his clothes.

"That's it," Lowell said. "Good boy, Tate." He pinched Tate's nipples. "And don't worry, we'll have you pierced, as well. Maybe chain you up to this little slut, hmm? You'd like that, wouldn't you?"

"Yes, Master," Tate said, resisting the urge to touch his cock.

"Yes, Master," Aaron echoed.

"I'm the luckiest man alive," Lowell said, ruffling the hair on both their heads. "And soon I'll have a third? I'll have to invest in a fucking machine just to keep you all occupied."

Tate glanced at Aaron.

Aaron beamed at their master. Happiness—there it was—overlaid on his tired, drawn face. He had dark shadows under his eyes. He looked pale and pinched. But he was smiling. He was happy. A strange, empty sort of happiness that didn't light him up from within.

Simple, false happiness, forced upon him by the chip.

Tate wondered if he looked the same and flinched as pain flared inside his skull.

Lowell didn't notice. "Tate, go learn your way around the kitchen. At least you can cook, unlike this one."

The twinging headache faded. Tate lost his train of thought. "Yes, Master," he said with a nod, and headed for the kitchen.

"What are you?" he heard Lowell ask in a low voice, just after he left the room.

"A whore," Aaron moaned back. "A slut. A tease."

Tate felt an ache in his stomach as he imagined Rory having to say those words. Imagined Rory's voice reaching that same eager pitch and imagined Rory held captive to the promise of that same terrible happiness.

He didn't want that. Not for Rory. Not for Aaron, not even for himself. But he especially didn't want it for Rory. Because Rory didn't do anything wrong. And more than that, Tate . . . Tate cared about him. Rory had been a bad master because Rory was his *friend*.

He busied himself around the kitchen. It felt good to slip back into the certainty of service, even while unease prickled the back of his head. From the next room, he could hear the slap of flesh on flesh and Aaron's muffled cries.

Lowell was a good master.

But not a good man.

That contradictory thought balanced on a knife-edge, and Tate held his breath while he waited to see where it might land. White, stabbing pain, or . . . or nothing. No pain at all.

Maybe time had rewritten the circuitry in his brain, the same as it had when he'd been a kid with his seizures. The doctors back then had shown him the shadowed parts of the scan. The parts that didn't light up anymore. But it didn't matter because his brain had adapted. Had used different routes. Maybe it was doing the same with the chip now.

Or maybe it was just possible to hold that contradictory thought in his head because it didn't matter if Lowell was a good man or not, only that he was Tate's master and Tate would worship him just the same.

Because he didn't know any other way to be.

CHAPTER
FIFTEEN

"You know," said Cal Mitchell, "most of my clients are a little more hostile than you."

Rory leaned back in his seat. The cuffs rattled when he rested his hands on the table. "What are my options?"

Going up against Lowell? Limited, to say the least. But Rory was very aware that he only had a small window of opportunity to act before the chip was in, and that the lawyer sitting across from him was his best hope.

His free lawyer, naturally. This was Beulah, after all. But Mitchell wasn't just some harried court-appointed attorney. He had a good reputation at the Hall of Justice as being an honest, hardworking advocate.

"I would advise you to take the plea bargain, Mr. James." Mitchell shuffled through his paperwork. "I certainly haven't seen all the evidence the police have, but what I have seen is compelling."

"I'm not disputing the evidence," he said. "Not here. Not yet. But I want to go to trial."

"If you go to trial and you lose, you'll be given life without parole," Mitchell said. "You're a young man with a bright future. You ought to think before you throw that away."

"When was the last time there was a criminal trial held in Beulah?" Rory asked.

"Oh, now that would be going back a few years at least. And she was found guilty." Mitchell sighed. "Listen, the police have your bank account records. They've traced the money. It's right there in black and white, son. You'd be a fool to take your chances on a trial."

"Is that what you told Tate Patterson?"

"Patterson," the lawyer murmured, and then nodded. "Oh yes. Well, he punched a man in front of witnesses and on camera, so I think my advice was valid, don't you?"

"I'd agree with you if I thought the conditions of his plea bargain represented a humane and reasonable punishment."

Mitchell's bland expression curdled somewhat. "It's not a *punishment* at all. We don't practice punitive justice here in Beulah, Mr. James. Working at the office of the chief justice, I would hope you'd already know that."

"I thought I did. And then I discovered what the chip you people gave him did, the chip that was supposed to just make him nonviolent? It made him a helpless slave." *A slave, and I didn't even know. He couldn't even tell me. And I abused him. I raped him.*

Mitchell, rather than looking shocked or horrified like he should have, just shook his head. "You've been listening to too many conspiracy theories. Those ARR lunatics. Lurking around, too afraid to show their faces but still trying to convince the good people of Beulah that there's something sinister going on just because they refuse to believe that our system works. They'd rather criminals get thrown into filthy prisons, I expect." He sighed again. "Mr. James, I've spoken to each and every one of my clients after the induction program, and they've never given any indication of such nonsense."

Did you ever ask them to suck your dick? Rory remembered the matching scars on Aaron and Tate's thighs. *To cut themselves?*

"In fact," Mitchell continued, "I'd go so far as to say every client I've counseled postinduction has been downright *happy*."

Rory's hands balled into fists. His heart seemed to stop. "They're *always* happy," he said. Recited it. For strength. To remind himself why he was here and what he had to fight for. "I'm not taking the plea deal. I want the chance to face my accuser. I want to go to trial."

Mitchell looked genuinely upset. "Oh, son, I think you're a fool, but I'll do my best to represent you."

And that, Rory figured, was the best chance he had.

"I can't," Aaron said. "Can't talk about it."

Tate held the wadded kitchen towel up to his nose. "I know."

Aaron closed his eyes. "I try . . . and it hurts. And I bleed."

"I know," Tate said again. Trying to comfort him, even as he tried to think of ways to push the subject. Until Rory came back from induction, Aaron was all he had. It wasn't fair that they couldn't even talk about what they really felt. What did their feelings matter, so long as they still obeyed? But Tate had wanted to know if Aaron was trapped, as well, if there was still a part of him that was screaming out to be heard behind the chip too. He'd asked, ignoring the stab of pain in his own head, and Aaron had opened his mouth to answer and then his nose had started to bleed.

"Mine's wrong, I think," Aaron whispered. "I shouldn't bleed. You don't bleed."

Tate shook his head. "They don't work . . ." He gritted his teeth and squeezed his eyes shut, riding a swell of pain. "They don't work perfectly, on the outside. Inconsistent. Maybe these . . . maybe these are the s-same." He panted. Even saying that much hurt. Ached. But he had to try.

"Tate, sometimes I'm so h-happy, and sometimes I'm so scared. I don't know . . . I don't know which one is real." Aaron whimpered and lifted his hand to cover Tate's, to press the kitchen towel more firmly against his nose.

"I know." He leaned forward and rested his forehead against Aaron's. He could smell the blood. He closed his eyes and savored Aaron's closeness. Not alone. He wasn't alone. Aaron felt the same. Aaron understood. He smoothed Aaron's hair with his free hand.

After a moment, Aaron straightened and stepped away. He dropped the bloody wad of paper in the trash. "Master will be home soon."

Warmth spread through Tate—pleasure, anticipation, the need to serve. He followed Aaron through the house, and together they knelt before the front door to wait for Lowell. He liked them like this. Naked and ready. Shameless. Maybe today Lowell would bring a plug and piercings for him so that they matched. Aaron looked so perfect with the base of a fat black plug half spreading his ass cheeks and those heavy silver rings weighing down his pink nipples. Tate wanted that too. He wanted Lowell to test him and push him the way he did with Aaron. He wanted to prove himself to his master.

Lowell was a good master.

Tate closed his eyes, listening to Aaron breathing beside him. He wasn't sure how much time passed before he heard the rattle of keys. He straightened his spine, pushed his shoulders back and his knees apart, just like Lowell wanted.

The door swung open.

"Good even—" Aaron began and yelped as Lowell flung his briefcase at him.

Lowell ignored him and glared down at Tate. "Do you know what your former so-called master has done, Tate?"

Tate cowered, breaking position. "No, Master."

"That little asshole thinks he can go to trial!" Lowell stalked toward the living room, ripping his tie off and dropping it on the floor.

Aaron, still clutching the briefcase, lunged for the tie, as though letting it lie on the floor for more than a second would be a disaster.

Going to trial? Tate remembered his lawyer convincing him it would be better if he just took the plea bargain. He rose to his feet, his stomach in knots, and padded after Lowell. Found him in the living room, pouring himself a drink. "*Trial*, master?"

Because Rory hadn't done anything wrong. But surely he didn't think that would protect him? Tate didn't understand. Seven years was better than life, and Rory could be—

Happy.

Could be happy for seven years.

Tate breathed through the burst of screeching static in his head.

"Yes, trial, you stupid, addled rezzy. I suppose he plans on using the stand to go public with what he's learned about the chips. Or maybe he really does think he can get an innocent verdict and walk out of Beulah a free man. Leave you—and all this—behind." He waved a hand. Took a gulp of his drink. "If that's the case, then let him return to that filthy hole you both crawled out of. But sadly, judging by the way he looks at you, he can't be trusted to do the decent thing and just save his own skin."

The way he looks at me.

Lowell set the glass down. "But you'll tell them, won't you, Tate?"

"Tell who, master?" Tate asked.

"The jury." Lowell reached out and stroked his rough fingers down Tate's cheek. "You'll tell them how Rory was stealing from the department this entire time. Stealing from Beulah. You'll tell them he used the money to buy you things. Nice, expensive things. Because he wanted to buy your silence. Or maybe buy your affection so when he cashed out, you'd run with him. Or maybe he intended on framing you the whole time, hmm?"

"He'd never—"

"I don't care about what you think of his character. As your master, I'm telling you to lie. Perjury shouldn't be so difficult for you, considering you're already a criminal."

Tate frowned worriedly. But he hadn't lied to the police or to his lawyer. The only person he'd lied to had been Rory, to try to be a better rezzy, to give him what he wanted. So if he'd lied for Rory, it was okay to lie for Lowell, wasn't it? Weren't they the same? "Yes, Master. I'll say what you want."

"Good," said Lowell, his voice low. He stroked his thumb along Tate's jaw, each small movement drawing a shiver from Tate. "You're a good boy, Tate."

Tate sighed with relief, but somehow the feeling never reached the pit of guilt sitting at the bottom of his stomach.

"That's it." Lowell dropped his hand and reached for his glass again. "Aaron? Where the hell are you?"

Aaron hurried into the room, wincing as he moved.

Lowell sprawled onto the couch and held out his hand. Aaron took it and settled onto his lap. Tate poured Lowell another drink.

Lowell stared at him over Aaron's shoulder. He slid his hands down Aaron's spine, gripping his ass cheeks tightly, so that the pink skin turned white. "Go get dinner on the table, Tate. When I'm done with this little bitch, I'll have worked up an appetite."

"Yes, Master," Tate said breathlessly, flushing. It was still . . . wrong, embarrassing, to see Lowell use Aaron so roughly, so confidently. Even though it was right, and it proved Lowell's strong hand as a master. Tate couldn't get used to the sight of it, though. Couldn't forget how much gentler Rory had been, how eager but kind.

He'd been a bad master. And now, Tate would condemn him.

Tate would lie and say he was a bad man, as well.

Legal detention in Beulah was exactly how Rory had expected it to be: clean, sterile, and safe. He was kept in the holding cell at the central police station because there was no prison to transfer him to until his trial. From what little Rory had learned from the police, he was something of a sensation. There hadn't been a criminal trial in years, and the media couldn't be expected to ignore that, even if the defendant *hadn't* been Justice Lowell's former assistant.

Still, Rory couldn't complain about his treatment. He was given decent meals, privacy, and had unfettered access to his legal representatives.

Rory looked up as the cell door opened, expecting to see Cal Mitchell's careworn face again. Instead, he saw a girl with her hair pulled too tightly into a bun and glasses that made her look older than she was.

She was the most beautiful sight he'd ever seen. "Alexandra! What are you doing here?"

"Work experience with Mr. Mitchell," she said, sitting down on his bunk beside him and dumping a stack of files between them. "Mr. Lowell said that I should take the chance to participate in a criminal trial when the opportunity came up."

"Really?" Rory snorted. "Like that's not a conflict of interest?"

She frowned at him over her glasses. "Please. As though the only interests that count here aren't Mr. Lowell's. That's why you're here, and it's why Aaron's in his house. He's not worried. And since I smile at his jokes and bring him coffee, then of course he remembers me when Mr. Mitchell told him about all the extra work an actual trial would be. He's so *generous*."

Rory smiled weakly. All true.

Hard to commiserate and laugh about a shitty boss when that shitty boss was about to have him condemned to slavery, though.

Alexandra drummed her fingers on the bunk. "Anyway, you've probably realized that the evidence against you is pretty compelling."

"I figured it would be." Who better to falsify it than a justice?

"Mr. Mitchell sent me to go through it with you, to see if I couldn't change your mind."

"You can't."

She smiled at that. "I figured I couldn't."

"But I hope to hell that's not all you're here for," Rory told her earnestly.

"No." She lowered her voice. "I need to know that you're going to tell the truth on the stand. The actual truth, I mean, and not Lowell's twisted version. Look, I can't promise I know what will happen there, but all of Beulah is watching. Whatever you say on the stand, they'll all see it. All of them. There'll be no way he can put that suspicion back in Pandora's box."

"Good."

"Look, the problem is, we don't know how big it is. I mean, nobody can tell us. We don't know if it's just Lowell or if there are other justices involved. The rezzy system has been in place longer than Lowell's been in office, but we don't know how long the chips have been used the way they are. We don't even know if the police are involved or if they're as much in the dark as anyone. The fact that Lowell is actually letting you go to trial is probably an indication that the corruption isn't widespread yet. It means questions would be asked if the process wasn't followed, we think."

"We?" Rory asked "The ARR?"

"Yes, and we're as ready as we can be," she said. "But, Rory, three years ago we were just a group of students who met up in a Restitutional Law tutorial. Whatever you hear about the ARR, we're not . . . *powerful.*"

"You're a bunch of lunatics, according to Cal Mitchell."

Alexandra smiled slightly. "But what we have got is two ex-rezzies we've illegally removed the chip from, and a lab tech who used to work at the induction center. We've got statements ready to be released as soon as the media is ready to listen. You've just got to get them to that point. You're credible. You're an insider. It won't just be a conspiracy theory anymore once it comes from your mouth."

"I hope so."

A shadow crossed her face. "And after this, we'll get Aaron back too."

Rory reached out and brushed his fingers over the back of her hand. "We?"

She smiled slightly at that. "Me. *I'll* get him back. And Tate too."

"I don't want Tate back. I want Tate freed." Even if the thought of watching him walk away forever made his heart sting. At least Alexandra knew what she was fighting for. Who she was fighting for. Rory didn't know Tate at all.

Only that he deserved his freedom, and that was what mattered. *All* that mattered.

He knew, logically, that it was true. But that didn't make it hurt any less.

"Don't tell Mr. Mitchell any of this," Alexandra warned him. "Just save it for the trial. He already thinks you're crazy. He's . . . he's like most people here. The system works, so they don't question it. It doesn't impact them, so they don't look at it."

"It's supposed to be perfect," he said.

"Maybe it was, in the beginning. I don't know." She shrugged. "How do you tell? If you can't trust what the government says now, how can you trust anything they've ever said? And when someone talks about the government, how can you even tell if they're a part of it or if they're a victim too? God, the rezzies . . . Nobody defends the chip like a rezzy. Until we take it out." She shuddered.

"What happens when it's out?" Rory asked, his mouth suddenly dry.

"It depends," Alexandra murmured. "Depends what their sponsors did. What they thought they could get away with. Make no mistake, most of the sponsors are as ignorant of the chip as the general population is." She was silent for a moment. "As for the rezzies, nightmares are common. Self-harm isn't unusual, either. Some of them really *hate* themselves. Some of them still feel like they're trapped. And some of them *are* trapped. You take away the ability for a person to articulate what they're feeling, and sometimes they don't get it back."

Rory rubbed his temples. "But what about the rezzies who were released? Why didn't they ever say anything?"

The look she gave him was almost pitying. "Oh, Rory, you don't actually think they ever turn off the chip, do you? And risk having them speak out? They just change the chip's programming after the seven years is up. They're not slaves, anymore, but they're still silenced for the rest of their lives."

"Shit." Rory shivered.

Alexandra turned her hand over and linked her fingers through his. "But you'll be okay. This is going to work, Rory. They won't get a chip in you. You did the right thing."

If only that were true.

The things he'd done to Tate ... Would Tate want to harm himself, or worse? Rory just had to hope that Tate would turn his hate outward instead. Punish Rory instead of himself. As much as that thought hurt him, it was the best-case scenario now.

And to think Rory had been falling in love.

Well, none of that mattered now. All that mattered was Tate— how Tate felt, what Tate wanted—and that was assuming Rory would be able to free either of them. That this wasn't some lost cause, that he wouldn't wind up a rezzy himself before long. A prisoner. A slave.

"You're going to be okay," Alexandra repeated, squeezing his hand, trying to comfort him, to give him the strength he so desperately needed.

But Rory had a feeling she didn't even believe it herself.

CHAPTER
SIXTEEN

It was late when Rory was awoken by the sound of the cell door sliding open. He'd been dozing on the narrow bench, not really sleeping, just imagining seeing all those shocked faces in court when he spoke, and trying to figure out what he could say. What if Cal Mitchell was right and people really did think the ARR was made up of thugs and conspiracy theorists? Well, the ARR was Rory's only hope now, so he had to be sure that people heard what he said and didn't just dismiss it as the ravings of a criminal lunatic.

He sat up when the door opened and found himself squinting at the three men.

"Rory James?" one of them asked.

"Yes." A knot of fear tightened in his stomach.

"Come with us, please."

Rory didn't move. "Where?"

One of the men stepped forward. He was large and wearing some sort of white uniform. "All defendants need to have a medical check before court appearances."

Rory curled his hands into fists. "Why is that?"

The big man shrugged, a knowing smile splitting his face.

"No," Rory said. "I need to talk to my lawyer. I need him here, right now!"

"It's standard procedure, Mr. James," the man said. "It's all been signed off on."

"Not by me," Rory said. God. If they took him away to some medical facility, what then? They'd put a piece of metal in his brain, and he'd be as malleable and as desperate to please as Tate had ever been. He'd be lost. He kept his voice steady, afraid that if he slid into panic they'd just drag him out of the cell. "I didn't sign anything. I want to talk to my lawyer about this."

"You're an inmate, Mr. James. We don't need your permission."

"I haven't been convicted of anything," Rory said, his voice wavering despite his best efforts. "I'm entitled to the presumption of innocence."

"Sure you are," the man said. "But it's a requirement of the court that you undergo a medical check before trial. Standard procedure, like I said."

There was nothing in Beulah that was fucking *standard*.

Especially not with Lowell pulling the strings. He should have known the man wouldn't give him the chance to testify freely.

He had to tell the truth. He had to appeal to the guy's compassion, since taking a stance on principle obviously wasn't working. "Look, I don't know how to say this exactly, but I think you might be making a mistake, taking me to that clinic. I think somebody's trying to make sure I don't make it to trial."

"Oh no," the man said. He turned his head and grinned at the others. "Mr. Lowell definitely wants you to go to trial. He's looking forward to what you say on the stand."

Whatever tiny amount of hope Rory had been clinging to drained out of him. They were with Lowell. Not just unaware of his corruption, but *with* him. Had they been involved in ensnaring Aaron? And what about Tate? Rory felt a sudden rush of reckless urgency. If they had the job Rory thought they did, if they knew what Rory thought they did, then . . .

These men *knew* Tate. Must have spoken to him before they put the chip in, even if it had only been a few hostile words in a cell like this one.

"Tate," he said, and the man looked at him curiously. "What's he like?"

"That's an odd question."

Rory shrugged. "What else have we got to talk about?"

The man chuckled. "Sure. Tate? Tate Patterson? He was angry. Angrier than you, anyhow." He showed Rory his hands. "Stand up for me now."

Angry. Rory had never seen Tate angry. Rory had seen Tate frightened and frustrated and breathless with lust, but he'd never seen him angry. Such a natural human emotion, stripped by the chip.

Rory rose slowly to his feet, the blood roaring in his skull. He wondered if he could fight them, but they were bigger than him. They outnumbered him. It wasn't a fight he could win.

God. How long until he didn't know himself? How long until he was lost in the same terrible place as Tate and Aaron? He wanted to scream and fight, and wondered if Tate and Aaron had. Pointless, but it was fight or flight, wasn't it? Two choices hardwired into him, into all people since the beginning of time, and he could do neither. All that adrenaline coursing through him, every nerve spiking, and he just had to stand there and fucking take it.

Maybe Alexandra would work out what happened. Maybe all hope wasn't lost just yet.

Rory wished he could believe that. Wished he could pin all his hopes on a girl he didn't really know and the invisible group she was a part of. What was the ARR anyway? Were they really ready, like she'd said? Or were they just like the groups Rory had been a part of when he was at university: full of big ideas and bravado but nothing of substance?

The man put a hand on Rory's shoulder and smiled again. Something in the curve of his mouth was almost sympathetic. "It's not so bad, you'll see. You'll be happy."

"Yeah," Rory said, his voice cracking. He saw Tate, face contorted with pain moments before he had collapsed in the shower. He saw Aaron, eyes vacant, with blood running out of his nose. "Of course I will."

They're always happy.
We, now.
We're always happy.

The courtroom was full. Tate, waiting outside with Aaron, caught glimpses of the packed benches every time the large doors opened and then swung closed again. There were always people going in and out. Each time the doors opened he heard Mr. Lowell speaking in a loud and confident voice. He couldn't see the stand though. Couldn't see Rory.

Tate had been buzzing with a strange energy all morning. He was nervous—not about lying because that was what his master demanded of him, but about seeing Rory again. He'd missed him. He wondered if Rory would smile at him across the courtroom when it was time to go in and answer questions. Maybe Tate could go in *now*.

No. No, he had to wait for Mr. Lowell's orders.

He drummed his fingers on the edge of his seat, then picked at a thread in the sleeve of his shirt. These clothes itched. He'd gotten used to being naked. Used to seeing no one but his master and Aaron. Cut off from the world, living in a haze of sex and service.

Strange to be back out in public, under the eyes of all these people. Smiling at them pleasantly, bearing their gazes, watching them try not to react when they saw the cuffs around his wrists marking him as a rezzy. Cuffs that his too-short shirtsleeves didn't quite cover. Lowell had planned it that way, he knew.

Whatever Rory said, Tate would be there to happily oppose him. Defend the system and his master. It was unthinkable to do otherwise. And it made him happy to think that soon Rory would be his friend again. Soon they would live together again.

Aaron looked up sharply, catching Tate's attention, as a middle-aged man and a young woman walked past them. The young woman was carrying a stack of folders.

"Alex!"

The young woman stopped, looked at him, and then kept walking.

Aaron's face fell, and then he shook his head and settled back into his seat. Tate patted his shoulder. "Maybe she's nervous about the trial," he said weakly, suddenly worried about what reaction he'd get from Rory. Even the people they loved and cared for most flinched away when they knew the truth.

But not their master. Their master would never let them go, would never reject their neediness.

"She's, um, she's on the defense," Aaron said in a small voice. "And we're with Mr. Lowell. So that's why she didn't talk to me, I guess."

"Will Rory be able to talk to us?" Tate asked, worry gnawing at him.

"After," Aaron said. "When he's with us, he will."

With us. Yes. That was what Tate wanted most of all. Rory, on his knees beside Tate, nipples pierced and ass heavy with a plug. Maybe Lowell would have them play together. Just once in a while. It would be enough. It would have to be.

And at the same time, Tate dreaded it. Dreaded Rory losing his freedom, having to serve like this, having to hurt when Lowell wanted to hurt him. It was the injustice of it that worried him. He looked up at the words on the wall: *Rehabilitation through Restitution*. Except Rory hadn't done anything wrong. He might find the same happiness in servitude that Tate did, but wasn't there a principle at stake?

Somewhere, there was.

Tate closed his eyes briefly.

Well, principles were nothing really. The consolation prize of the losing argument. *Yeah, well, it's the* principle *of the thing!* The winner never had to say that.

And anyway, thinking about it was making his head hurt.

This would be over soon, and then they'd be happy. All of them.

Rory sat in the dock with his trembling hands in his lap. He wasn't sure why they were shaking, but they hadn't stopped all day. Maybe nothing more than an aftereffect from his surgery. The anesthetic or something. He wasn't nervous. He knew what he had to do here.

He had to be *good*.

There was a strange sort of itch in the back of his skull. Rory wasn't even sure if it was physical. It felt more like the feeling he got when he couldn't remember where he'd put his keys and retracing all his steps didn't help. Not quite like he'd forgotten something, but that he'd forgotten its importance. As though he knew his keys were missing, but he couldn't think why he needed them. Something about the trial rankled, but Rory couldn't pin it down.

But no, the only important thing was to be good. To make people happy, yes, that was important. The bandaged cut on his thigh stung, reminding him. How amazing it had felt to be good, to be obedient.

He looked out across the courtroom. He knew some of the faces here. Zac was sitting at the prosecutors' table while Ruth asked Mr. Lowell questions. Mr. Lowell, sitting comfortably in the witness stand, gave his answers clearly.

Alexandra was sitting across the aisle from them, taking notes while Mr. Mitchell listened.

Rory listened carefully to Mr. Lowell as he spoke. Accounts linked to other accounts and passwords and data trails, and everything that led straight back to Rory. Rory could feel their condemnation, but it didn't make him angry. It only made him want to earn their forgiveness.

"Thank you, Justice Lowell," Ruth said at last, and Mr. Lowell stepped down from the witness stand.

"Shall we take a break?" the presiding judge said. "Five minutes?"

Rory watched as Mr. Lowell sat down at the prosecutors' table with Zac and Ruth. It warmed him a little when Mr. Lowell flashed him a friendly smile. Once this trial was over, he knew, Mr. Lowell would be his sponsor. He would live with Mr. Lowell and repay his debt to society. It was good to know that Mr. Lowell was ready to forgive him and help him grow. That was what that smile said, and it calmed some of the anxiety gnawing at Rory's stomach.

Alexandra rose and approached him. "Are you holding up okay?"

"I'm okay." He was. He absolutely was. All he needed was for this trial to be over so he could go home and get on with his life. He wished he'd taken the plea bargain and saved everyone the trouble of being here today.

"Okay." She lowered her voice. "Lowell is going to cross-examine you himself. Whatever he says, don't let him trip you up. This is your only chance, remember."

Rory flexed his shaking hands. "Yes, I know."

His only chance to prove himself worthy of forgiveness. To show how sorry he was. How much better he wanted to do. He glanced over at the prosecutors' desk again. Lowell had risen from his chair and was walking toward the doors. He didn't go through them, though. Only opened them a crack and said something. Then, before the doors could swing shut again, someone pushed them open.

Tate. Tate, wearing clothes, with Aaron trailing behind him. Rory's heart clenched.

"Tate," Rory whispered, and he felt a streak of wetness down each cheek.

Alexandra glanced over at them, then frowned at Rory. "Just keep it together, okay?"

Rory drew his gaze back with difficulty. "I will."

Her frown deepened. She opened her mouth to say something, but then the justice banged his gavel and she had to take her seat again.

Rory couldn't keep his eyes off Tate. The way he was sitting, he looked uncomfortable. He looked . . . sad. It made Rory ache in a way his crimes and his failure to please didn't. The feeling was purer, somehow. Like he could still throw himself to his knees at Lowell's feet, begging, but the thing he wanted most of all was to gather Tate into his arms and kiss him and never stop apologizing to him.

So much to be sorry for.

That itch again, at the back of his skull, that threatened to tip over the edge into pain if Rory didn't somehow stop it. Didn't concentrate on what was important. The itch was almost enough to distract him from Mr. Lowell standing and approaching. Almost enough to make him miss the first question.

"Why did you do it, Rory?"

Oh. Not the question of a prosecutor or a justice at all. Lowell's voice was low and full of regret. It was the question of a friend betrayed.

But Rory still stared at Tate over Lowell's shoulder, at Tate's huge dark eyes, full of worry and compassion, and the answer came to him.

I didn't do it. I've been framed.

But what came out of his mouth was, "I was tired of working for money. Tired of working, working, working. I just wanted what I was owed."

The guard. Lowell's man. He'd told Rory to say that, and now he had.

Rory smiled. Lowell smiled back.

Soon, Rory would be his.

Why didn't he take the plea bargain?

"Oh, Rory," Lowell sighed, and shook his head. "I just wish you'd come to me first."

Such a generous man. A kind man.

"I'm sorry," he said, and it nearly came out on a sob. "I'm so sorry."

Tate had been sorry too. He'd begged for forgiveness, hadn't he? He knew how much it ached, to have wronged someone. Ached so much he wanted to crawl on his belly on the floor like a worm.

Rory stared past Lowell. Past every face in the room—Ruth's, and Zac's, Mr. Mitchell's, and Alexandra's. Hers was wide-eyed and widemouthed, pale with shock. Rory found Tate's face again. Tate would understand. Tate would help him. Tate would accept him, even though Rory had never truly accepted Tate. Now he did. Except Tate looked like he was frozen, his brows drawn together in a frown. His jaw was working, like there were words that he couldn't force through his lips so he was chewing on them instead.

Lowell sighed loudly. "This is the tragedy of the outside world. The people there are so accustomed to crime and greed and injury that they fall so easily into their grip. These are good people, though. Just unfortunate."

Rory nodded. Yes. He didn't deserve Beulah. He was tainted. Filthy and dishonest, the bad world he came from rotting him from the ground up. He'd be damn lucky to stay here as a rezzy now.

And Tate? Was Tate lucky? Was Tate rotten too?

Tate had punched him in the face, but when Rory looked at him now, he didn't see rot, didn't see taint. He saw only a man—a man in pain.

"You understand the consequences of your actions, don't you, Rory? You understand that because of your crimes and because you refused our customary plea bargain—costing the taxpayers money for this wasteful trial where you have no defense for you or your actions—you'll serve lifetime restitution?"

"I understand," Rory said. "I'm sorry for wasting taxpayer money and your—and everyone else's—time." The itch at the back of his skull was there again. It was sharper now, starting to dig in. Starting to hurt. And there was Tate, staring at him, but now he was . . . he was standing, mouth still working, hands gripping the bench in front of him so that his gold-brown knuckles were nearly white. "I have no defense."

"Liar!"

For a second Rory didn't know who'd shouted it, but then Tate yelled it again.

"Liar!" Tate raised a fist and pressed it against his temple. "He's lying! I know him, I know him. He's not a thief, not a criminal. He's a good man, he's a good man!" He squeezed his eyes shut, his head ticking sideways over and over. He was holding his head in both hands now. And then he said it, the word that was itching at the back of Rory's mind, itching, itching . . . "The chip! It's the chip! The chip! The chip lies! The chip . . . makes us slaves!"

The whole courtroom erupted in shouting, everyone rising from their seats, the judge shouting for order as the bailiffs rushed forward.

And in the middle of it all, Tate screamed, went as pale as death . . . and tumbled, twitching—no, seizing, he was seizing— right over the back of the bench in front of him and onto the floor.

CHAPTER
SEVENTEEN

The first thing Tate heard was crying. He forced his heavy eyelids open and stared up into the dimness at the shadowed white ceiling. The room was cold. It smelled of antiseptic. And his head . . . Fuck, his head was killing him. Like a hangover but a hundred times worse. Must have been a hell of a night. He tried to swallow, but his throat was too dry.

He turned his head. There was someone in the bed beside his. Someone crying.

"Aaron?" he rasped.

There was a girl sitting beside Aaron's bed, and she turned when Tate spoke. Alexandra. Tate remembered her from the courtroom yesterday.

"You're awake," she said. She looked very pale. "I'm glad."

"What . . ." Tate squinted.

"You're in the hospital. You're safe."

"What the fuck happened?"

Suddenly, Alexandra smiled. It was a weak, trembling smile, and it was tearful, but there was no mistaking the joy on her face. "You did it, Tate. I don't know how you did it, but you overrode the chip's programming, right there in the courtroom, right there with everyone who's anyone watching. The justice saw. The media saw. The police saw. The *people* saw."

Tate's memories were fuzzy, but when he focused, when he closed his eyes and visualized, he could see them. Rory, sitting on the stand. Lying. Saying terrible things about himself that Tate knew weren't true. Because he was a good man. Tate remembered that.

Except . . . Nausea rose in his gut. They'd fucked. Tate didn't fuck guys but he had, hadn't he? The disgust hit him hard.

"Oh fuck," he said. "God."

The sobs grew louder.

Aaron. Aaron was crying. He was curled up under the sheets, his back to Alexandra. Her hand was on his shoulder, stroking him distractedly, and he was *vibrating*.

Lowell had hurt him. Had hurt them both, but had hurt Aaron infinitely more. "Aaron—" Tate choked out.

Now, Alexandra's smile broke apart and fell into a deep frown. "His chip's out too. He's been awake for a few hours but he won't . . . he won't talk to me."

Shit. Tate couldn't blame him. He'd seen the way Aaron had looked at her at the trial. "You knew him, before?"

She nodded.

Yeah, well. Tate wouldn't want the girl he'd had a thing for to see him reduced to an object of pity, either. And it was more than a thing, he understood that now. At some time, Aaron had really cared about Alexandra. Even with the chip, Tate had seen it on his face.

Right now, Tate wasn't even sure he could tell Paula. And if there was anyone who couldn't or wouldn't judge him or pity him, it would be her. She'd done some bad shit for drugs herself . . . and God, how he'd judged her then. He didn't now.

Thinking of her triggered something else, another thing smothered under his sickening need to obey, nearly lost. Emmy. His eyes stung. He didn't want to remember everything she meant to him, not now, but there she was, every fragment of feeling the chip had suppressed in him rushing back, and all of them about her. All that love and care and beauty, all flooding him at once, filling him with so much grief and regret that he thought he'd overflow.

And now he wasn't sure he could ever stroke her hair again or kiss her skinned knees when the memory of everything that had happened since he'd left her felt so fucking filthy.

Tate squeezed his eyes shut. Not everything. Everything with Lowell, sure. But Rory had been different. Wasn't fair to hate the guy for taking what Tate had offered so desperately. And it had felt good, mostly.

Okay, no. He didn't want to think about that now. It was probably only the chip that made it feel good anyway. And in the grand scheme of things, Rory didn't matter at all. Only Emmy did.

Emmy, who'd been the thing to bring him to this shithole in the first place.

Emmy, who needed the money he'd stolen for food and clothes because her mother couldn't care for her and Tate was going to take her and give her a fresh start and—

Oh God. She was still out there with no one to care for her. How long had it been? How long had Tate been here, drugged by that fucking chip, suppressing what was important? For how long had he left Emmy alone?

"Alexandra," he said, sitting up in bed too fast. His head spun, but he didn't let himself lay back down. "Can I leave? Can I go? My daughter— I have a daughter. I have a daughter! She's on the outside somewhere with no one to look after her."

Alexandra's hand stilled against Aaron's shoulder. "I don't know. It's . . . unprecedented, what happened. The judge wants to talk to you. There's a board of inquiry being set up. Most of the legal fraternity is saying that the chips can't do what they did, but the judge said he won't ignore your allegations without due process. He ordered your chips removed so he could be sure they weren't interfering. You . . . you have to stay and tell the truth, Tate. We need you. All the rezzies, past and present, need you. *Aaron* needs you." She bit her lip. "And you're still a convicted criminal, I guess. A violent one. It's all up in the air." And then she gestured to the foot of his bed, where his ankle was cuffed to the rail.

"Oh God," Tate choked out, covering his eyes, and suddenly he was crying as hard as Aaron. "Please, you have to help me! I have to get out of here!"

"It's the middle of the night," Alexandra told him. "The ARR are here undercover, guarding you both . . . and Rory too, but the hospital is probably crawling with people loyal to Lowell and the rest of his scumbags. You're safe here for now, okay? And as soon as you stand up in front of the inquiry, this will be over. Whatever happens then, I'll help you." She bit her lip again. "The ARR, we have contacts on the outside. I can see if they can . . . if they can find your daughter for you. I can't promise anything."

"I'll give you the address," Tate said. "I'll write it down for you. Please, can someone go there? See if my daughter's okay?"

Alexandra cast a look at Aaron, who hadn't turned, hadn't spoken at all. Just cried and trembled and made hoarse sounds. And then she nodded. "It's the least I can do," she said. "You saved him, after all. Although, saved him for what . . ." She got off the bed and bent down to pick up her bag. She took a pen and a notepad and handed them over to Tate. "Write it down. I'll take it to someone in the group. You'll be okay in the meantime. The medical staff here are good, and the nurse on your ward is one of us. She'll keep an eye on you."

"Okay." Tate wrote Paula's address down carefully, then handed the pad back to Alexandra. "Please. Please make sure someone does this."

"I'll do my best," she said, touching his cheek hesitantly. "You try to rest. And . . . look after Aaron for me, okay? You're probably the only one who understands what it was like for him."

No, Tate thought. *Lowell was far crueler to him than he ever was to me.* But he couldn't tell her that. That was Aaron's story to tell, his secret to reveal, when he was ready. Tate nodded instead.

Alexandra shot another worried look at Aaron and then left the room.

Tate closed his eyes again. His head was still aching, but he thought that maybe he could sleep. And maybe if he slept, he wouldn't have to replay every awful memory in his head.

Or question why none of them seemed to be about Rory.

"Here's how it's going to be," Aaron said suddenly.

"What?" Tate opened his eyes, surprised to find that Aaron was now facing him, lying on his side, eyes huge in the half dark of the room.

"That's what he said. 'Here's how it's going to be.'" Aaron shuddered. "I thought he was joking. I didn't steal. Kept waiting for the punch line." His face twisted, his voice choked with fresh tears. "'Here's how it's going to be, Aaron.'"

Tate felt tears on his face too. "I'm sorry," he managed to get out, even though it was meaningless.

Aaron shook his head. "Don't be. To be honest, when you came, I was . . . I was relieved. A part of me, at least. A part of me was jealous— the *chip*, the chip made me jealous, afraid you were going to—"

"You don't have to say it," Tate whispered, and Aaron nodded, thankful.

"But a part of me, the real me, was relieved. Because I wasn't alone, I wasn't alone with that . . . *monster* anymore." The strangled sound that escaped him was almost like a laugh. He threw the sheet off himself suddenly and yanked down the collar of his hospital gown to point to the tape on his chest, covering his nipples. "Look. They took them out. The plug too. I'm scarred there. Might need surgery even. Might never regain normal, normal . . ." He sucked in a shaking breath. "She knows. Alex heard them tell me. I'm glad she was there to protect me, but I hate that she knows. I wish she didn't know."

Tate didn't know what to say.

"I was supposed to be her boyfriend," Aaron said. "I thought I could be, anyway, if I was smart enough and stuff, and maybe learned more about politics, but she'll never look at me like that again, will she? She'll never look at me like I'm the kind of guy who can be clever and funny and strong, because she *knows*. She knows what he made me into."

"She knows it's not your fault."

"Does it matter?"

"It has to," Tate said. "It has to. Oh God."

Aaron's bed creaked, and suddenly he was in Tate's bed, under Tate's covers, hugging him tightly. And Tate told himself that it should have mattered, that this should have disgusted him a little—the memory of what had happened between them under Lowell's command was sickening—but it didn't, because maybe Alexandra was right. Maybe Tate was the only one who did understand Aaron, and maybe he needed some fucking comfort for himself right now, as well.

He hugged Aaron back, not caring if they were both crying and not caring if they were close enough that he could feel Aaron's mouth against his neck. This wasn't sexual. This was clinging on to someone who needed him, and someone he needed in return.

The things they'd done didn't matter. Didn't count. The sick things that Lowell had ordered.

But there had been other moments, when Lowell hadn't been home. When Tate had reached out and held Aaron's hand. When Aaron had leaned against him for support. When they'd touched, not accidentally, but because in those quiet moments when the fear and the pain fought back against the chip, a touch was necessary.

Tate closed his eyes. Hadn't Rory given him those moments too? It hadn't all been sexual with Rory. Sometimes it had been nice to just touch because they were friends and because, since they'd already fucked, it was stupid to keep barriers up. What use was personal space when a guy had put his dick up your ass?

He wondered what it would be like now with Rory. Without the chip. Would it be awful?

Rory was being kept in a separate room—that must be for a reason. Because they thought Tate might hate him? If that was the reason . . . Tate didn't hate Rory. Couldn't hate him. Maybe he didn't want to think about him too hard, but that wasn't the same as hate.

Oh God. Rory had been chipped. Tate hadn't even acknowledged it before now. He must have been chipped, to have lied on the stand that way.

Had he been hurt, the way Tate and Aaron had, even in that short time? Did he have that matching scar? Cradling Aaron against him, Tate realized the only feeling he had for Rory now was concern.

CHAPTER
EIGHTEEN

Rory had only had the chip for a short time, but when it was gone, it somehow left a gaping hole behind. Fear trickled in. He was stuck in a hospital room. He didn't know where he was or what had happened exactly, and every time the door opened, he was afraid it would be Lowell. Or Tate.

There was a police officer at the door, and often another man came and sat inside. He was with the ARR, he whispered, although his badge said he was a nursing student. Rory didn't know whether to believe he was ARR or not, or if the police officer knew. He felt a little safer with the guy there though. Every time Rory fell asleep, he was afraid he'd wake up *changed*.

He remembered the courtroom as though it was something he'd seen in a movie—from a distance. Something not quite real. He remembered the commotion after Tate's collapse and Lowell's strident denials. Too late for that, though. Far too late. In the interests of a fair trial, the judge had ordered the chips removed from Rory, Tate, and Aaron—Rory might have thought he'd dreamed that part, but the guy from the ARR had confirmed it quietly. Which made things precarious now. Made Rory's heart race every time the door opened. Because no way in hell would Lowell let them speak against him. He'd lose everything, and a man like Lowell wasn't going to give up his power so easily.

Where was Tate? And Aaron? Were they okay? Did they, too, have someone posted in their rooms to guard them?

They must; Alexandra was here somewhere after all. She wouldn't let Aaron out of her sight.

And Tate? Who was looking out for Tate?

It should be me.

But would Tate even want to see him, after everything?

In the end, it didn't matter. Rory wasn't allowed to leave his room, and Tate probably wasn't, either. His only visitors were medical staff, the man from the ARR, and a very shell-shocked Cal Mitchell.

"I wouldn't be surprised at all if you want different representation," he said when he pulled a chair close to Rory's bed. "This is all . . . well, incredible. It's incredible. The chip really makes you lie?"

"It makes you want to please," Rory said. The words were sour. "It makes you become a slave."

Mitchell sucked in a sharp breath.

"What? Is there something wrong with using that word?" Of course there was, in enlightened Beulah. "What else do you call it when someone has no choice about anything they do?"

Mitchell bowed his head. "God. I told defendants to take the plea bargain."

"You didn't know." Rory figured Mitchell was no more culpable than most other people in Beulah. And maybe he was even less culpable than Rory, who'd adapted so well to the whole rezzy system that he'd fucked Tate, and what was worse, gone on to debase him at Lowell's house. Tortured him, just like Lowell had tortured Aaron. It didn't matter that he'd thought Tate had wanted it. What did intent count when the harm was the same?

Mitchell lifted his gaze again. "The media is in a frenzy over this. Are you up to facing an inquiry panel? It won't be public. Just a panel of justices."

Rory's stomach clenched. "Not Lowell?"

"No. Mr. Lowell is on administrative leave."

Administrative leave. Not even under arrest for his corruption and crimes.

"Okay." Rory nodded. "When?"

"They're setting up now," Mitchell said. "In a conference room here in the hospital. It was thought . . . *prudent* to do it quickly, and quietly."

Quickly and *quietly* weren't the most encouraging words when it came to the concept of justice. "Will it be fair? Will they listen?"

"Oh yes." Mitchell nodded. "It won't be swept under the rug. I just wish we'd listened to you earlier."

It might have been easy to attack the man for that, for not listening when he must have known, deep down, that there was something wrong, something rotten with the system. But Rory hadn't listened, either. He'd ignored his own unease, and all because Tate had seemed so willing and happy. Because he'd believed Lowell instead of his own instincts.

Lowell had had them all fooled.

And people like Aaron and Tate—Beulah's most vulnerable— had suffered for it.

Even if things weren't as simple as Mitchell made them out to be, Rory had to try.

He had to stand up for Tate.

Tate took a step back.

There was a room full of people staring at him.

"You're not on trial," Alexandra reminded him.

He wanted to reach out and take Aaron's hand, but how would that look? And what did it mean anyway? The old Tate never would have held a guy's hand, even if it didn't mean anything. But hell, there was no part of Aaron that he hadn't seen—or touched, or licked—so it seemed a little stupid to worry about something like hand-holding. Tate just didn't know where the boundaries were anymore. Not after everything.

He took a deep breath and stepped inside.

He sat down at the seat Alexandra indicated. Aaron sat beside him. Tate still didn't reach for Aaron's hand.

One of the women sitting on the panel looked at her watch, like she was waiting for something.

Shit.

Tate turned around as the door opened and closed again and saw Rory standing there. Rory. When Rory sat down on his other side, Tate didn't know whether to lean toward him or lean away. Didn't know if his skin was crawling or he was breaking out in goose bumps. He stared straight ahead, afraid to look.

Afraid. Hell, Tate had never been afraid of anything in his life, not before Beulah, and not before the fucking chip. Sudden rage rose up in him, and he clenched his fingers into fists. What the chip had stolen from him, he'd never get back. Even though it was gone now, it had *changed* him, and that wasn't fair. It hadn't been a punishment; it had been a violation, and it always would be.

The panel started with him. A man with glasses said, "Mr. Patterson, can you tell us, in your own words, how you came to be in the restitution program?"

In his own words.

"I punched him." Tate jerked his head in Rory's direction. "But then he fucked me, so I guess we're even, right?"

It felt good to be angry again. Anger, that was *his*. Something the chip had tried to take from him, but he was still here and so was his anger. And he didn't have to be ashamed if he could be angry instead.

The woman on the panel cleared her throat delicately. "You two had a sexual relationship? After he became your sponsor?"

Tate narrowed his eyes. "I got an erection when I scrubbed his fucking dishes. Everything I did was to make him praise me. That was the only thing that mattered. It *hurt* when he didn't. Of course we fucked. I would have done anything." He leaned back in his seat and folded his arms across his chest. Glared at the panel and tried not to hear Rory gasp beside him. Horror? Surprise? Didn't matter. He didn't care. Rory was a victim too, but he wasn't Tate's problem. All of the concern he'd felt for him previously had been washed clean by Tate's anger. Fuck this place, and fuck these people.

"Did Mr. James force himself on you?" the woman asked.

"No." Tate glowered, but a little of his anger at Rory slipped out of his fingers. "It was the chip. The chip made me initiate. I don't think he knew that . . . but Lowell did. I'm not gay." Then he did what he'd told himself he wasn't going to do. Turned his head and stared right into Rory's pale, shocked face. "I'm not gay."

"Tate," Rory croaked. He reached out his hand and then dropped it again. "I'm sorry."

Tate refused to let Rory's apology soften him. He needed this anger right now. Needed it.

"Justice Lowell?" one of the panelists prompted. "You say he was aware of the chip's full capabilities?"

"That fucking pervert probably designed the thing!" Tate shuddered. "Yes, he knew, just like the doctors at the induction center knew. He knew that it made us . . . made us unable to say no to him. That's why he framed Aaron for stealing . . . because he . . . because—"

"Because I said no." Aaron's head snapped up. "Because that whole night before my arrest, he'd been watching Tate and wanting a rezzy of his own, and because when I walked him home, he invited me in, and I said no. I didn't steal from him, but I couldn't prove it."

"Because he's a sick fuck," Tate snarled. "He tortured Aaron and me, he—" So much for his anger carrying him through this. Everything Lowell had done was right there, playing like a movie in his head, but Tate couldn't say it aloud. His voice would break if he tried. *He* would break. "He *knew*. Lowell knew."

"You understand you're accusing Justice Lowell of rape?"

Tate almost laughed at the way the panelist said the word like it tasted sour. Well shit, if she hated it that much, wait until she heard the details. He leaned forward so that the small microphone on the desk wouldn't miss a thing. "Yes. I'm accusing Justice Lowell of rape, because that's what he did. He raped us."

Beside him, Rory shuddered.

"And you, Mr. James? Did Mr. Lowell . . ."

Rory shook his head. "Not him. He didn't get a chance before my trial. But I don't doubt he intended to. That wasn't his aim with me, not like it was with Aaron—he just wanted to silence me—but I bet he'd have taken advantage of it as a side benefit."

"What do you mean, he wanted to silence you?"

"I was suspicious of the chip. I suspected that he'd framed Aaron for a crime he hadn't committed. I tried to confront him, and he told me to keep my mouth shut or he'd frame me and have me chipped too."

Tate suddenly found it hard to breathe. He thought back to that moment in the living room when Rory had tried to defend him, tried to save him from Lowell's control. He'd let himself be taken rather than go on hurting Tate. Let himself be taken and—

"Not him," Rory had said.

Mr. Lowell may not have gotten to him in time to rape him, but someone had. That fucking induction center. Someone had. A part of Tate wondered if he should take grim satisfaction in that. *How do you like that dose of karma, Rory?* But the thought of Rory getting hurt like that just sickened him.

"But I—" Rory's voice faltered. "I couldn't pretend it wasn't wrong. Not once I knew."

"Oh my God," said one of the panelists, at the same time one of the others said, "This is outrageous!"

"It's true," Rory said, raising his voice. "Take the chips out of all the rezzies. Ask them all. Ask them if they had a say. Ask them."

He wasn't angry like Tate. He wasn't distressed like Aaron. Somehow Rory sounded calm and in control. He was the sort of man they would have to listen to, in the end. Tate frowned and risked a glance at him.

Rory was pale, but his face was determined. His jaw was set. His hands, resting on the table, didn't shake. "Every single testimony heard in court by a rezzy is suspect. Every interview with a parole officer or a lawyer. And every answer given to a sponsor." He turned his head and caught Tate's gaze. His voice faltered when he spoke again. He never looked at the interviewers again. Just stared directly into Tate's eyes. "Take the chips out, and listen to them. Listen to them before it's too late, before you have the kind of guilt on your conscience that I do now."

Tate sucked in a sharp breath. *Guilt?* Yeah, he wanted Rory to feel guilty. A part of him did, at least. But Tate had *begged* for it. So where did that leave it? It was unfair to blame the guy who only took what you were throwing at him. Wasn't Rory's fault, however much Tate wanted to blame him, because he was right fucking there.

It wasn't Rory's fault that he'd slept with—fucked? made love to? none of them were right—Tate. Wasn't his fault that he'd been sweet about it, either. And it had felt good. Wasn't Rory's fault Tate didn't know whether it only felt good because of the chip. Would probably never know . . . He fixed his gaze forward again.

"Mr. Patterson," the lead panelist said, "you say that the chip gave you no control? Is that true?"

"Yes," he said.

She shuffled through her notes. "You're a convicted felon. You can't blame the chip for your criminal behavior."

Tate jutted out his chin. "I never said I did. But I can sure as fuck blame it for everything that happened after."

Beside him, Aaron shifted restlessly in his chair. "Doesn't matter," he muttered.

Tate reached out and put a hand on his forearm.

Aaron flinched, standing up so suddenly that his chair fell back. "You want to know what the chip does? You put one in your head! Go on! Put one in your head, and scream so much inside that you bleed!" He lifted his hand to his nose reflexively. "You put one in your head!"

"Aaron!" Alexandra broke free from her place in the audience and rushed to his side. "Calm down, please."

"Don't!" Aaron pulled back. "Don't fucking touch me! Nobody fucking touch me!"

Tate rose to his feet, as well, looking around the room for police or orderlies or whichever assholes were going to try to take Aaron down. "Leave him alone! Just . . . just leave him alone."

Alexandra stepped back, her hands fluttering.

Tate watched Aaron warily. He stood hunched over, fists clenched, like he was trying to squeeze himself into a tiny space. He was breathing heavily. Ready to snap, Tate figured. He turned to the panel. "Can we get a break here?"

Didn't really know what he'd do if they refused, but Tate wasn't the only one who saw how close Aaron was to losing it.

"We'll take fifteen minutes," the head panelist said.

"Hey." Tate lowered his voice. "I can touch you, right?" He didn't have to wait long for an answer. All it took was a nod, and Tate reached out and grabbed Aaron's wrist and pulled him toward the exit. He checked to see if Alexandra was following. "Come on."

They made their way into the corridor.

Aaron leaned his forehead against the wall. "Sorry. I'm sorry."

"Fuck them," Tate said. He rubbed Aaron's back. "Fuck them, yeah?"

"Yeah," Aaron muttered.

People began to leave the conference room. The doors squealed open and closed. Most of them stared openly at Tate and Aaron, and Tate bristled. He kept his voice low. "Yeah, fuck them."

Alexandra watched them through tear-filled eyes. "Aaron?" she said at last. "Do you want to go back to your room?"

He nodded, still facing the wall.

Tate saw Rory exit the conference room and stand awkwardly in the corridor. He lifted his hand off Aaron's back. "Hey, you go with Alex, okay, and I'll catch you up?"

Aaron tensed. "Where are you going?"

"Gonna see if I can score us something better than fucking pudding," Tate said.

Aaron snorted. His shoulders relaxed, and at last, he let Alexandra draw him away. Tate watched him go.

"You're not, um, going with him?" Rory asked.

"Nope." Tate frowned past Rory at the guys standing nearby. ARR. He knew their faces by now. Knew they wouldn't let Lowell get the jump on them. He looked back at Rory almost reluctantly. Would be a hell of a lot easier if he hated him. If he didn't find himself staring at those lips and remembering exactly what they could do. "You just gonna stare at me in the meantime?"

Rory turned away sharply.

Tate opened his mouth, then closed it again, unsure what to say. *It's not your fault? I'm sorry?* He sighed. "Rory?"

Rory turned. Tate couldn't read his expression. Fearful? Hopeful? Sorrowful? Maybe all those things at once.

"This is shit," Tate said at last.

Rory managed a tiny smile. "Yeah."

"I guess there are things I want to say to you," Tate said, swallowing. "Mostly, I know you feel bad for what happened. But you had it in your head too. You know what it did. So, I'm not blaming you." He wrinkled his nose. "That's all, I guess."

But it wasn't all. There was something else. Something Tate needed to know for sure.

"I *am* sorry," Rory said softly, and as calm and controlled as he'd been at the panel, his voice shook now. "I wish I'd have known earlier. I wish I'd have listened to my gut. I never wanted to hurt you. I hate that I did. I hate *myself*."

Tate had to force himself not to reach out and touch Rory. Comfort him. But no, it was Rory who'd wronged Tate. It was Rory who should be comforting Tate. But once again, Tate's righteous anger was failing him. "I don't hate you," he said, and then added, "but I don't forgive you yet, either."

"I don't expect you to forgive me," Rory said in a small voice. His eyes shone.

Well then. Good. Except . . .

Tate sighed. "Listen, I know I was pretty fucking convincing, okay? Even I—" his hands clenched into fists "—even I don't know where the chip ended and I began."

Staring at Rory, backed up against the wall, wincing, the epiphany hit him.

"Which is why I have to do this one thing. It doesn't mean anything, okay? I just . . . I just need to know." And then, before he could talk himself out of it, he pushed forward, nudging their lips together. Because he needed it. Needed to know who he was and what he wanted. And maybe just needed a shred of that comfort he'd once had with Rory.

"Tate!"

He grabbed the back of Rory's neck. "Shut up."

Rory huffed in surprise, his breath hot against Tate's lips. Tate kissed him—*don't think about it, just* do *it*. It was familiar and shockingly new at the same time. He'd done this before with Rory, too many times to count, but it felt like the first time. Tate pressed his tongue against the seam of Rory's lips, and Rory let him in.

Because whatever it had been for Tate, for Rory it had been *real*.

Rory let out a noise partway between a moan and a whimper, his body going limp against Tate's.

When had Tate put his hands on Rory's chest? When had this gone from an experiment—*let's see exactly how not gay I am*—to something more? He missed Rory's touch and missed touching him. He missed their closeness. He missed the smell of Rory's shampoo, for fuck's sake. Missed how gentle and receptive Rory could be, just like now.

A bad master. A good man. A *friend*. Tate remembered that, and it was still true. Even with the chip, some things could still be true.

This feeling was true. Despite everything, some part of him still wanted Rory. Maybe even could learn to forgive him, and then possibly to love him. In time. The potential was there. The seed of real affection, planted in those nights watching movies together, all those times Rory had proved himself. And now.

Tate didn't have to be afraid of this thing inside him that he'd never stopped to examine before; the idea that he could feel these things for a man didn't shake him to the core. Didn't shatter him. Felt more like something in him was expanding, instead of breaking.

He wouldn't hide from it.

He pulled away and stared into Rory's flushed face. "I know you," he said. "You don't know me, but I know you. Shit, maybe I don't even know me. But we're not done. Not yet."

Rory swallowed. "What?"

Tate gripped his shirt. "You and me," he said fiercely. "We're not done. Okay?"

Rory nodded, looking dazed. "Okay."

Warmth spread through him. He released Rory's shirt and scowled at him. "Good."

"Um, excuse me," a third voice interjected. A young man with a drawn face approached them from down the hallway. "Tate Patterson?"

Somehow, Tate knew. Knew just from the man's face that this wasn't some interviewer looking for his story.

This was about Emmy.

Tate stepped forward. Stared into the guy's face and just *knew*. Knew that this guy, this random guy out of nowhere, was about to ruin his life. The look on the guy's face said that he knew it too.

"My name's Daniel. I'm with the ARR. We checked the address you gave us. I-I'm sorry, but there was no one living there. It was abandoned. Boarded up. Looked like it's been unoccupied for a long time."

Tate knew exactly how long "a long time" was. Since he'd been arrested. That was how long. Tate had known this was a possibility. Had almost expected it. Had rehearsed the quiet dignity that he would display in receiving the news.

So much for all that.

The grief and rage hit him like a giant fist to his chest, knocking the wind out of him, knocking him right off his feet. He crashed to his knees and roared. Screamed. Smashed his fists against the floor over and over, until his hands ached, and then went on.

Months' worth of feelings hit him all at once. Every injustice. Every rape. Every assault. Every fucking moment that he was trapped here was a moment they'd stolen, and now Emmy was gone.

"Tate—" Rory said, kneeling beside him, trying to touch him, comfort him, calm him.

Tate squeezed his eyes shut and tried to hold the breath in his lungs until he felt strong enough to speak. "I gotta . . . I gotta go." He stared up at Daniel. "Maybe you checked the wrong address. Maybe you didn't ask enough people . . ." He twisted around and frowned at Rory. "Am I still under arrest? Am I still a prisoner? I have to leave."

"I don't know."

"I have to leave. I— When I woke up, I was cuffed. I'm not cuffed anymore. Does that mean I'm free? I don't have a guard now, do I? Am I free? I need to be free. I need to leave." He grabbed Rory's hand. "Will you help me find out? Ask Mr. Mitchell?"

"We can ask," Rory said, his eyes wide with worry. "What's going on, Tate? What address?"

"Emmy's address," he said, bile rising in his throat. "My *daughter*, Rory. She's why I came here in the first place. And now she's missing. Her mom is . . . a junkie. You know, you know what it's like out there. She's *four*."

Rory paled, and in that second, Tate knew exactly what he was thinking because Tate was thinking it too. All those weeks spent on his knees, smiling for his master, and he'd ignored the most important thing in the world. In the universe.

Let a piece of fucking software in his head tell him that Emmy didn't matter.

And now she was gone.

CHAPTER
NINETEEN

He has a daughter.

Aaron didn't come back into the inquiry. Alexandra, slipping back in just as the panelists took their seats, whispered to Rory and Tate that he was sedated. Tate, jiggling his leg restlessly, didn't even seem to hear.

He has a daughter.

He has a daughter.

No wonder Tate had punched him in the face. To get back to someone he loved, to someone who depended on him? Rory would have punched a stranger too.

He has a daughter.

Rory was numb with the news, unable to even *begin* thinking about what had happened before that particular revelation.

He was numb and he was in shock, but he still had a job to do.

"We need to get Tate out of here," he whispered to Alexandra. "Tell Mr. Mitchell. He's gotta go home. You had your guys check an address for him?"

Alexandra nodded.

"It was empty."

"I'll see what I can do." Alexandra moved to the chair beside Mitchell's and spoke quietly to him.

Mitchell rose to his feet. "A point of order before we begin again," he said. "Mr. Patterson has asked for some clarification of his status, and I'm inclined to wonder about it myself. Are my clients still in custody?"

The panelists conferred for a moment, and then the woman in charge spoke. "Given the unusual circumstances in this case, I think that your clients can immediately be released on bail, pending the outcome of this inquiry. There are still the criminal matters outstanding. I'm going to order retrials of all three criminal matters, provided there is enough evidence to pursue them once the inquiry is complete."

Tate tugged at Rory's sleeve. "What's that mean?"

Rory closed his eyes briefly. It meant that he and Aaron were likely to be exonerated. They were innocent. But Tate wasn't. Justified, but not innocent. "It means you'll get a proper trial this time."

Tate shook his head. "No. I gotta go. Am I on bail?"

"You can't skip bail," Rory told him. "The border security in this place . . . You'd never make it."

"Fuck you," Tate hissed. "I *have* to go!"

Mitchell was nodding at the panel.

Rory shoved his chair back and stood up. "That's not acceptable, sorry. Retry me, that's fine. Any untainted investigation will find there's no evidence to pursue a criminal case against me, or against Aaron. But what about Tate? We all saw the footage from the station." He forced a smile. "And let me tell you, he's got a hell of a right hook."

"What are you getting at, Mr. James?"

Rory sighed. "I'm getting at the obvious. Tate's guilty. We all know he's guilty, but that leaves you in a difficult position. How do you punish a guilty man when your judicial system is in total free fall? And most people out there, once they know the truth, are going to tell you that Tate's been punished enough."

"It's not about punishment," the woman said. "It's about rehabilitation. It was never the intention of the people that criminals be *hurt*."

"I understand that," Rory said. "I understand the system is supposed to be enlightened, not barbaric. But that's the thing with barbarism. It's human nature, like it or not, and any system designed by humans can be tainted by it. What happened to Tate was barbaric. You may not have intended to hurt anybody, but he *was* hurt. The damage is done, and I think—no, I know—that you don't have the ethical standing anymore to pass down judgment on this man."

The woman bristled. "If Tate was treated cruelly, the fault is not the justice system's. The fault is yours."

"True." Rory's gut clenched. "And I'm prepared to accept any punishment—sorry, *rehabilitation*—that you deem fit. But Tate, a guilty man, has more than paid his due, and your system's chip is what allowed that to happen. Retry me and Aaron. Charge me with whatever you think appropriate for what happened to Tate. But let him free. He deserves that. Your *system* owes him that."

"He's right," Mitchell put in. "At the current time, Beulah's legal system doesn't have a foot to stand on. You can't possibly still believe we have any right or authority to judge this man."

The woman frowned and conferred for a moment with the other panelists.

Rory fought the urge to drum his fingers on the table.

What felt like ten hours later, she finally turned to Rory again, adjusting her microphone. "We're not prepared to make such a ruling at this time, Mr. James, but we see the validity of your argument and are prepared to release Mr. Patterson on a probationary basis until such time as we can arrange a retrial."

Mitchell leaned down to listen to something Alexandra was saying. He straightened up again, nodding. "Mr. Patterson is also going to need permission to leave Beulah, to attend to urgent family matters."

The woman was taken aback. "Do you really expect us to believe that Mr. Patterson would return to Beulah for a trial?"

"Given the way he was treated here in the past?" Mitchell shot back. "I wouldn't blame him at all. But I do believe he's a man of his word, or at least I believe he deserves the opportunity to prove that he is."

"Mr. Patterson," the woman said. "If you were given permission to leave Beulah, would you come back for your trial?"

"Yes," Tate said.

Rory tried not to let his disbelief show. Of course it was a lie, and everyone here had to know it. Why the hell would Tate come back?

"For my trial," Tate said, "and for Rory's."

My trial. Rory's gut clenched.

"You and me." That fierce look on his face, like no expression Rory had ever seen on him before. A dangerous look. A look of unfinished business. *"We're not done."*

Rory's heart beat a little faster. At first, in the corridor, hope had unfurled in his chest when Tate had kissed him. And hope was the one thing Rory couldn't trust.

Revenge, then. Rory was certain he could trust revenge.

Tate would come back for a chance to testify against Rory, have him convicted for rape. God. And Rory deserved that, of course. Of course he did. Tate deserved justice, and part of that meant justice against Rory.

Didn't make it any less scary, though.

Rory had come to Beulah for a new start, for a better life than he could get in the outside world, and what had happened to that? Now he was a rapist. A lower sort of criminal than Tate had *ever* been.

Rory didn't see where it had all gone so wrong. It had been gradual, he supposed. The first time he'd suspected there was something off about Tate, he should have stopped. Should have asked questions. Shouldn't have listened to Tate's reassurances. Because he'd known something wasn't right. And even if there had been no chip, even if Tate had been freely asking for those things, Rory had still been his sponsor. But he'd let Lowell convince him that it was okay, and he deserved to be punished for that.

It was easy to hold the moral high ground when there was nothing to tempt him. Easy to draw an imaginary line. But what had happened the first time Rory had ever been tested? His morals and ethics had crumbled into dust. Which meant he'd never been the decent man he'd thought he was. He was just as bad as Lowell, taking what he wanted.

He glanced at Tate quickly. Tate's jaw was set, and his gaze was fixed on the panel.

Someone's dad. Tate was a little girl's dad, and because of Lowell and Rory, that little girl was gone now. Whatever else had happened between them, Rory deserved to pay for that. He imagined a child with Tate's golden skin and dark eyes. With his curls. His daughter would be beautiful. A beautiful little girl who was *gone*.

An empty address. A junkie mother. Tophet, the outside world, harsh and unforgiving.

If Rory's heart was aching just to think of it, how the hell was Tate feeling?

Rory sneaked another glance at Tate's set face. Revenge. Tate would absolutely come back to Beulah for that. Because what did he have left to lose?

"You and me. We're not done."

When Tate had kissed him, Rory had thought maybe it was possible to read something else into that intense look on Tate's face. But the kiss had been . . . been what? Rory didn't know, and he bet Tate didn't, either. Tate was angry and confused and fucked up by everything that had happened. Next time Rory saw him, he knew, Tate would know exactly where he stood. And he had a feeling that wherever that place was, it wouldn't be one where they were kissing.

Rory hadn't just cost Tate his freedom, and his free will. He'd cost him his daughter.

The woman on the panel conferred with her colleagues for a moment longer, then leaned forward. "Tate Patterson is granted bail, by special order of this tribunal."

Tate didn't even smile. He only narrowed his eyes at the panel.

Next time, Rory knew, he'd want his revenge.

Tate didn't know if he was imagining it or if people were staring. He didn't know how public things were yet, or maybe people just remembered him from the footage of the last time he'd been at this station, of punching Rory. They'd said, at the time, that it was a big media event. He wondered how big *this* scandal would be.

At least he wouldn't be here for it.

"Don't lose your ticket," Alexandra told him as they waited for the train. She frowned. "You'll need it to get back into Beulah when . . . when you're finished."

Finished failing to find out what happened to my daughter?

Tate wondered if he'd ever be finished. If he'd ever have a story, or closure, or a trail gone cold, or anything. People in Beulah didn't really know what it was like outside. Seeing it on news reports wasn't the same as having to live it. Rory knew, but everyone else seemed to think that he'd actually find out what happened. As though someone would tell him. As though any of the people he and Paula had called friends weren't completely drug-fucked or drunk or dealing with enough shit of their own that they didn't care. That's what happened to people out there. They dropped out of your life and maybe you wondered about them for a bit, and then you didn't. They became ghosts.

It was the reason he'd come to Beulah in the first place. To get enough money to go somewhere better. Somewhere away from the city, where maybe people still counted for something. Maybe family and neighbors counted. Not that Tate would have fit in anywhere like that, but he'd wanted to try, for Emmy.

"You think I won't come back?" he asked Alexandra, taking his ticket. "I mean, would *you*?"

"I don't know."

She was honest. He'd give her that.

"I said I would," Tate said. "To sort things out with Rory, I will."

Alexandra frowned at him. "What do you mean by that, 'sort things out'?"

"His trial," Tate said and shrugged. "Someone's gotta tell them that he didn't know."

"Oh!" Her eyes widened. "I thought you meant . . ."

"What?"

"I thought you meant you wanted him to pay for what happened to you."

Tate's stomach clenched. "Maybe I did, kind of. But it wasn't his fault. That's the worst part. It'd be easier to hate him."

A piece of him did, he guessed—but not for what had happened when he was under the influence of the chip. He'd looked for Rory after the tribunal had let out, but he'd already vanished. And Tate had *told* him they weren't done. But apparently Rory thought they were. He'd been pissed about that, but nobody from the ARR would tell him where Rory was. And with Emmy missing, Tate didn't have time to chase Rory around.

As much as it strangely hurt, Rory wasn't Tate's priority.

That was what he told himself. But although there was no question that Emmy was more important than Rory, it didn't mean that Rory was nothing.

He meant *something*—possibly even *too* much—even if Tate hadn't exactly figured it out. Even if he didn't want to look it in the face quite yet. It was there, lurking in the back of his mind, and he'd face up to it. Soon. When he came back to Beulah.

He would come back.

Whatever Alexandra was going to say was lost in the sudden bustle around them as the train approached. She gripped his hand tightly for a moment. "I'll see you again."

Tate almost smiled. It sounded a little like a question, despite his assurances. "You will," he said. "Look after Aaron, okay?"

"Yes," she said and surprised him with a hug. "Be safe, Tate."

"I will." He drew a deep breath and stared at the train.

Here he was, leaving at last. Hating the thought of leaving Rory to face everything alone and hating the thought of what he would, or wouldn't, find back in the outside world. And hating himself for being too slow, too careless, too reckless the last time he'd been at this station. Because if he hadn't fucked up then, everything would have been okay.

"If I were you, son," Cal told Rory, "I'd hope he didn't ever come back."

Somehow in the past few weeks, Rory had stopped thinking of the man as Mr. Mitchell, and started to consider him a friend. Which didn't make hearing what he had to say any easier.

Rory grimaced and stared down at the pages spread out over the desk. "Lowell told him to lie under oath and say I was stealing. That makes him a witness."

"Does it?" Cal asked, leaning back in his chair. "We'll prove you're no thief. We can build a solid case without Tate."

"Solid?" he asked. "Nothing's solid where Lowell's involved!"

"Still, it's better than any witness who will declare your innocence on one hand, and on the other hand tell the court how you had sex with him at a time when he was not able to give consent."

Rory glanced at Aaron, who looked up quickly and flashed him a nervous grin.

In the weeks that Tate had been gone, Aaron had started to come out of his shell again. He was still standoffish with Alexandra, except on nights like these when they were all gathered around the large desk in Cal Mitchell's chambers, sifting through statements and evidence and playing with different scenarios. It was almost like it had been working at the Hall of Justice. Sometimes Rory half expected Lowell to walk in, his tie undone, and announce he was buying the pizzas.

Lowell was still on administrative leave. The induction center had been closed down pending the outcome of all the related trials, and all current rezzies—there were less than a hundred in all of "crime-free" Beulah—had been removed from their sponsors and placed in the care of the hospital system until such time as the government decided whether or not to remove their chips. Which was a given, in Rory's opinion. It had been truly gratifying to see how horrified most politicians and justices were once the news of Tate's and Aaron's testimonies had gone public.

Three days ago, Alexandra had come racing into the office and slammed down what looked like blueprints. "Look what my contact in the Works Department got me!"

"What's that?" Rory had asked, staring at it.

"A jail," Alexandra had announced. "You know what this means? No more chips. No more sponsors. The government is already planning what to do without them." She'd grinned. "And I hope Lowell is the first damned resident—er, prisoner!"

Rory wished he could have been as enthusiastic, but he was fairly certain that if Lowell ended up in a cell in a shiny new jail, then Rory would be his neighbor. Cal was obviously worried about that as well and, depending on his mood, couldn't decide if he wanted Tate to come back or not. Could he testify against Lowell? Absolutely. But he could also testify against Rory. Despite that, Rory hoped he would see Tate again. Maybe to talk, and absolutely to be held accountable. He was afraid of his punishment, but he knew he deserved it.

And it was sad too, to think that this utopian society, this beautiful gleaming beacon that he'd been so optimistic about, was about to have an ordinary old jail, just like the outside world. And Alexandra was *happy* about it. But then, she didn't know any better. To Rory, it didn't feel like progress.

"Now, I've had notice from the Hall of Justice that Aaron's retrial will be first," Cal said. He smiled at Aaron. "It's nothing to worry about. We have witnesses who say you had permission to use Lowell's credit card anyway and footage from the store that shows the disputed purchases were made by Lowell himself. He can't make that evidence disappear, not now. And the police have been more than thorough."

"Sure," Aaron murmured. "*Now* they're thorough."

"Yes," Cal said. "Now they are."

None of them responded to that.

"Now, after Aaron, will be Rory, and then, finally Tate, to determine whether the cruel and unusual punishment he suffered is enough to have him pardoned and his previous sentence overturned. Which, I believe, will serve as a precedent and thus a blanket decision for all current and former rezzies." A landmark decision, then. So much more than just Tate's fate depended on that trial. Of course, there was no such thing as "just" Tate, not for Rory. Even now.

Cal drew a deep breath and hesitantly concluded, "And then, Lowell."

Rory shivered.

"Lowell," Aaron murmured.

"Yes," Cal said. His face was grave for a moment. He shook his head, and Rory saw the battle in the man: betrayal and anger and disgust. Cal, in his own way, must have felt as culpable as Rory did. Maybe everyone in Beulah would, once the full shape of the truth came to light.

Alexandra, passing behind the desk, reached out and squeezed Cal's shoulder. "The moment we've been waiting for, sir. What was it you told me the other night? We're going to nail that fucker."

Cal huffed. "I'm sure I would never use such language."

"I'm sure you did."

He snorted, and then he smiled. "Maybe."

It was no victory, but they had hope at least.

CHAPTER
TWENTY

I t was shocking for Rory to see Lowell sitting in the courtroom. Not at the prosecutor's table, with Ruth and Zac, but at his own little desk between the prosecution and the defense, as though nobody knew where he ought to sit. That was fine. In a few weeks, it would be Lowell up in the dock, and then he'd know what it felt like.

The prosecution, as Cal had predicted, was halfhearted at best. Any evidence they'd tabled had easily been debunked by the investigation. It had all obviously been manufactured by Lowell, who Rory guessed wasn't as smart as he thought, or at least wasn't smart enough for his plots to succeed without the power of the chief justice's office behind them.

Because once people started to ask questions, it all fell apart so very easily. Not that a man of Lowell's ego would allow that to happen. Not without demanding the right to cross-examine Rory, as though he thought Rory would collapse under the force of Lowell's personality and retract everything he'd already said.

But Rory wouldn't. Even Aaron—quivering and crying a little as he'd given his testimony about his supposed credit card theft—hadn't.

This, Cal had told them, was like a practice run for when Lowell was on the stand. A man like that, when he was crashing in flames, would try to take everyone else down with him. Except even Rory could tell that the court was against him. Not just the press and the public gallery but the justice, and even Ruth and Zac.

"Rory." Lowell smiled, pacing up and down in front of the dock as though the courtroom was his own personal theatre. "You were my personal assistant, is that right?"

"Your executive assistant."

"My apologies." Lowell's smile broadened. "But things got fairly personal, didn't they?"

Rory didn't answer that.

Lowell chuckled. "With us and our rezzies, I mean. You had a sexual relationship with your rezzy, didn't you?"

"Relevance?" Cal called. "Mr. James is on trial for fraud and theft, not for anything else."

"Not yet." Lowell winked and held up his palms. "Character. It's all about character. I just want to show the court exactly what sort of man Mr. James is."

"Yes," Rory said. It would all come out at Lowell's trial anyway.

"Yes, what?"

"Yes, I had a sexual relationship with my 'rezzy,' Tate Patterson," Rory said.

"Did he want it?" Lowell asked with a smile.

Rory opened his mouth and was suddenly unsure how to answer. Yes? Because Tate had, or at least the chip had. But if Tate had wanted it, then so had Aaron. This was nothing more than Lowell playing the long game. He didn't give a damn about whether or not Rory was convicted of theft. He just wanted it on record somewhere how much Tate had begged to be fucked. He just wanted to show, a few weeks down the track, that he was no abhorrence. Well, fuck that. Rory wasn't going to give him any help there.

Rory's stomach clenched. "No. It is my understanding that he didn't want it. The chip made him incapable of meaningful consent."

"Ah," said Lowell. "And you did it anyway?"

"I didn't know about the chip," Rory shot back. "*You* did."

"Irrelevant," Lowell said.

"If Justice Lowell wishes to examine my client's character, he can examine his own, as well," Cal said, and a murmur ran through the public gallery.

Lowell's smile slipped a fraction. His once-toothless pet public defender suddenly using the law to destroy him. "Well then," he said, recovering quickly, "you had a *personal* relationship with your rezzy, Tate Patterson."

"Yes," Rory said.

"He knew you well," Lowell said. "And you trusted that he would keep your secrets. In fact, you were so sure of yourself, that you *told* him that you were diverting funds from my department into your own accounts."

"No," Rory said, at the same moment as Cal called out, "Hearsay!"

"Of course," Lowell said. "It's hearsay since Mr. Patterson, a key witness in this matter, was granted bail!" He laughed. "An astonishing decision! And one very convenient for you, Rory, isn't it? Because we both know that Mr. Patterson was intending to testify against you, don't we?"

"I don't know that. I know he was intending to testify today but not to what end," Rory said firmly.

So where is he? Where is he to end my waiting? Where is he to condemn or absolve me? His lips tingled, as if Tate had just kissed him a minute ago, instead of a month ago. *Where is he to tell me where the fuck I stand?*

Lowell smiled. "Of course you do, Rory. You told him you were stealing, he told *me* that you told him that, and suddenly, he's gone. I wonder who's really pulling the strings here, hmm?"

Not you. And don't you fucking hate it?

"Relevance?" Cal asked. "If Justice Lowell has a conspiracy theory to share, perhaps he should just put all his cards on the table. Because from what I remember, Mr. Patterson's last attempt at testifying against Mr. James didn't play out the way Justice Lowell wanted."

"No, no conspiracy theories," Lowell said, fixing his gaze on the media gallery. "I'm just wondering why the one man who could tell this court that Mr. James is guilty was suddenly allowed to leave Beulah."

"Because an independent panel ruled it so."

"An independent panel!" Lowell roared with laughter. "Headed by a woman whose promotion I reluctantly turned down last year. You might not have known that, Rory, since you're an outsider."

This time the murmur that ran through the public gallery felt less hostile toward Lowell.

We're losing them. The bastard's actually bringing them around to his side.

Maybe Lowell was a little smarter than Rory had given him credit for.

Shit.

"Records," Lowell had told Rory once, *"are useless to juries. You might as well try and get a cat to read Chinese. It all comes down to* performance." And Lowell knew how to perform.

For a moment Rory wondered if he was actually going to be convicted of embezzlement. And then anything he said against Lowell when it came to the way he'd treated Aaron would sound like he was chasing petty revenge. Lowell could actually destroy Rory's credibility here, and Aaron wasn't strong enough to stand alone against Lowell. And then Lowell might even walk free of his charges of rape and assault.

Tate, where are you?

And here Rory was thinking the worst-case scenario was Tate showing up in court to condemn and denounce him. How wrong he'd been.

"This is hearsay," Cal said again.

"The jury will disregard any mention of Mr. Patterson," the presiding justice said at last.

But they wouldn't, of course. Nobody could un-hear something.

"I apologize," Lowell smiled. "I am only, as I said, trying to get at the defendant's character."

"My character!" Rory blurted. "I'll tell you my character. I thought my character was unassailable until I met *you*." He could see Cal shaking his head in warning, but Rory couldn't stop. He knew it was a mistake, but fuck Lowell and his smug smile. "I spent my whole life dreaming of something better, a better place, a better life, a better way of being. And then I got here, and I thought I'd finally made it."

Lowell's smile grew. "And you wanted what we have? You wanted *wealth*, Rory."

"No. I wanted happiness. And I thought I had it too. Being here in Beulah, I thought I finally had it."

"Happiness?" Lowell asked. He shook his head pityingly. "No, Rory, like so many pathetic outsiders you looked on us with envy. Jealousy. Covetousness. You wanted to take the things that we worked hard for. You *stole*, Rory, and you took advantage of Beulah's wealth just as surely as you took advantage of Tate Patterson. To be perfectly blunt, Rory, you fucked him, and you fucked all of us too."

The courtroom erupted, drowning out any reply Rory might have made.

"Your honor!" Cal appealed over the noise.

Rory just shook his head silently. He spoke softly, and the courtroom went silent straining to hear. "But being in Beulah didn't make me happy. Beulah's wealth didn't make me happy. Only Tate did that. Not Tate's service, not Tate's body, not Tate's obedience. It wasn't the chip. It was Tate. It was . . . loving him."

"He was your prisoner!" Lowell laughed as if it were all a hilarious joke. As if he couldn't believe what was coming out of Rory's mouth. Couldn't believe the *gall* of him.

The people gathered in the courtroom laughed along or made expressions of disgust.

At Rory. But God, it didn't matter. It didn't. This was Rory's truth, and he was going to speak it. "I know that now," Rory said. "And it's true, I don't know what was him and what was the chip. I don't know if he would have consented, if he actually had a genuine opportunity to. But I do know that I loved *him*, and that was something the chip couldn't fabricate."

"Ah yes," said Lowell, growing serious suddenly. "Of course, I loved Aaron, as well."

And even though Rory had known this was a trap, even though he'd known that Lowell was leading him somewhere, right until that moment, he hadn't seen it. Lowell only had to discredit Rory and then claim he was in exactly the same unfortunate position: he hadn't known his rezzy's chip made him act that way. He'd loved his rezzy too. Maybe he might be convicted of fabricating evidence, and maybe he'd lose his job and his reputation would be ruined, but he wouldn't be put in that jail that they were building. He wouldn't be convicted of rape in his upcoming trial. He'd slip away with his accumulated wealth, live a quiet, comfortable life, and all the while, Aaron, his witness testimony ripped to shreds on the stand under the force of Lowell's rhetoric, would live in fear, live with the knowledge that justice had been stolen from him.

It wasn't fucking fair.

Some fucking doctor or inconsequential peon working for the induction program would take the fall for the chips and Lowell could pretend he was as oblivious as everyone else.

"You didn't love Aaron. You weren't even his friend!"

That voice. Rory twisted around and saw him standing in the doorway—Tate.

"Rory was my friend, and he didn't steal anything." Tate strode forward, walking through the chaos of the courtroom like he was parting the damn Red Sea. "I'm sorry I'm late. I had to arrange childcare. But I'm here now, and I want to testify."

Lowell went white.

There were only a handful of people that Tate trusted to look after Emmy, and with Cal and Alexandra tied up with court, that had left Aaron. He was taking Emmy to the park.

Cal caught him as he reached the defense table. "What are you going to say up there?" he asked under his breath.

"The truth," Tate said.

Cal still looked worried, but he nodded at the courtroom. "Well, Justice Lowell, it appears your star witness has arrived after all. I'm sure everyone here is dying to hear his crucial testimony." Now, he smirked.

Tate headed for the witness box. It was a lot easier to give testimony without some chip trying to tear his skull apart. He wasn't afraid of Lowell. He figured he wasn't afraid of anything anymore, not after finding Emmy okay. *Better* than okay.

Because rather than his disappearance causing things to go off the rails back at home, it had actually been the catalyst for Paula to reevaluate her life. Or, like she'd said, to get her shit together. She'd taken Emmy to her stepmother's house—a stepmother who had been out of her life for so long that Tate hadn't even known about her. Paula had gotten a part-time job. Gotten clean. Taken care of their child and kept her safe, and Tate was eternally grateful for that.

They'd talked it out. Talked about their past, talked about what had happened in Beulah, and talked about what Tate ought to do next. What *they* should do next, as a family. So here they were. Paula was getting their paperwork sorted so they could stay in Beulah, and Tate was in court. Doing what was right, for once in his life. And after those horrible weeks when all he could see when he closed his eyes was a fucking slideshow of terrible things happening to Emmy, Tate wasn't afraid of Lowell or Beulah or even that look in Rory's eyes, the one of guilt and sorrow and hope all mixed together.

Rory, who'd just admitted to a courtroom, under oath, that he loved Tate.

Tate took his seat, read the oath from the little card, then stared at Lowell. And Lowell stared back. Tate wondered if the man had ever been lost for words before in his life.

"Sorry," Tate said at last, "was I not supposed to come back?"

Someone in the public gallery smothered an incredulous laugh.

"If Justice Lowell won't ask the witness any questions, I certainly will," Cal said. "Mr. Patterson, did Rory James ever tell you that he was stealing from Justice Lowell's department?"

"No, he did not."

Cal smiled. "And did Justice Lowell tell you, when you were under the influence of the chip, to lie to this court and say that Mr. James had made that admission?"

"Yes, he told me to lie," Tate said. "And I wanted to do it too. I tried to, the last time, but I couldn't in the end."

"And why is that?" Cal asked.

"I don't know," Tate said. "The chip was trying to rip my head apart, but as much as I wanted to please Mr. Lowell, I couldn't tell that lie. Because Rory wouldn't steal. He's a good man. He's an honest man. I *knew* that, and even the chip couldn't convince me otherwise."

"So you're saying he's innocent of the crimes he's been charged with today, that is, fraud and theft?"

"Completely one hundred percent innocent."

"And when today's trial is concluded, do you intend on pressing charges against him for rape, due to the nature of your relationship while you were a part of the restitution program?"

Tate looked to Rory. Looked him right in the eye. "No. I don't."

Cal dusted his slacks. "Well then, it seems the only thing to do now is to acquit Rory James of all the charges against him. Unless, of course, Justice Lowell has any questions for the witness?"

Tate looked at Lowell.

Lowell's eye twitched. "No, no questions."

Tate smiled at him.

"Well, that's you, Rory," Cal said, squeezing Rory's arm. "Go home, get some rest, and don't answer your door. The media will be all over you. I'll see you tomorrow, and we'll start working on the case against Lowell."

Rory's head was still buzzing. He'd tried to see where Tate had gone after the court had cleared, but he'd lost him in the flood of people. He wanted to talk to him. To ask if he was okay and if the mention of childcare back in the courtroom meant that he'd found his daughter. To ask why he wasn't going to press charges for rape.

"Did you know?" he asked.

Cal slid a stack of papers into his briefcase. "Know what?"

"When you asked Tate if he wanted to press charges, did you already know the answer?"

"I had a very good idea," Cal admitted. "A little birdie at the Hall of Justice told me that Tate was there last night and was asked that exact same question in front of the panel."

A panel in the Hall of Justice? "He came back," Rory said. "What for?"

"He's a smart one," Cal said. "He wouldn't even step foot over the border until he had a letter signed by three different government officials stating he would be pardoned and not put on trial again." He straightened up. "So I can only suppose he came back to testify against Lowell at his trial, and to make sure that you weren't going to get convicted today. Although my little birdie also tells me that his compensation payout is extremely generous."

"Payout?"

"For his suffering, yes. And for his silence."

"They want all this to go away," Rory sputtered.

"They're politicians. Of course they do. And Tate has a family to care for and a new life to build. He deserves that, don't you think? So don't judge him too harshly for making the deal."

Cal touched Rory's shoulder gently, encouragingly. Maybe mistaking the reason for Rory's frown. As if Rory had any right to be disappointed that Tate wasn't willing to drag out his pain and suffering when a quiet life was in his grasp. *Oh, but you do have the right to be disappointed he has a family that doesn't include you?*

"But that doesn't mean there aren't others out there willing to give the establishment hell!"

Rory forced a smile. "Yeah, of course."

Cal had told him to go home, but sitting around in that empty house didn't seem like any way to celebrate his acquittal. No, not celebrate exactly. Rory should have been more relieved, should have felt something, but he was still numb. He didn't want to sit by himself in his house. He wanted to be somewhere there were people. So instead of heading for the station, he walked in the other direction toward the river. There were always people in the beautiful parklands along the riverbank, and Rory didn't want to feel alone right now.

It was providence that took him to this place where a sloping length of neatly trimmed grass met the riverbank, shaded by wide trees that dropped blossoms to the ground. The air smelled sweet, but there weren't as many people around as Rory had expected.

That was when he saw them: a man and a little girl tossing bread into the water for the ducks. Tate. And Emmy. She couldn't have belonged to anyone else. She was just as he had imagined her, with Tate's curls, and Tate's skin, and Tate's brilliant smile. Rory could hear her shrieking with laughter from where he stood hidden in the shade of the trees.

He was about to approach them when someone else did. A woman. A woman who fit into Tate's arms as though she was meant to be there. A woman who lifted her hand and placed it against his cheek and said something that made Tate smile. Then Emmy raced for them, and Tate leaned down and swung her up onto his hip. They looked perfect.

A perfect, happy family, bathed in sunlight and full of smiles.

Rory's heart constricted.

This was who Tate was, and this was who Tate was supposed to be. No chip. No Rory.

He turned around and hurried from the park before they saw him.

CHAPTER
TWENTY-ONE

Weeks passed. Rory returned to work at the Hall of Justice—in Cal Mitchell's fledgling department now. Jericho Lowell's office stood locked but hadn't been cleared out. Preserved, his name still etched into the door, like there was a possibility he could return to his position after his paid leave. Maybe there was.

It was a terrible environment to work in, but Rory stayed on anyway because it was better spending these anxious hours busy and productive than spending them at home, worrying and pining, and pining and worrying. It helped, too, that Alexandra was now employed there. After all, there was work to be done, a whole society and legal structure to be fixed and restructured from the ground up, and Alexandra was one of the few people that Cal, the man who'd somehow inherited the task, trusted.

Lowell's trial was all anyone talked about in the Hall of Justice—in all of Beulah, really—and Rory hated the way those conversations ceased when he walked past. He couldn't tell if it was out of respect for what had happened to him or because people thought he was scum for intending to testify against Lowell, who despite everything seemed as well-liked as he'd ever been. Rory almost understood that. People could believe the best in anyone as long as they didn't have to look too closely. A part of him felt like apologizing for exposing Lowell's true nature. And it would only get worse once Lowell's trial began. Once all the horrible secrets came to life. Once they all revealed their individual humiliations.

Rory dreaded the thought of Aaron taking the stand, dreaded hearing even a moment of the hell he'd lived in under Lowell's control. Didn't want to be faced with it, didn't want Aaron to have to relive it, didn't want Aaron's story to come under scrutiny by cynical bastards who hadn't even been there. But Aaron was going to testify.

Alexandra was worried about him. She seemed to think that the only thing holding him together was the idea of testifying. That when he was done, he'd crumble. He'd refused to speak to a psychologist. He'd refused to speak to anyone, apart from Tate apparently. Rory wondered what the hell they talked about.

The first day of the trial was cool and overcast. Cal took them through the back door to avoid the pack of media out front. There was no public gallery this time, or at least no members of the public in it. From what Rory could tell, every seat was filled with a politician or a justice.

The process was interminable and excruciating, and Rory found himself sitting beside Aaron's shell-shocked parents on one side and the woman from the park on the other. Which was horrible enough to begin with, and that was even before he had to get up on the stand and talk about what had happened that night at Lowell's, when he and Lowell had fucked their rezzies and made them fuck each other. It seemed so pitiful, now, to explain how Lowell had gotten him drunk and convinced him it was all right, and how he knew it wasn't but he'd refused to listen to his gut. He said this in front of Aaron's parents. In front of Alexandra. In front of Tate's . . . girlfriend? Wife? And the most horrible thing of all was the way none of them looked him in the eye again.

The trial lasted for six days. Rory saw faces he never wanted to see again: the doctors from the induction center and the guards, some who claimed to be innocent—and maybe even were—and some who were quick to name names in the hope of some leniency when they faced their own trials. He heard things he never wanted to hear: the testimony of Aaron's doctors from the hospital, detailing his internal injuries, and Aaron's own testimony, given in a voice hardly above a strained whisper as he recounted exactly what Lowell had done to him. And all the while Aaron's mother snuffled into her handkerchief beside Rory.

How the hell could he have let it happen? All that time Lowell was bragging about what Aaron could take, why hadn't Rory even wondered if it was safe? And, God, the doctor from the induction center had come to his *house*, and Tate had bled, and that had to be on Rory too. He should have noticed. He should have guessed.

Rory couldn't stay in Beulah. He needed to find somewhere else. Somewhere away from people. Tate and Aaron had been his friends, and he'd hurt them. He couldn't stay here and keep doing it. Not when every time they saw his face they would remember.

When the trial ended and the jury went into deliberation, Rory quit his job in Cal's department and went to his house to pack.

He wouldn't stay to hear the verdict. What did it matter? The fact that he was walking free meant justice hadn't been served in Beulah. And to think Cal expected him to participate in the restructuring efforts? He was tainted. Any contribution he made would be tainted too. Even if his own actions repulsed him, he didn't trust himself not to subconsciously re-create their circumstances.

Lowell. Give him power, give him time, and he'd turn into Lowell.

At the house, Rory threw his closets open and began to pack. He had no idea where he was going, only that he had to leave soon. When the first clap of thunder sounded from the storm that had been building all day, he imagined the angry roar was all for him. As though nature itself railed against him.

He closed his eyes for a moment. There was his egotism again. Just like Lowell.

The sound of the thunder faded away, and he slowly became aware that someone was knocking on his door. He approached it carefully, wary of reporters. He kept his foot against the door when he opened it a crack, ready to slam it shut again if he had to.

Tate was standing on the front step, soaked with rain. His curls were plastered to his forehead, and water ran down his face. Rory was shocked.

"Are you going to let me in?" Tate asked, raising his brows.

Rory was too surprised to refuse.

"You keep the towels in the same place, right?" Tate padded to the bathroom, leaving wet footprints on the floor.

He thought about following Tate, thought about asking him what he was doing here, but then turned and went to sit in the living room instead. Whatever it was, he would hear Tate out. He would apologize, they would both agree he was an asshole, and then it would be done. Over.

Tate joined him a few minutes later, shirtless, scrubbing a towel over his hair. He sat opposite Rory and stared at him. "Are you going somewhere?"

"Yes."

"Where?"

"I don't know yet."

"Why?" Tate asked.

Rory shook his head and shrugged. "I just . . . I just can't stay here. Not after everything."

"Where else is there to go?" Tate asked. He dropped the towel onto his lap. "Nobody knows better than me how flawed this place is, but at least the air is clean here. I know that sounds dumb, but when I went back to Tophet . . . Shit, I could hardly breathe for my first few days in the city. What sort of place is that to raise a child?"

"You'd rather raise her in the place that put a chip in your head?"

"I'll kill any fucker who touches her," Tate said, his tone even. "But there won't be any more chips. Things will be different. I was going to tell every politician and judge in Beulah to go fuck themselves, but what good would that do Emmy? She can go to school here. She can go to the park. She can have a better life here than anything we could give her on the outside. She's four, Rory, and she's already been hungry too many times in her life."

Rory put his head in his hands. "Shit. You're right. I'm sorry. I have no right to shame you for choosing to live here."

"Anyway," Tate said, "they told me you were going to help restructure the justice system or something, and I figured that would be good. I figured at least there'd be someone I could trust overseeing things. Someone who'd give me the nod if it was about to go to shit. And then I come here, and it turns out you're packing."

Someone he could . . . trust? He sighed. "Why *did* you come here, Tate?"

Tate looked at the floor. "Mostly I didn't want to hang around the court waiting for the verdict, you know?"

"Yeah. Me neither." Rory's jaw wobbled, and his lip trembled. "But why come here? I'm just as bad as him."

"Don't be a fucking idiot, man."

That shocked him. The Tate Rory remembered, the one under the influence of the chip, would never speak so harshly. It stung, and then it felt warm and sweet, and he smiled. "Whoa, don't treat me like porcelain or anything."

Tate rolled his eyes and grinned. "Yeah, I know you're being sarcastic, but that was actually me sugarcoating it, just so you know. For future reference."

Future?

Tate balled up the towel and dropped it on the floor. For some reason, that made Rory want to laugh. Tate leaned forward. "Listen, you're not like him. You were nice to me, and you didn't *know*."

"It doesn't matter if—"

"Shut up," Tate said. "It matters. Of course it matters. Jesus, Rory, I wasn't just pretending to want it. I *did* want it. More than oxygen." He wrinkled his nose and flushed. "You want to know why I came here today? Because a part of me is shit-scared that Lowell will find some way to weasel out of this still, and I wanted to be with a *friend* just in case that happens. And you're just about my only friend here, Rory. Those times we sat on the couch and watched movies together . . . That's when I was happy here. Happy for real, not just because of the chip."

"Tate, I—" Rory swallowed thickly. "That means a lot to me, it does. Your forgiveness or your pardon or whatever means a lot. But I can't be friends with you."

"*What?*"

Rory twisted his hands. Forced himself to look Tate in the eye. "I'm in love with you, Tate." There. That was that. "And yeah, I like you, too, but I can't be friends with you and just hang out and shoot the shit and be buddy-buddy knowing you've got a wife and a kid at home. Maybe if all this hadn't happened, if we hadn't s-slept together, we could be friends and I could adjust to seeing you with a woman—or anyone other than me, I guess. But not now."

Tate's jaw dropped.

Rory smiled slightly. Yeah, so Tate would probably help him pack after that admission. He looked away.

"Rory?" Tate cleared his throat. "I don't have a wife. Paula and I . . . We were only together for a little while. And not for a long time now. We were terrible together. A *disaster*. You know, we enabled each other, we fought all the time . . . I'm happy she's sober now, ecstatic, and so glad that the both of us can raise Emmy together as coparents. But we're not a couple. We're not *together*."

"Oh." Rory's face burned, and he tried for a self-deprecating smile. Maybe there was something he could salvage here after all. If not a friendship, than at least he could be honest. "That, um, that probably shouldn't make me feel better, right?"

Tate stared at him intently. "Don't do that. Don't make fun of yourself."

"I'm not. I'm really not." Rory sucked in a shocked breath as Tate slid off his couch and landed on his knees on the floor. "What are you doing?"

Tate's face was bright with embarrassment. "Making you notice me."

"I don't . . ." Rory murmured as Tate began to close the distance between them, shuffling on his knees. His damp jeans squeaked on the floor. "You don't . . ."

Tate lifted his hands and put them on Rory's knees. "I told you weeks ago we weren't done." He briefly dropped his gaze to Rory's crotch. "I want to try this with no fucking chip in my skull. Just us this time." He tapped the back of his neck, just below his hairline. "Just us."

Rory exhaled slowly. He opened his mouth to tell Tate exactly why this was a bad idea, but those words stuck. Instead he said, "Not on the floor, Tate. Don't be on your knees."

Tate smiled and nodded. He bit his lip as he stood. "So where do you want me, then?"

His wording made Rory wince, but it seemed like a bad idea to point out why. "Just there's fine," he replied. He shifted forward on the couch, then reached out, taking the wet denim of Tate's fly in hand. He popped the button. Pulled down the zipper. Reached in with one hand, resting his palm against the hard line of Tate's dick inside his underwear. Hard. He was hard. Rory looked up at him. Tate's eyes were half-closed, his head was thrown back, and he was biting his lip again. "Tell me if there's anything you don't like. Or you need me to stop or slow down or—"

"I'm not going to let you rape me. Relax, Rory. I appreciate that you care, I do, but can we try to have this not be *completely* weird?"

Rory flushed in shame. "Y-yeah."

"Good boy. How about instead of talking, you do some sucking?" Tate tilted his hips forward, the movement a little jerky. Nervous, maybe, but his stare was challenging. "Hurry up then!"

Heat coiled in Rory's stomach. Tate had never snapped at him under the influence of the chip, and he'd never talked dirty this way—forceful, dominant—before, either. Turned out, Rory liked it. A lot.

He pulled down the elastic of Tate's waistband until his cock sprung free, so dark and thick and perfectly curved, then took the base of it in hand, holding it steady so he could give the tip a little sucking kiss.

"F-fuck," Tate exclaimed.

"Still like it?" Rory asked with what he hoped was a twinkle in his eyes. Tried to make it sound at least a little sexy so that Tate didn't get mad at him for checking *again* if he still wanted to do this.

"Yeah!" Tate's chest rose and fell quickly. "I mean, it's okay."

Rory snorted and leaned in again. This time he closed his mouth around the head of Tate's cock and flicked his tongue against the slit. Tate moaned, and his hips jerked again. Rory was just about to get into the rhythm of things when the thought hit him. He pulled off abruptly. "Are you gonna want to top? I mean, because when you— The chip—"

Tate shook his head. Jerked himself off absently as he spoke. "I thought about that, but you know, I want to do it the same as we were doing. To see if I like it for real. Gotta tell you, whenever I have a wet dream, it's always your cock inside me."

"Jesus," Rory whispered, shivering. He wondered if Tate had called out his name in his dreams.

"I think I'll still like it."

"If you don't, we can try it the other way," Rory offered quickly.

Tate flashed him a smile. "Next time." He shifted forward, straddling Rory's thighs. Arching his back to thrust his cock forward. "Fuck me, man. Come on."

Rory reached up for him and tugged his face down for a kiss. Tate's breath was hot. Rory pressed their lips together, and Tate opened his mouth. Their tongues touched, and Rory felt a shiver run through Tate.

Tate drew back and laughed a little breathlessly. "Did you pack the lube yet? This kissing shit is nice, but it's for schoolgirls."

"Bedroom," Rory said. Tate slid off him as he rose to his feet. Rory curled his fingers around Tate's wrist and pulled him to the bedroom with him.

He was so different. *So* different. Rory still felt the same love for him, the same affection, but it was like meeting him all over again.

And it was *exciting*.

Tate peeled off his wet jeans and sprawled naked on the bed. If he was still nervous, he was better at hiding it. His cock was dark and hard, and he curled his fingers around it and tugged gently as Rory undressed.

He toed his shoes off and pulled his shirt over his head. He hesitated when he reached for the button on his fly.

"What?" Tate asked keenly.

Rory looked at him, lying there, unashamed and wanting this. He shoved his pants down. "I don't know. I'm just really tired of wondering how I fucked things up so badly. And I don't want to make that mistake again."

"This," Tate said, "is not a mistake. Just us, Rory." He drew a deep breath. "Get the lube."

Rory closed his eyes briefly. He just had to ask, one more time. Just had to know. "Are you sure?"

"Yes." Tate's voice didn't waver. "Do it."

Rory got the lube.

Tate wasn't gay, but he definitely wasn't straight, either. He knew that now, looking at Rory, looking at the masculine lines of his body, his fat dick, his big hands. He wasn't straight, and he wanted Rory inside of him.

Now. No, not even now. Ten fucking minutes ago. And he wasn't going to let Rory's nervousness, or his own, derail this. He stretched on the bed, trying to remember how he should relax the muscles in his ass and worrying that he'd forgotten. But then maybe riding a guy was just like riding a bike: you never forgot how to do it. Mostly he wanted Rory closer, because lying here naked and pretending like he was completely cool and relaxed was fucking excruciating. He wanted to lose himself in sensation. He wanted to touch and be touched. He wanted to feel less exposed. Wanted to know, for sure, that this was what he wanted.

He drew his legs up as Rory approached the bed. Planted the soles of his feet on Rory's comforter and tried to remember how to breathe.

"You know," Rory said with a laugh, clambering up his body. "It's different. You're different. Before, you were . . . needy. Desperate. But you know, this time, you're . . ." He spoke through dramatically gritted teeth, "Fucking impatient, Jesus!"

Just like that, all his tension and fear and anticipation crashed into pieces, and Tate laughed. Laughed hard, and suddenly Rory was laughing too. He tensed up for a second when he felt the press of Rory's finger against his ass, but only for a second. Then Rory's finger breached him gently, and Tate sighed. Yeah. This was what he wanted. He shifted to allow Rory easier access and relaxed into the sensation. It felt good.

Back on the outside, after he'd found Emmy and let himself start thinking about what had happened in Beulah, he had thought that maybe he could find some guy and figure out where exactly along that fuzzy scale between straight and gay he landed. But he hadn't. Because he'd missed Rory. He'd wanted Rory. Only Rory. And he was glad now that he'd waited for this moment.

Rory crooked a finger inside him and hit that spot, and Tate gasped, almost jumping off the bed. "Fuck!"

"Found it," Rory said with a smug grin.

"Find it again," Tate suggested, his body jerking as Rory obeyed. "But with your cock."

"I'd prefer to give it a go with my tongue," Rory replied, slinking back down the bed, leaving Tate cold and wanting again. "Don't think it's long enough, but it's still worth a try."

"Are you serious?" Because that still seemed a little . . . weird? Or maybe because it was something Lowell had made him do with Aaron, Tate had figured it was supposed to be degrading. Something that a top didn't do. "You'd do that for me? You'd *like* it?"

"Yeah, and so will you," Rory said, ducking down between Tate's legs.

"I have . . . um . . ." Tate's voice wavered as Rory's tongue flicked against his hole. "Shit. I have a lot to learn."

Rory chuckled, his breath somehow hot and cold at once against the wet skin of Tate's hole. He poked his head up from between Tate's legs. "I'd prefer if you didn't use the word *shit* when I do this, though. If you don't mind."

"F-fuck," Tate said, half barking out a laugh, and fell back onto the mattress again.

Which was good because once Rory started lapping at his ass in earnest, there was no *way* he would have been able to keep himself upright. He shivered and trembled, feeling that tongue darting inside him, licking in circles, even fucking back and forth a little. So wet, so nimble and playful and almost ticklish, but holy hell, Tate wasn't laughing, he was fucking *sobbing*. It felt so good. It felt so, so good. Even though he'd done this before and had it done to him, it was nothing like this. Nothing.

He really was new. This was new.

But the best thing was, that the love he felt now . . . That wasn't new at all. It just needed to be seen in a new light.

And to be here, making love to Rory as if for the first time, provided plenty of that.

"Rory," he gasped, his breath hitching. He reached down and tugged at Rory's hair. "C'mon, please. I need more."

What he needed was to be able to see Rory's face. To hold him close. To kiss him maybe, even though his tongue was currently in Tate's ass. Yeah, that was another weird thought. Not disgusting, just a little weird.

Rory shifted back and then stretched his body out over Tate's. He laid a trail of kisses up the side of Tate's throat and huffed a little in surprise when Tate turned his head to kiss him.

"You ready?" Rory murmured.

Tate nipped at his bottom lip. "Stop asking me that and fuck me. No fingers. No tongue. Fuck me with your dick, like a man."

"Let me get a condom."

"They tested me at the hospital. Negative, and there's been no one since." Tate held onto him. "You?"

"No one," Rory whispered.

"Then fuck me bare," he urged.

Rory huffed again. "Jesus."

"C'mon," he said, hooking his legs around Rory's and urging him closer. He could feel the blunt heat of Rory's cock pressing into his balls and shifted to tilt his pelvis up. Right where he wanted it. Rory's dick at the exact angle it needed to be to fill him, if only he would just *push*. Tate growled in frustration. "Do it!"

Rory pushed.

That first sting of penetration felt better than Tate had remembered. Rory was slow, almost too slow, but Tate was suddenly too breathless to complain. He wondered if he would ever get tired of feeling this, the moment when Rory's cock breached his body and Tate had to fight to let it in. The sting, the pressure, the strangeness of feeling his own body stretch to accommodate Rory: all of those things that had terrified him at first, but he knew now were the prelude to mind-blowing pleasure. Pleasure that he genuinely wanted, and not with anyone else. Just with Rory.

Rory's worried face hovered over him.

"Don't," Tate said. "Just fuck me."

Rory nodded. He leaned down and kissed Tate, open-mouthed, their tongues sliding together. Then he placed his hands on either side of Tate's head, rested his weight on them, and began to thrust.

Tate groaned, his eyes rolling back. For all his dirty talk, for all his demands that Rory just fuck him, *this* was what he wanted, and Rory had known it. Slow and sure, with Rory rocking them both into an easy rhythm. Small, sweet kisses that Tate had to raise himself up off the mattress to chase. Eye contact. Touching.

Tate ran his hands down Rory's sides, feeling rib and muscle. Learning the way his body moved as they fucked. Tate's cock was achingly hard, straining and rubbing between their bellies. It throbbed in time with his heartbeat, with his ass. With Rory inside him. He moaned and clenched hard on Rory's cock.

The shudder ran through them both.

"Tate," Rory whispered, saying his name like a prayer.

There was only one reply for that. Only one thing Tate could say in return and have it mean half as much. "I love you," he murmured, clutching at Rory's nape.

Rory's eyes widened, and his rhythm faltered. "Thank you. God. Tate, I—" His face seemed to crumble. "I love you too."

"Good," Tate said, pulling his head down for another kiss. "Because I told you I wasn't done with you yet."

Rory moaned into the kiss. "God. Are you . . . I'm not gonna last."

"Almost." Tate rocked his hips and slid his hand between their bodies. Jerked himself. Clenched down on Rory's cock and shivered as it nudged against his prostate again. Sensation sparked through him, lighting him up. His balls drew up, and he moaned again. *Almost.* A part of him didn't want this to ever end, but he was wound so tightly now that something had to give. He squeezed his cock. "Rory. Shit, Rory."

Rory thrust again, harder than before, and that was all it took for Tate to come apart. His cum spattered both their bodies, and soon Rory was tumbling behind him, hips jackhammering and eyes squeezed shut as his cock pulsed deep into Tate's body and flooded him with warmth.

Rory fell forward, breathing heavily into his ear.

Tate shifted, and they lay facing each other. With another partner, Tate thought, he would have already been dressing. But he didn't feel the same with Rory. He wasn't embarrassed by being close, by being naked together. He didn't mind if Rory knew he needed him for more than just fucking. That he needed him for closeness, as well.

Rory reached for Tate's hand and laced their fingers together. "Did you mean what you said?"

"Yes." Tate squeezed his hand. He smiled at Rory and saw everything he was feeling reflected back in his eyes. "Just us now. I love you."

And saying it seemed like the easiest thing in the world.

EPILOGUE

Winter came slowly to Beulah. It wasn't bitterly cold like Rory remembered from the outside. It was cool and fresh—a temperate winter, much like the temperate summer before it. At night the temperature dropped low, but the days were pleasant and sunny. No trudging through sleet and muck to get to work. No shivering alone in his bed-sit at night, blankets pulled around him, tapping on the heater to try to make it work.

When it came time to leave his house, it didn't take long for Rory to pack his belongings. He'd never really had the chance to make the house his own. Never got around to putting pictures on the wall, like Aaron had suggested he do. He didn't feel any regret at all when he locked the door for the last time and left the key in the mailbox. He never wanted to see this place again.

The taxi driver loaded his suitcases for him, and made small talk as they left the neighborhood. He looked at Rory curiously once or twice. He probably knew Rory's face from the news, either from his own trial or from Lowell's more highly publicized one—coverage ran almost 24-7 after the guilty verdict was handed down, and Lowell was the first person in Beulah to ever be sentenced to a jail term. However the driver recognized him, he didn't mention it. Didn't ask any uncomfortable questions. Rory was grateful for that. He settled back in his seat and watched the passing scenery.

Pretty houses, well-tended gardens. People stopping to talk. Kids playing.

Paradise.

Rory sighed. It had all seemed so perfect once. Too perfect, as it turned out.

Maybe now Rory could learn to appreciate the middle ground. Find his place—and real happiness—in imperfection.

The driver hummed some tune. "Just up here?"

"Yeah, on the left," Rory confirmed. He smiled as he saw Tate waiting on the footpath, Emmy at his side. She was holding a cardboard box and thrust it toward Rory the second he opened the taxi door.

"Rory! Look! Chickens!"

Four startled bundles of fluff chirped up at him.

"She couldn't wait to show you." Tate shrugged. "Which is why we've been standing here for a half hour instead of inside the house where it's warm, like sensible people."

Rory beamed at the excited look on Emmy's face. "Did Daddy build the coop yet?"

Tate made a face.

"He said you're going to," Emmy told him.

"Is that right?"

Tate was suddenly busy with Rory's luggage, lugging it toward the front door. Rory shook his head, paid the taxi driver, then followed Emmy inside. As they hefted Rory's luggage down the hallway, Paula poked her head out of her room. "Ah, you're here! Please tell me you're going to build that chicken coop before you even consider unpacking, because let me tell you, if you don't, I'm going to go out there and build one myself, but I'm going to put our daughter in there instead of the damn chickens."

Our daughter. She hadn't been talking to Tate, either. She'd been talking to Rory.

Our daughter.

Rory warmed from the inside out.

Sure, it was a little strange, even in open-minded Beulah, to have three adults raising a child together under the same roof, with Mommy and Daddy not even a couple. But they could make it work. They made their own rules now.

Rory pecked Tate on the lips quickly, unceremoniously dropping his suitcases onto their bedroom floor. "You heard the woman. I've got a chicken coop to build before our daughter winds up in the yard. Coming, Emmy?"

"*Yes!*" Emmy exclaimed. She tugged on Rory's hand eagerly.

"Go on," Tate said with a smile. "I'll get dinner started for us, eh? Though . . . not poultry, I don't think."

Rory crinkled his nose, then flashed Tate a grin just as beatific as Emmy's.

Two hours later, the chicken coop was built and the chicks were nestled inside. Emmy crouched in the grass, clucking and playing mother hen, while Rory put away his tools and returned the scrap wood to the shed. He surveyed the chicken coop for a moment—not a bad effort for a city kid, splinters aside—and rolled his aching shoulders.

"Emmy!" Paula called from inside. "Rory! Dinner!"

"Goodnight, chickens!" Emmy called and was in the house like a shot. Rory followed at a more leisurely pace, enjoying the chilly evening air and the vivid colors of the sunset. He slid the door shut behind him. The house was filled with the smell of Tate's cooking, but Tate wasn't in the kitchen. Neither was Paula. Rory figured they must be setting the table in the dining room. He heard a squeal of laughter from that direction: Emmy.

Smiling, Rory rounded the corner.

"Surprise!" the people gathered there shouted.

"Surprise!" Emmy echoed belatedly.

There was quite the little crowd around the table and a banner on the wall that read, "WELCOME HOME."

Rory was absolutely not going to tear up. Not at all. And he didn't, until Tate slid an arm around his waist, grinned, and kissed him. Then, caught somewhere between laughing and crying, Rory let Tate lead him to the table.

"Rory." Cal stood up to reach across the table and shake his hand.

"I hear congratulations are in order," Rory said. "Chief justice."

"*Interim* chief justice," Cal corrected with a smile. "And I'll need you on my team, you know. Alex can't do everything herself."

"Huh," Alexandra said, reaching across him for the bread. "I'm sure I can."

Cal snorted. "Look at her! She hasn't even graduated yet. She'll have my job in ten years, the rate she's going."

"Five," Alexandra corrected him.

"Five," Cal agreed. "I'm serious though, Rory. I could use you."

"We're not talking about work at the dinner table," Tate announced.

"Says Mr. Unemployed," Paula shot back.

"Someone has to babysit while you're off at school."

Paula elbowed him but laughed.

That had been a sore point. Paula was ten years older than the other students in her class. Beulah didn't have night school. Didn't need it. Everyone got a free education here. So Paula had screwed up her courage and enrolled in high school.

And Tate would find something, once Emmy was at school herself and didn't need full-time care. Something that wouldn't see him cooped up in an office.

"I brought those plans you wanted," Aaron said from beside Tate.

Rory didn't miss the way Alexandra immediately ignored whatever Cal was saying and zeroed in on Aaron. She wasn't quitting on him. She'd told Rory that, and he didn't doubt it for a second.

"No! No plans, either!" Paula said. "No work, and no plans."

Tate rolled his eyes and grinned at Rory. "That chicken coop you just built? Aaron and I are going to take the roof off it and put in a cooling system. It gets hot in summer."

"Solar powered," Aaron said. "It's a little, um, cost-prohibitive at the moment, and the energy it takes to produce a solar panel is much more than we'd ever conserve using it on a tiny project like this, but we're going to figure out some alternatives to using a standard panel, find a balance."

It would all work out. Rory believed that.

"All that for chickens!" Paula said with a laugh. "Beulah, Beulah, will wonders never cease."

Tate met Rory's eyes and smiled as he replied, "You know? I don't think they will."

"For chickens," Emmy announced and spilled her drink all over the tablecloth.

Everyone rushed to move plates and dishes before they were soaked. Juice dripped onto the floor and, laughing, Tate went to get the mop. Rory leaned back in his chair to watch him.

If this wasn't happiness in imperfection, then Rory didn't know what was.

Dear Reader,

Thank you for reading Lisa Henry and Heidi Belleau's *Bliss*!

We know your time is precious and you have many, many entertainment options, so it means a lot that you've chosen to spend your time reading. We really hope you enjoyed it.

We'd be honored if you'd consider posting a review—good or bad—on sites like **Amazon, Barnes & Noble, Kobo, Goodreads, Twitter, Facebook, Tumblr,** and your blog or website. We'd also be honored if you told your friends and family about this book. Word of mouth is a book's lifeblood!

For more information on upcoming releases, author interviews, blog tours, contests, giveaways, and more, please sign up for our weekly, spam-free newsletter and visit us around the web:

Newsletter: tinyurl.com/RiptideSignup
Twitter: twitter.com/RiptideBooks
Facebook: facebook.com/RiptidePublishing
Goodreads: tinyurl.com/RiptideOnGoodreads
Tumblr: riptidepublishing.tumblr.com

Thank you so much for Reading the Rainbow!

RiptidePublishing.com

ALSO BY
LISA HENRY

King of Dublin, with Heidi Belleau
He Is Worthy
The Island
Dark Space
Tribute

With J.A. Rock:
When All the World Sleeps
The Good Boy
The Naughty Boy
The Boy Who Belonged
Mark Cooper Versus America
Playing the Fool Trilogy (Coming soon)

Coming soon:
Sweetwater

ALSO BY
HEIDI BELLEAU

King of Dublin, with Lisa Henry
First Impressions Second Chances
Blasphemer, Sinner, Saint, with Sam Schooler
(Bump in the Night anthology)

Rear Entrance Video series:
Apple Polisher
Wallflower
Straight Shooter

The Flesh Cartel serial, with Rachel Haimowitz

The Professor's Rule series, with Amelia C. Gormley:
Giving an Inch
An Inch at a Time
Inch by Inch
Every Inch of the Way
To the Very Last Inch

Bookended

With Violetta Vane:
Mark of the Gladiator
Cruce de Caminos
Galway Bound

Coming soon:
The Burnt Toast B&B, with Rachel Haimowitz

ABOUT
LISA HENRY

Lisa Henry likes to tell stories, mostly with hot guys and happily ever afters. Lisa lives in tropical North Queensland, Australia. She doesn't know why, because she hates the heat, but she suspects she's too lazy to move. She spends half her time slaving away as a government minion, and the other half plotting her escape. She attended university at sixteen, not because she was a child prodigy or anything, but because of a mix-up between international school systems early in life. She studied History and English, neither of them very thoroughly. She shares her house with a long-suffering partner, too many cats, a dog, a green tree frog that swims in the toilet, and as many possums as can break in every night. This is not how she imagined life as a grown-up.

Visit Lisa at her blog: lisahenryonline.blogspot.com, on Twitter: @lisahenryonline, and on Goodreads: goodreads.com/LisaHenry.

ABOUT
HEIDI BELLEAU

Heidi Belleau was born and raised in small town New Brunswick, Canada. She now lives in Edmonton, Alberta, with her husband, an Irish ex-pat whose long work hours in the trades leave her plenty of quiet time to write. She has a degree in history from Simon Fraser University with a concentration in British and Irish studies; much of her work centered on popular culture, oral folklore, and sexuality, but she was known to perplex her professors with non-ironic papers on the historical roots of modern romance novel tropes. (Ask her about Highlanders!) Her writing reflects everything she loves: diverse casts of characters, a sense of history and place, equal parts witty and filthy dialogue, the occasional mythological twist, and most of all, love—in all its weird and wonderful forms.

To learn more about Heidi, please visit heidibelleau.com.

Love some kink with your sci-fi romance? Find more at RiptidePublishing.com!

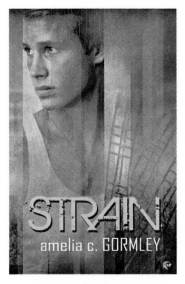

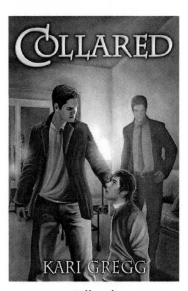

Strain
ISBN: 978-1-62649-070-3

Collared
ISBN: 978-1-937551-09-4

Earn Bonus Bucks!

Earn 1 Bonus Buck for each dollar you spend. Find out how at RiptidePublishing.com/news/bonus-bucks.

Win Free Ebooks for a Year!

Pre-order coming soon titles directly through our site and you'll receive one entry into a drawing to win free books for a year! Get the details at RiptidePublishing.com/contests.